FULL SCORE

Books by Fred Urquhart

Novels

Time Will Knit
The Ferret Was Abraham's Daughter
Jezebel's Dust
Palace of Green Days

Short Story Collections

I Fell For A Sailor
The Clouds Are Big With Mercy
Selected Stories (Hour Glass Library, 1946)
The Last G. I. Bride Wore Tartan
The Year of the Short Corn
The Last Sister
The Laundry Girl and The Pole
Proud Lady in a Cage
A Diver in China Seas
Collected Stories 1: *The Dying Stallion*
Collected Stories 2: *The Ploughing Match*

Books edited by Fred Urquhart

Modern Scottish Short Stories (with Giles Gordon)
No Scottish Twilight (with Maurice Lindsay)
Scottish Short Stories
W.S.C.: A Cartoon Biography of Winston Churchill
The Cassell Miscellany 1848–1958
The Book of Horses
Everyman's Dictionary of Fictional Characters (with William Freeman)
Scotland in Colour (with Kenneth Scowen)

AUP Titles of Related Interest

INTO THE EBB
a new collection of East Neuk stories
Christopher Rush

A TWELVEMONTH AND A DAY
Christopher Rush

TWO CHRISTMAS STORIES
Christopher Rush

THE LAIRD OF DRAMMOCHDYLE
William Alexander
Introduction by William Donaldson

GRAMPIAN HAIRST
An Anthology of North-East Prose
edited by William Donaldson and Douglas Young

GLIMMER OF COLD BRINE
A Scottish Sea Anthology
edited by Alistair Lawrie, Hellen Matthews, Douglas Ritchie

FULL SCORE

Short Stories

FRED URQUHART

edited and introduced by
GRAEME ROBERTS

ABERDEEN UNIVERSITY PRESS

First published 1989
Aberdeen University Press
A member of the Pergamon Group

© Fred Urquhart 1989

The publisher acknowledges subsidy from the Scottish Arts Council towards the publication of this volume.

British Library Cataloguing in Publication Data

Urquhart, Fred, *1912–*
    Full score: short stories
    I. Title
    823'.912

    ISBN 0 08 037719 X

PRINTED IN GREAT BRITAIN
THE UNIVERSITY PRESS
ABERDEEN

Contents

Introduction

It is more than fifty years since Fred Urquhart published his first short story in 1936. During the next two decades he produced no fewer than seven volumes of stories, as well as three novels, and earned the accolade from Alexander Reid of 'Scotland's leading short story writer of the century.' The publication of his *Collected Stories* in 1967–8 won for his work the admiration of a new generation of readers and critics. Since then the appearance of three more volumes of stories in the early nineteen-eighties has consolidated Urquhart's reputation as 'Scotland's finest contemporary writer of short stories'.

Born in Edinburgh in 1912, Urquhart spent his boyhood in Fife, Perthshire and Wigtownshire before returning to complete his schooling in Edinburgh. Leaving school at the age of fifteen, he then worked for seven years in a bookshop near the University, where, he recalls, 'in the long intervals between customers, I read an enormous amount. It was, I like to think, a better grounding for a writer than any university; the customers certainly taught me a lot about human nature.'

It was, however, Urquhart's portrayal of the female of the species which caught the attention of early admirers, such as Compton Mackenzie, who praised his 'remarkable talent for depicting women young and old'. 'He does girls very well.' remarked the poet Stevie Smith of his first volume of stories. Two of the stories that Stevie Smith singled out from that volume for particular praise, *Sweat* and *We Never Died in Winter*, have been included in this selection.

The first is about a young woman desperate to escape from the basement sweat-shop where she works, who spends her hard-earned overtime pay on a bottle of perfume in the hope of disguising the 'sour acrid odour' of her sweat and thereby enticing her boyfriend into marriage, only to discover that he is completely turned off by the smell of her 'cheap scent'. Besides its narrative economy, harsh realism and ironic concluding twist, *Sweat* also displays the kind of craftsmanship and polish—what Stevie Smith calls the 'diamond style'—that one associates with earlier American masters of the genre.

Longing for escape from the monotony and drudgery of working-class life is a characteristic theme of several of Urquhart's stories about young women, as well as of his second novel, *The Ferret was Abraham's Daughter* (1949). Sometimes that longing ends in bitter disillusionment, as in *The Bike*, where a girl employed in a wine merchant's warehouse saves for three years to buy a gleaming red racing cycle, sacrificing everyday treats and enduring the jeers of her workmates in order to own this symbol of freedom and escape. 'And so she saved and dreamed. Dreamed of the time when she would be able to dash along freely without feeling crushed on the crowded pavements.' Her joy of ownership is short-lived, however, for her bicycle is damaged beyond repair by the carelessness of her drunken boyfriend, who runs over it in his lorry and then adds insult to injury by his 'derisive grin' and 'scornful words': 'She knew that something more than her bike had been broken. Nothing would ever be the same again.'

The fragility of youthful happiness is also explored in *Tomorrow will be Beautiful*. On one level this story is a re-working of one of the stock themes of romantic fiction: a young girl's discovery of love in the most unexpected place. Eve is reluctant to accompany her relatives to an 'At Home' at the barracks, since she despises soldiers and those their uniforms attract: 'Catch her making eyes at a soldier!' she remarks scornfully, 'Only common girls go with soldiers.' Nevertheless, she becomes enamoured of the handsome artilleryman she meets in the stables. What raises this story above the level of adolescent wish-fulfilment is the way Urquhart captures the comic mixture of frustration and embarrassment the heroine feels at the behaviour of her relatives, and reveals the element of terror that accompanies sexual awakening. For Eve's moments of peace and contentment as she listens to Scotty's optimistic words of reassurance which give the story its title, are brutally interrupted by a burst of machine-gun fire, a stark reminder of the anxiety that awaits the girl who gives her heart to a soldier.

Another early story which displays what Alan Bold describes as Urquhart's characteristic emphasis 'on the way dreams are defeated by hostile circumstances' is *Washed in the Blood*. Its young heroine, Thomasina, longs to be saved by an exotic black revivalist like the rest of her school-fellows, whose 'religious ecstasy' and sense of vocation she envies and yearns to share: 'They were the Elect, and I wanted passionately to become one of them.' However, when she finally plucks up courage to defy her mother's ban on attending the evangelist's Sunday School, her childish faith is rudely shattered by the discovery that 'The Lord Jesus was a carpenter'—just like the drunken village joiner, McKendrick, whom she has previously identified as the personification of evil. The effectiveness of this story depends on the way Urquhart carefully maintains an ironic distance between the naive childish self whose experiences are recorded and the knowing adult self who narrates them. It is this distance that enables him to present the child's point of view with great sympathy and understanding, yet avoid any trace of sentimentality.

But perhaps the finest of Urquhart's early stories about working-class girls whose 'dreams are defeated by hostile circumstances' is *We Never Died in Winter*. This moving account by a TB patient of the nine months she spent in hospital is a remarkable study of courage and resilience in the face of physical discomfort and disappointed hopes. Its tragic power is due in large measure to the rather flat, matter of fact, almost banal tone of the narrative, which by playing down the pathos inherent in the heroine's situation, sets off the cheerfulness and wry humour, epitomised by the story's title, with which she adjusts to her illness and faces the loss of love, hope and ultimately life itself. The gradual falling away of her erstwhile friends and the inevitable disintegration of her relationship with her dull boy friend are treated without bitterness or recrimination: 'At first, everybody that I wrote to answered, but pretty soon I didn't get any answers. So I stopped writing and spent all my time knitting.' Nor is there any trace of self-pity in the account she gives of her simultaneous receipt of the two letters which announce her fellow patient's death, which foreshadows her own fate at the end of the story, and Roddy's final rejection of her. It is Urquhart's achievement in stories like these to transfigure the commonplace by realising the tragic potential of shopgirls and factory hands.

Urquhart's later treatment of the theme of romantic yearning, however, tends to be robustly comic, as in the case of the slatternly Norma in *The Last Sister*, writing fan letters to her favourite male film stars and ogling every farm hand in sight; or Lizzie, the servant lass in *Beautiful Music*, who in spite of her wall-eye, dung-splashed legs and fingers 'like rationed red sausages', dreams of being fought over by the Polish officers billeted on the farm where she works, yet happily settles for a 'small and stunted' Glaswegian from the HLI, much to her mistress's amusement.

John Pudney once remarked that Urquhart's specialities were 'good dialogue and bad women'. Certainly the malicious Rosie, shamelessly maligning her morose but inoffensive friend in *Win Was Wild*, is brought to grotesque life by the idiomatic vigour of the story's vernacular dialogue, in this case Cockney rather than Scots. Urquhart's fine ear for dialect speech and his ability to reproduce it on the printed page has been much admired by other writers, such as Orwell, Muir and Crichton Smith: as Naomi Mitchison says, 'He seems to be fascinated by the corruption of language.'

In the Introduction to his selection of *Scottish Short Stories* (1957) Urquhart attacked what he saw as the vogue for 'slick, popular, emasculated stories', stories that sacrificed truth to sensation, sentiment, or mere gimmickry. Although his own stories, like those of Angus Wilson and Flannery O'Connor, often deal with bizarre characters or outrageous behaviour, one rarely feels that he is out to make an impression at any cost. Mrs Crichton emptying two jars of home-made jam into Norma's trunk at the end of *The Last Sister* is giving understandable, if extreme, expression to an all-too-natural anger at her feckless and sleekit servant; and the fatal road accident at the end of *Maggie Logie and the National Health* adds a final touch of comic irony to the heroine's reckless pursuit of the benefits of the new welfare state. Even a well-told anecdote like *The Moley was a Diddler*, in which a city-bred farmer's wife is tricked by the local mole-catcher— 'the biggest diddler in the whole countryside', and which exploits the difference between the Scots and English senses of 'diddle', has more to it than the ironic reversal at the end.

It was part of the war years, however, years that he spent in Kincardineshire, that provided the insights into North East rural life as well as the subjects and settings for what are arguably Urquhart's best stories—those set in and around the fictitious town of Auchencairn in the Howe of the Mearns, whose colloquial 'speak' he reproduces with such fidelity and to such good effect.

Three of Urquhart's Auchencairn stories feature Italian prisoners-of-war captured in North Africa and sent to Scotland to work on the land. The best of these, *The Prisoners*, like Jessie Kesson's *Another Time, Another Place* (1983), explores the impact they have on a North East farmer's wife. Not only do the Italians seem to bring 'an exotic note into the drab life of the farm', but she also finds herself identifying with them: 'For after all, she was as much a prisoner as they were. A prisoner bound by her love and fear of Will', her domineering and secretive husband. The choice of Mary as the focaliser of the narrative enables Urquhart to explore in detail the dynamics of her ambivalent relationship with Will. Indeed, the effectiveness of the ending, in which Mary discovers an unexpected vein of sympathy and under-standing in the husband she thinks 'so callous, so cruel, so unimaginative', depends on our being limited to her single, restricted perspective.

At one point in *The Prisoners* Mary alludes to 'that man, Grassic Gibbon, who wrote the books about the Mearns folk and who was so disliked by them because of it'. The best of Urquhart's Auchencairn stories do indeed bear comparison with the work of Gibbon. One critic to link the two writers is Alexander Scott, who claims that Urquhart's 'sympathetic insight and unobtrusive skill' result in 'the best of the localised stories becoming works of universal relevance'.

Insight, indeed, is the hallmark of Urquhart's best stories, insight which is the product not only of observation and imagination, but also of careful attention to details of language and tone. It is this care that enables him to avoid what he described as the 'sentimental clutch of the Kail Yard', particularly in his Auchencairn stories. Nowhere is it better exemplified than in *The Ploughing Match*, which won the Tom–Gallon Award for 1952-3.

Annie Dey, the story's central character, has for years dreamed of holding a ploughing match on her Mearns farm, ever since the day she met her late husband at the contest held on her father's farm. Now at last her girlhood ambition is about to be fulfilled, but she is paralysed and bed-ridden, restricted to watching the match through 'a square window' with the aid of a pair of spying glasses, and forced to relinquish to her son's 'ill-gettit quaen of a wife' the glory of playing hostess to the local gentry and presenting the prizes. Moreover, instead of the 'horses with beribboned manes and tails' that she remembers from the past, this contest has only tractors—'a lot of new-fangled dirt'. And though she lies all day in her downstairs room waiting to receive visitors, arrayed in her best pink silk nightdress, as befits one of the 'Miss Soutars of Kethnot', none of her dead husband's friends or the gentry whose laughter and voices she can hear in the sitting-room takes the trouble to pay their respects or pass the time of day with her.

Summarised in this way, the irony inherent in Annie's situation seems likely to be drowned in a welter of pathos. That this does not in fact happen is due not only to Urquhart's conception of Annie's character, but also to his control of language and tone. The sheer physical helplessness of Annie, deprived by a stroke of the use of both tongue and limbs and compelled to communicate her needs to an impudent servant girl by means of paper and pencil, is brought into sharp focus by a single image:

> The old woman sucked in her lower lip, clamping down her hard gum on it. She looked at her set of false teeth in the tumbler beside the bed, and she closed her eyes in pain. To be beholden to other folk to get them put into her mouth . . .

This expresses Annie's impotence and the disgust which her awareness of it arouses far more exactly than references to her spilling tea over 'her shrunken bosom' or 'trying unsuccessfully to keep the yolk from running down her chin'. As this passage suggests, it is the blow to Annie's pride that is hardest to bear. This is also expressed with economy and precision in a couple of vivid vernacular phrases:

> She that had aye had a tongue on her that would clip cloots to be lying here speechless! It was a judgement, folk said. She knew because Hannah, the maid, had reported it to her. And the old woman writhed as she thought of what the grieve and the ploughmen childes must say out there in the tractor-shed: 'Only an act o' God would make the auld bitch hold her tongue!'

The peasant humour, vigour and candour of these comments establishes the unsentimental narrative tone at the very start of the story, enabling Urquhart to introduce a whole series of potentially pathetic situations without producing a maudlin effect. When in the final paragraph 'a tear—of rage, self-pity or loneliness, the old woman did not know which'— rolls down Annie's cheek, it is a very moving climax indeed.

Three of Urquhart's Auchencairn stories deal with man–animal relationships. The first, *The Red Stot*, describes a series of incidents from the working day of an orra loon: feeding the cattle before dawn, driving them to the local mart, his encounter with a girl, the embarrassments caused by the beast that gives the story its title, and their return journey through the driving snow. More of a sketch than a story, it not only depicts in faithful detail the coarse realities of farm life and its speech, but examines the feelings of a young lad in his first job, particularly towards the animals in his charge: 'The loon held his face away from their slobbering, fawn-coloured muzzles, slimy with saliva, and their great walloping tongues. "Keep yer stinkin' breaths oot o' ma face, damn ye!" he cried.'

The other two stories, by contrast, focus on the feelings of an old farmer and the perennial antagonism between youth and age. In *The Dying Stallion*, a maimed horse becomes the emblem of a vanishing way of life: 'The old man wanted to stretch out his hands and touch the animal, willing to give all his own dying vigour to revive it, but he was afraid of the ridicule of the young men.' Indeed, the lack of compassion in his sons-in-law for the old stallion—'Ye'd better cut him,' advises one, 'and yoke him to a cart'—mirrors their contempt for the old farmer and his outmoded values.

In the final story, *Elephants, Bairns and Old Men*, published six years later, the same farmer, deaved by his nagging daughters, their bragging husbands and spoilt children, and haunted by the memories of his dead son, takes refuge from the festivities of Hogmanay in the stable. There, 'leaning his thin body against the beast's massive presence', old William Petrie finds physical and emotional comfort in the warm, sympathetic presence of his favourite horse, symbol in the story of the old intimacy between man and nature which is threatened by the new inanimate, mechanical world of his brash sons-in-law.

Urquhart's classic treatment, however, of the foibles and frailties of family life, particularly as these come to the surface on special occasions, is *Alicky's Watch*. This story of a nine year old's preoccupation with his treasured watch which has tragically stopped on the morning of his mother's funeral, is framed by the 'continual genteel bickerings between his two grandmothers, each of them determined to uphold the dignity of death in the house, but each of them equally determined to have her own way in the arrangements for the funeral'. Particularly comic is the argument Granny Peebles uses to veto the cremation of her daughter: 'We have the ground, Sandy! It would be a pity not to use it.' Their subsequent jockeying for position at the funeral tea and the gradual thawing of the atmosphere after the minister leaves and the drink begins to flow, culminates in the miraculous re-starting of Alicky's watch amid the laughter and reminiscences of his relations, and his escape to the pictures with his younger brother. Treading a delicate line between comedy and pathos, Urquhart has produced a marvellous portrait, at once satirical and sympathetic, of urban Scots family life in the mid twentieth century.

The four stories which conclude the present collection illustrate Urquhart's work since the publication of *Collected Stories* in 1967–8, and indicate something of the variety and range of his writing, including his ghost and historical stories. It is, of course, impossible to do justice to the achievements of fifty years in a single volume, but it is to be hoped that *Full Score* will show why Fred Urquhart deserves his title of 'one of our greatest short story writers'.

J Graeme Roberts
University of Aberdeen

1 Sweat

SHE WAS TERRIFIED people would feel the smell. It didn't matter so much in the workroom, for each of the girls sweated; a heavy pungent cloud of perspiration penetrated to every corner of the small room. But in cinemas or in tramcars she was afraid always that people would feel the sour acrid odour. If she heard anybody sniff she grew sick with shame. They might say that she was too lazy to wash. And that wasn't true. God alone knew how often her parents and her brother raged at her for spending so much time in the bathroom. It seemed such a waste of energy, for her nostrils never seemed to become quite free of the smell. Sometimes she tried to delude herself into believing that the smell came only from the other girls; that it was their odour lingering in her nostrils like a half-remembered tune. But every time she pressed her arm to her side she could feel her dress wet under the arm-pits. And she knew then that she was like the girls in the advertisements for B.O. in the American magazines she sometimes bought out of Woolworth's.

None of the girls seemed conscious of the smell in the workroom. Of course, most of them had worked there for years. She had been at it only six months: it was her first job. She supposed she too would get used to it in time. But it was awful in this hot, sultry weather. Almost unbearable. The workroom was below the level of the street, and the only light came from electric globes. The fanlights were open, but the air outside was so heavy that no fresh current of air ever seeped in. The big fire for heating the irons made the atmosphere even more oppressive. It was as repellent as a morgue. She often wondered how she would manage to stay in it for as long as some of the others had done.

Maggie, the girl who sat beside her, advised her to get married. She said: 'Don't you stick in this dump, Jeanie. You that's got a boy an' all. Get married and get out of it while you've got the chance.'

'But I don't know if Harry wants to get married,' Jeanie said.

'You make him,' Maggie said. 'Get him warmed up till he takes the plunge. Don't make the same mistakes I made. Waitin' till I thought somethin' better would turn up. I waited so long I got dried up

1

waitin'. And I'm still here in this bloody sweat shop, workin' for less 'n some o' the women pay for the frocks I help to make. What're you gettin', Jeanie?'

'Fifteen bob a week.'

'Well kid, it's not worth it. And you know it as well as I do. Snap out o' it afore it sucks all the energy out o' you. Lookit Joe.'

Jeanie looked at Joe.

Joe was the message-boy. He was about twenty-five, a powerfully-built young man beginning to grow flabby. He sat in the corner beside the big fire, oblivious to the heat and the sweat, reading *The Beasts of Tarzan*. He moved only when the electric buzzer summoned him upstairs to deliver a parcel.

'Lookit him,' Maggie said. 'When he came here ten years ago he was full o' go. He wanted to get on. But now he sits there readin' all the time. He's content now to be a message-boy. All the life's been sucked out o' him. Don't you make the same mistake, kid.'

She wouldn't, Jeanie vowed. She didn't want to be here always. Harry hadn't a very big pay, but it would be better to be his wife than to stay here among the sweat and the dirt. Stewing in her own juice. Sewing until her eyes ached and her mind grew so numb that she couldn't think of anything but *Gee, I wish it was half-past six; if it was only half-past six. . . .*

'Oh, my, I don't want to die, I want to go home!' Maggie sang in a shrill tuneless soprano.

One of the tailors from upstairs, who was waiting at the fire for his iron to heat, passed a rude remark. Maggie took no notice; she went on singing. The man spat in the fire.

Jeanie hated him. He was tall and he had a thin cruel face with very red lips. Once or twice when Jeanie had encountered him in the passage he had pinched her behind as she passed him. And once he had tried to kiss her and she had slapped his face. Ever since then he had sneeringly referred to her as the Virgin. He said something now to Joe about the stink of sweating women.

All Jeanie's hatred for the man flared up afresh at this. Did he think that women were the only ones who sweated? Any time she had been in the tailor's room she had noticed that there was a smell of stale sweat there too. Perhaps it wasn't so insistent as the women's smell, but it was there.

'You get to hell out o' this, McArthur,' Maggie said. 'You'd sweat too if you worked as hard as us.'

It was Friday, pay night. Jeanie had a shilling overtime. It represented almost two hours' heart-breaking and back-aching toil. She knew she should use it for extra car-fares instead of walking to the penny-stage and making herself sweat all the more. But on the way home she spent it on a bottle of scent: *Flowers of Passion*. Maybe this would help to warm Harry up a bit. Anyway, it would make the smell of sweat always a little less noticeable.

She hurried with her tea, but she wasn't quick enough to get into the bathroom before her brother. She sighed wearily; she knew he'd be there for almost half-an-hour. She went to the scullery-sink and filled it. Then she shut the door and started to peel off her dress.

'What're you shuttin' that door for, Jeanie?' her mother cried. 'Leave it open and let some light into the kitchen. Your father can't see to read the paper.'

Jeanie swallowed something in her throat. She didn't want to wash her breasts and her armpits with her father sitting there. She pulled on her frock again, and she contented herself with washing only her face. It couldn't be helped: she couldn't wait till Peter came out of the bathroom. In her bedroom she took off her dress and sniffed at her armpits. She shuddered with disgust and, pouring some *Flowers of Passion* into the palm of her hand, she smeared it on her armpits and in the hollow between her breasts. She sniffed appreciatively. If that didn't warm up Harry nothing would.

Harry took her for a walk in the King's Park. They sat on a seat well away from the crowded pathway. Harry started to paw her.

'Don't,' she said.

But she made no move to resist him. She had a clear vision of the sweaty work-room and the haggard women who worked there. Its horrors were stronger than respectability. At the remembrance she felt again the strong sour smell. . . .

Suddenly Harry lifted his head from her shoulder and sniffed. And as she watched his nose wrinkle disdainfully, Jeanie's stomach shrivelled with fear like a little worm at the root of a flower.

'Why the hell d'you put on all that cheap scent, Jeanie?' Harry said.

SWEAT was published in *Fact*, a series of sixpenny monthly monographs under the general editorship of Raymond Postgate. It was one of eight stories in *Fact Number 4: Writing in Revolt* edited by Arthur Calder-Marshall, published in 1937. It was Fred Urquhart's fourth published story. It was in his first collection *I Fell For A Sailor* (Duckworth, 1940) and was republished in 1948 in an anthology *Writers of Tomorrow* edited by Peter Ratazzi.

2 *We Never Died in Winter*

THE FIRST MONTH I was in the Royal Georgian Hospital for Tuberculosis the girls in Mathiesons' visited me regularly, but when winter came I got fewer and fewer visitors. Soon, Roddy was the only one I could depend upon. He came on Saturday and Sunday afternoons. At first he used to say: 'When are you going to get out of here?' But after a while he stopped asking: he must have realised how foolish his question was. Sometimes I had the feeling as he sat beside my bed that he blamed himself because I was there. If it hadn't been for him I wouldn't have gone to see the doctor in the first place. But early one morning when we were coming home from a dance he said: 'Can't you walk a bit quicker? You're trailing along there as if you couldn't help it.'

'Neither I can,' I said.

And honestly I was dead-beat. It wasn't the result of the dance, for I'd felt like this before I went to it. I'd felt like this for such a long time that I couldn't remember when exactly I'd first noticed it. Indeed, I hadn't noticed it at all. It was so much part of me that it was as natural as any other feeling. I was always tired and dispirited. I used to think it was boredom.

'Snap out of it,' Roddy said. 'You'd better see a doctor if you're not going to brighten up a bit.'

I tried to walk more quickly, but that only made me cough.

'That cold of yours never seems to get any better,' Roddy said. 'You'd better see the doctor. Maybe you need a tonic.'

'Maybe, ' I said.

Next day I went to the doctor, and the first thing he said was: 'Good God, girl, why didn't you come to see me sooner?'

'I thought it was just an ordinary cold,' I said.

'How long have you had it?' he said.

"About three years,' I said. 'On and off.'

'Good God!' he said.

I must have looked shocked, for he said: 'Some of you people would make a saint swear. Why don't you go and see a doctor when there's anything wrong with you? What do think we doctors are here for?'

And straightaway he ordered me off to the Royal Georgian. I was put into Ward Five beside the other Artificial Pneumathorics patients who were on 'Strict' bed. It was August: lovely warm weather. I had been looking forward to going to Blackpool for the first fortnight in September, and I was mad at having to go to my bed. It wasn't as if I felt ill, really ill, that is. Still it'll be for only a week or two, I said to myself, then you'll be better and you'll get home. The first day I was so miserable that I hardly spoke to anybody, but I soon cheered up. What was the good of moping anyway? I had T.B. so that was an end of it. And I got talking to the other girls in the ward.

I discovered that there were three other Marys beside myself—Mary Thompson, Mary Gibson and Mary Coates. We often used to sing that old song that Mary, Queen of Scots and her ladies-in-waiting sang: *Last night there were four Marys, Tonight there will be but three.* But after a few weeks we didn't sing it anymore. It made us feel sad, and made us think that maybe it might turn out to be true.

Mary Gibson had been in the R.G. for six months; Mary Thompson for two months; and Mary Coates for three months. This was Mary Coates' second visit, though. Eighteen months ago she had been in for six months. 'But it's my own fault that I'm here again,' she said. 'I didn't do what the Chief told me. I'll know better this time. No smoking, no dancing, no pictures, no nothing. When I get out I'm going to be a blooming plaster saint!'

We all laughed, but somehow or other we didn't think it very funny, because Mary's face was almost blue and her sputum-bottle was hardly ever out of her hands.

I came in on a Wednesday, and Roddy came to see me on the first visiting-day, Saturday. When he came he sat and glowered. He was uncomfortable at seeing so many girls in pyjamas and bed-jackets. All the men who visited the ward had that 'lost' look the first two or three times they came, but they always lost it sooner or later. Roddy wanted to know exactly what the doctor had said and what they had done to me and how long I'd be in.

So I tried my best to tell him. I said: 'He says that one of my lungs is touched, and that all I need is a rest. The work in Mathiesons' is too confining and he says I'll have to get another job where I'll get more fresh air when I get my discharge.'

'When will that be?' Roddy said.

'Maybe six weeks,' I said. 'I dunno. It depends on how long they keep my lung collapsed.'

'Your lung collapsed?' he said.

'Sure,' I said. 'It's collapsed, and I'm getting Artificial Pneumathorics treatment.'

Everybody who came wanted to know what Artificial Pneumathorics was, and I got fed up explaining it to them. Nobody in the R.G. ever called it by its full name; we all said that so-and-so was an A.P. case, and we left it at that. Life, we felt, was too short for such long words. But all my visitors were interested and wanted to know everything about my illness. They looked at me as if I were some kind of beast in a cage when I told them that one of my lungs was collapsed.'But you *look* all right,' they said. 'You look so healthy, you really shouldn't be lying in your bed at all.'

I laughed and said that it was the air in my 'Summer Residence' that did the trick. They all thought that 'Summer Residence' was a good one, and they said to each other: 'Mary keeps wonderfully cheerful, doesn't she?' as if they were disappointed at not finding me in tears.

Each patient is allowed only two visitors at a time in the wards, but you can get as many as you like when you're in the shelters. Or as many as will come to see you. Usually by the time the patient gets into the shelters her visitors are tired of coming to see her; the novelty of visiting a consumptive friend has worn off. That's what happened to me, anyway. Often in the winter when I was in one of the shelters I wished that some of the visitors I'd had at first hadn't been so anxious to come and see me then, but had waited till I really looked like an invalid.

These first two or three Sundays, for instance, I had so many visitors that they had to take turns to come in to see me, five or ten minutes at a time. They all brought me sweets and flowers and fruit and pretty soon my bed began to look like a shop-counter. I got tired telling each of them all the ins and outs of the treatment I was getting, so I wasn't sorry when four or five of them sneaked in at once. But they weren't there for long before Sister came in and said in her snippy way: 'Only two at a time allowed.'

Roddy got annoyed because all the girls were there. 'I can't get a chance to speak to you at all,' he said. And he asked away from his work and came on Wednesdays, too. Mother always came on Wednesdays, and she and Roddy sat and stared at each other and things were so uncomfortable that I had to do most of the talking myself.

But mother wasn't so quiet when Roddy wasn't there. She grumbled because I needed so many things when I came in and because I wanted something else every week. 'Your middle name should be *Want*,' she said. 'Where do you think I get the money?'

My pay hadn't been very big, but she missed it. When I came into hospital I applied for National Health Benefit, but I was told that, although I was eligible for it, I wouldn't get anything until I got my discharge from the R.G. Then I'd get it in case I wasn't able to start work at once.

'Why can't they give it to you just now?' Mother said.

'Because they say the R.G. supplies all I need,' I said.

'Well, in that case why did you ask me to buy a dressing-gown and pyjamas and a bed-jacket?' she said.

'Who was going to wear the flannel nightgown the R.G. provides?' I said, laughing. 'I didn't want to look like Little Orphan Annie.'

'You're like your father,' she said. 'You never think of where the money's to come from. Oh, the lord will provide! You're jack-easy, both of you.'

'What's he saying about me being in here?' I said.

But I knew before she told me. I knew that Dad's remark when things were looking blackest was always *We never died in winter yet!* He never worried; he left that to mother. 'One worried face is enough in the house at a time,' he said.

Dad didn't come to see me till the third Sunday I was in the R.G. He sat uncomfortably at my bedside and he looked around.

'You're getting plenty of fresh air, anyway,' he said, nodding at all the wide-open windows. 'A change for you, eh?'

'You bet,' I said.

'It's funny to see you lying here,' he said.

'Is it?' I said. 'You wouldn't think it so funny if it were you.'

'I mean that it's funny to see you lying practically in the open-air when you think of how you always wanted all the windows shut at home.'

'Isn't it?' I said.

'Your mother says you're eating well,' he said.

'You bet,' I said.

'You were always such a pick,' he said.

'Wasn't I?' I said.

'Changed days!' he said.

'You bet,' I said.

And honestly it was changed days. When I first came in I ate every-thing they gave me. Perhaps it was due to the fresh air and to not working, but I think it was mainly because of the greater variety that the R.G. kitchen offered. You simply don't feel hungry when you know that at home you get stew on Mondays, mince on Tuesdays, sausages on Wednesdays, and so on.

Dad looked from bed to bed: from Mary Coates' blue face to Liz Jerome's white one. 'You look all right, anyway,' he said, and I thought there was a note of relief in his voice. 'See that you do everything the doctor tells you,' he said.

'You bet,' I said.

And honestly I did what I was told. I was a model patient. Every time he examined me the Chief was pleased. I put on weight. I was only seven and a half stones when I came in, but it wasn't long before I was nine stones. 'I'm going to get a job as a fat lady in a circus when I get out of here,' I told my visitors.

I was on 'Strict' bed for six weeks, and in a way I passed the time pleasantly enough. It was very restful to lie there by the open window and to look out at the lovely gardens, and it was fine to know that I didn't need to rush and go to work. It was just like being on holiday. The R.G. was more like a hotel than a hospital. And once I had got used to the idea of having T.B. I was prepared to make the best of it. It wasn't as if I had any pain. Not like Mary Coates, who was sometimes so bad that she couldn't speak; she just lay and stared at the ceiling. But the rest of us passed the time in talking and knitting and writing letters. I wrote so many letters that the house-doctor asked me if I was writing a book. At first, everybody that I wrote to answered, but pretty soon I didn't get any answers. So I stopped writing and spent all my time knitting.

I knitted myself a lemon jumper and I started to knit a mauve one, but I stopped when I found that my clothes didn't fit me the same. 'I'll need to wait till I stop expanding!' I said. And I knitted a jumper for mother and socks for Roddy. I began to knit him a pullover for his birthday, but I never finished it. It's lying in my case now. Sometimes I think I'll unravel it and knit something else, but I haven't the heart. I can't bear to look at it after what happened.

At the beginning of November, when I was allowed up most of the day, I was put in one of the shacks. Or the shelters, as Matron called them; she was annoyed when one of the few letters I got was addressed to Shack Number Four. There were twelve shacks, and they lay in a half-circle at the top of the lawn. They had only three sides and there were windows in each side, so we got plenty of fresh air. They were on swivels, and the nurses turned them round whenever the wind changed. We weren't allowed to turn them round ourselves, though sometimes when the wind changed through the night we got up and had them shifted before the Night Nurse got our length; we preferred the risk of being reported to the Chief to the risk of having the wind drive the rain on to us, for though we had waterproof covers on our beds there was always the chance that the wind would blow in such strong gusts that it would drive the rain in as far as our pillows.

Usually the shacks faced the road, so that we saw all the traffic that passed. Sometimes Mathiesons' big van passed, and Alfie the driver, always waved to me. Once or twice I spoke to him over the wall, and he told me all the latest news of the shop. But I was never able to speak freely to him; I always had to keep my eyes skinned for Sister; we weren't supposed to speak to anybody over the wall. Especially men. We weren't even allowed to speak to the male-patients. We did, of course, We wouldn't have been human if we hadn't spoken to them. And the fact that it was forbidden added to the fun.

There were some awfully nice boys amongst them. You'd never have thought, to see some of them, that there was anything wrong with them. Sometimes I used to think that it was even harder on them than it was on us; a woman can be a chronic invalid all her life, yet she can manage to muddle through some way or other because she's usually dependent on somebody else, but a man simply can't afford to be an invalid if he has his living to make like those boys. It was a pretty black outlook for them. All the same they managed to keep cheerful.

It was a terribly severe winter. Folk said it was the worst they'd ever experienced. But they didn't really know anything about it. If they'd been in the R.G. they'd have died. Sometimes I wonder why I didn't die myself. But it's funny that none of the patients died in the winter, though some of them have died since. The few people who came to see me huddled themselves in their heavy coats and gave exaggerated shivers. 'I don't know how you stand it,' they said. 'I'd be dead within three days.' But I just laughed and said: 'You get used to everything but hanging!' And sometimes I used to sing *I wouldn't leave my little wooden hut for you! I've got one lover and I don't want two!*

All the same it was no joke when the Night Nurse wakened us in the mornings. Especially on those mornings the snow lay thick on the ground for weeks. We used to wake and find it lying three or four inches thick on our waterproof covers. We were supposed to get up at seven o'clock, but Nurse usually wakened us at ten to seven, so that gave us a few minutes to pluck up courage. We always lay to the very last minute and then we would begin to count, and as soon as we had reached twenty we'd jump out of bed and pull on our coats over our pyjamas. Then Wilma would race me to the bathroom in Ward Five. We weren't supposed to run, but we knew that it wasn't likely that either Sister or Matron would see us at that time in the morning.

I don't know what I'd have done without Wilma. She was a real cheery case, and she and I got along fine. She had been in for two

months longer than I had, and she was always talking about getting
her discharge, for she was engaged and she hoped to get married as
soon as she got out. But she didn't keep moaning about it and make
both herself and me miserable, as Liz Jerome would have done if she
had been in Wilma's place.

When I think of it, I realise how lucky I was to get Wilma for a
shack-mate and not Liz Jerome, who was put in the shacks at the
same time as I was. Liz was awful sentimental, and she cried at the
least thing. Every time we played the gramophone in the Recreation
Room she cried at all the sad records. The first time she heard *When I
Grow Too Old To Dream*, you'd have thought she was at a funeral, and
when I laughed she said: 'You've got a brick for a heart, Mary Orr.'

But I just laughed all the more. If I hadn't laughed I'd have cried
even more than Liz was crying herself. For I'd just got a letter from
Roddy that morning.

If I'd known that Roddy was looking for another job I wouldn't have
got such a shock when I got his letter. But I had no idea that he was
dissatisfied with his work; he seemed to be getting along all right.
That is why I took it so hard, him doing it behind my back. I felt that
either he hadn't been interested enough to tell me or that he had been
afraid to tell me in case I tried to stop him—though God knows I
wouldn't have done that; I was too keen for him to get on so that we
could get married. Or was he afraid that I was in the R.G. for 'keeps'?
It was only then that I realised that I'd been there for nearly five
months, and that there was no likelihood of getting out soon. I tried
not to worry about it, but all the time the feeling was there, and
however hard I tried I couldn't escape from it.

Not that Roddy had ever shown that he thought I was in the R.G.
for good. Every Saturday and Sunday up to Christmas he visited me
regularly. Some time before that he stopped coming on Wednesdays
since I hadn't so many visitors and he could get me all to himself
when he came. I was glad of that, but sometimes I couldn't help
wishing that somebody would come in and give us something to talk
about. For Roddy had absolutely no conversation whatsoever. He had
never been a great talker, but I had always managed to find
something to interest him. In the R.G. however, I was simply lost. It
was just what I'd imagine prison would be like. Sometimes we didn't
see newspapers for days. There was always the wireless, of course, but
we never listened to anything but dance-music; as soon as we heard
talking we switched it off. So I didn't know very well what to say
when Roddy came, unless it was to talk about the other patients, and
he wasn't very much interested in them. All he seemed interested in

was how long I was going to be there. He never seemed   able to realise that I had T.B. 'You shouldn't be in here,' he often said. 'Why, you look as well as I do.'

At Christmas and the New Year he was busy at his work so he could come in only for a little while on Christmas and New Year's days. He came the first Sunday in the new year, but he didn't come on the following Saturday or Sunday. I had no idea of what could have kept him, and when I didn't get any letter on the Monday I began to be worried. I knew that he wasn't a great hand at writing letters, but I thought that he might have let me know what was wrong.

The letter came on the Tuesday. It was very short and said that he had suddenly got a job in London and that he'd had to go very quickly and hadn't had time to come in to see me before he went.

Of course, I found plenty of excuses for him. But, at the same time, I knew that he could easily have come in, even although it had been only for a few minutes. And not being on a visiting-day wouldn't have mattered. Matron would have allowed him in at once if he had just asked. After all, it wasn't as if I were a prisoner or anything like that. I shut myself in the bathroom and started to cry, but I stopped when I remembered that I hadn't any powder with me. I didn't want any of the girls to know that I'd been crying. In case they thought it strange about Roddy not coming to visit me any more I said casually that I'd known that he was going to a job in London but that I hadn't thought of mentioning it to them.

Roddy wrote to me every week at first, and told me all about his new job; he was always anxious to know if I was feeling better and if I'd be able to get out soon. In one of his first letters he mentioned that he hoped to get a raise after he had been there for six months, so this would mean that we'd be able to get married. And in a letter two or three weeks after that he said that he was thinking about putting his name down for one of the new houses in a Building Scheme that was going up. Of course, I made a lot of plans in the letters I wrote to him, telling him the kind of house I thought we should have and things like that, but sometimes I couldn't help wondering if those plans would ever come to anything. For my discharge seemed as far away as ever. I had stopped putting on weight; somehow or other I just didn't have the same appetite as I'd had when I came in. And at the end of January I got a cold and didn't seem able to throw it off. Apart from those things the Chief always seemed well enough pleased with me, but whenever I mentioned discharge he would shake his head and say: 'There's time enough for that, my dear young lady.'

All February, March and April I got letters regularly twice a week from Roddy. Then he told me not to be surprised if he didn't write so often as he was going to be very busy before the Coronation; his firm had a lot of contracts and he was working overtime. 'I'm saving up,' he wrote, 'so it will be better for us both in the long run.' I didn't mind at all so long as I knew he was well enough. And, although he wrote only one short letter every week and then towards the Coronation only once a fortnight, I wrote to him regularly twice a week. I told him all the funny things that happened in the R.G. so as to show him that I was keeping my pecker up and wasn't losing hope after being there for nearly nine months. And really there were quite a lot of funny things that happened just about that time.

For instance, there was the time that some of the male-patients climbed the wall and went off for the afternoon. They often did that, and nobody ever found out. But this afternoon they went to Princes Street Gardens and the first person they met was Sister. It was her afternoon off, and that was one of the reasons why they had been bold enough to go that far. They didn't know what to do; it was too late to cut and run. But Sister just smiled sweetly at them and said: 'Good afternoon, boys,' and walked past as if they were just casual acquaintances.

After that none of the males would hear us say anything against Sister. They said she wasn't a bad sort, but we told them that it was only because she was an old maid and had a soft spot in her heart for men.

She wasn't bad to us either, sometimes. It all depended if you got the right side of her. She could be real mean sometimes, but there were times when she was quite human.

One of these times was on the day of the Coronation of George VI. She came into the Recreation Room when we were listening to the broadcast from Westminster Abbey and she said: 'Have any of you girls got any sweeties?'

'No, Sister,' I said, and it was the truth.

'Have you?' she said to Wilma.

Wilma had, but she thought that Sister was going to confiscate them, so she said: 'No, Sister,'

'Have you?' Sister said to Liz.

'Y-Yes, Sister,' Liz said in a low voice.

'You might bring them,' Sister said. 'I feel like eating a sweetie.'

Liz was so flabbergasted that she brought two tins. Sister took them and sat down with them on her lap. She ate continually for the next hour while listening to the service, and at the long bits where there was nothing but the pealing of the organ she told us all about her life when she was a girl.

But Sister could be real mean, too. Like the time when she reported Wilma and me to the Chief for talking to the males, and she didn't report any of the males. She said that they had run so that she wasn't able to see who they were! But the Chief said that as neither Wilma nor I had run we were to be commended. So that was one in the eye for Sister. Some of the girls said that the reason why Sister was so changeable was that she had been in love with somebody who had jilted her, but I don't know if that was the reason or not. I don't think that anybody who had been jilted could be so mean to other folk. If you can't eat your cake yourself there's no sense in keeping it from others.

I got a letter from Roddy a few days after the Coronation. I got two letters that morning. I kept Roddy's to the last like a kid with a fancy cake. I didn't know who the other letter was from, but when I opened it I found that it was from Mary Coates' mother.

All through the winter Mary Coates coughed and spluttered and her face got bluer and bluer. Soon she couldn't sit up in bed at all. In February the Chief wanted to send her to another hospital where she would get more specialised treatment (he said this though he knew there was no hope) but her mother wouldn't hear of it; she said that if Mary was going to die she'd die at home. And though the Chief said it was a mistake Mrs Coates took Mary away.

This was a letter to say that she was dead. I sat and looked at it for a long time. I knew that it was the best thing for Mary, but I thought how unfair it was, after she had struggled so hard all winter, to die just then when the summer was going to begin. I felt that I should pray for her, but it was such a long time since I had prayed that I didn't know how to start. I just sat on the edge of my bed and slowly I ripped open Roddy's letter.

I read it twice before I realised what it meant, and then I sat and stared at it, not thinking. I was sitting like that when Wilma ran into the shack. She was roaring and laughing and she collapsed on her bed. I looked at her for a while before I could manage to say: 'What's wrong?'

She was laughing so much that she couldn't answer me, and she nearly choked when she started to tell me. 'It's Liz Jerome,' she said. 'She's roaring and crying.'

'That's nothing to laugh about,' I said.

But Wilma laughed all the more when she heard the tone of my voice. 'Oh, it's funny,' she said. 'You should go along and see her.'

'I don't think it's funny at all,' I said. 'Maybe when the Chief examined her yesterday he told her something that she didn't tell us.'

'No, it's not that at all,' Wilma said. 'She's reading a love-story and it's that sad that she can't help weeping.'

I stood up slowly and held out the two letters. 'Take those along and let her read them,' I said. 'Maybe they'll give her something to cry about. Mary Coates is dead, and my boy-friend has given me the heave.'

That was three months ago. I'm back home again. Mother made me come home; she said I wasn't getting any better in the R.G. The Chief and she had an awful row about it; he said that she wasn't giving me a chance, nor him either; he wanted to study my case to find out why I had such a relapse after getting so far along the road to recovery the first few months I was in. But mother wouldn't hear anything he said, and she bundled me home. 'She'll spend what time she has left among her own folk,' she said. But Dad told her to shut-up. 'You're always looking on the black side, woman,' he said. 'We never died in winter yet. Did we, Mary?'

WE NEVER DIED IN WINTER was written in August 1937 and published in December 1938 in *Penguin Parade*, number 4, edited by Denys Kilham Roberts. It was in Urquhart's first collection of stories *I Fell For A Sailor* (Duckworth, 1940) and in *The Ploughing Match*, volume two of his *Collected Stories* (Rupert Hart-Davis, 1968).

3 *The Bike*

THE BICYCLE COST her seven pounds ten. It took her almost three years to save the amount. She did without the pictures and new stockings and sweets and lots of other things to get it. The other girls in the wash-house laughed at her determination to save. When they sent Tammy for pies and ice-cream and lemonade they always tried to coax her to get some, too. And they laughed at her refusals and said she was mean. They could not understand her desire to have a bike.

'What dae ye want a bike for, onyway?' Lizzie the forewoman said. 'What guid's it goin' to dae ye?'

'I don't know,' Annie said. 'I just want a bike.'

She could not put into words her longing to sail along superbly, skimming like a yacht in full sail. The only argument she could find in its favour was that it would save car-fares. 'It costs me fourpence a day to get here,' she said. 'I'd save that if I cycled. Five fourpences and twopence on Saturdays. What's that?'

'Guidness knows,' Lizzie said. 'I never was ony guid at coontin'.'

'Twenty-two pennies,' Annie said, her brows wrinkled with the effort of calculation. 'That's one and—one and tenpence.'

'Ay, it's a guid bit oot o' ten bob a week,' Lizzie said. 'Well, it's time we got on! Harry's yellin' aboot thae Domingo Souza bottles no' bein' labelled yet.'

Still, although the other girls in the Wine and Spirit Merchant's warehouse saw that Annie's reasons for wanting a bicycle were good, it did not prevent them from jeering at her for saving. They said she was a mug not to get it on the instalment system. Annie refused to do that, however. It was too much like getting a thing 'on tick'. And so she saved and dreamed. Dreamed of the time when she would be able to dash along freely without feeling crushed on the crowded pavements.

But the three years were long when she saw the number of pies the other girls consumed and the bottles of lemonade they tilted to their dry mouths. Sometimes she thought it wasn't worth it: the bike seemed as far away as ever. And she would look at the little penny bank-book that was all that she had to show for her scrimping, and

15

she thought often of blowing the whole amount on a new coat or on a trip to Blackpool. But she sternly set her mind against the temptations that the other girls whispered to her. And at last she got her bike.

It was a lovely bike. A low racer, painted a bright red, with cold gleaming chromium-plated handlebars. The first morning she passed her hand proudly over its shining mudguards before she jumped upon it and whisked along to her work. She wouldn't need to steal any more rides on her brother's bike! Here was something of her own: something she could clean and oil and tend; something she could keep shining and spruce. Her heart sang with exhilaration and proud accomplishment, keeping time with her feet working the pedals and the wheels going round. She had a bike! *Oh, Georgia's got a moon, and I have got a bike! The one I've waited for, and I have got a bike!* And she waved gaily as she passed Lizzie and Meg and Bessie walking to the warehouse.

She put the bike behind the barrels at the back of the wash-house. It was safely out of the way there.

Everybody in the warehouse came to admire it. 'It's a nice wee bike,' said one of the lorry-drivers. 'Ye look real smart on it. I saw ye wheech past the tram-car I was on this morning, and I said to masel' "Is that Annie?" Ay, ye're a real smarter!'

'What did ye say ye paid for it!' asked Charlie, the youngest lorry-driver.

'Seven pounds ten,' Annie said shyly.

'Oh boy!' Charlie whistled with astonishment. 'Some capitalist made a pile out o' that. Ye were a mug to encourage him. Fools and their money!'

Charlie was always talking about the capitalists and about wage-slaves and socialism and the revolution. He was a loud-voiced, swaggering young man, rather good-looking in a flashy sort of way. Although he was never properly shaved and always wore a muffler instead of a collar and tie, Annie was very much attracted by him. But he never encouraged her either by look or by word, and she was too shy to show that she liked him.

That afternoon as Annie returned to work, she overtook Charlie at the gate of the warehouse. She jumped off her bike and walked with him towards the wash-house.

'Ay, it's a nice bike,' he said, eyeing it critically. 'How much did ye say ye paid for it again?'

'Seven pounds ten.'

Charlie whistled tunelessly. He slouched along with his hands in his pockets. At the door of the wash-house he made no move to leave her. He leaned against the door-post. Annie stood, holding the bike, watching him, admiring the yellow curls that dangled over his low brown forehead.

'Seen that picter at the Gaiety?' Charlie said.

Annie shook her head. She caressed the bike's leather seat.

'Like to see it?'

"I was goin' tonight,' she said.

'Yourself?'

'Uhuh.'

'Mind if I chum you?'

'Okay,' she said.

All afternoon Annie could hardly work for thinking about going to the pictures with Charlie. Even the bike was overshadowed by this wonderful happening. She could hardly take her tea for thinking of what lay ahead, and she was at the corner of Commercial Street ten minutes before the time.

She hardly recognised Charlie when he mooched up to her with his hands in his pockets. He was wearing a collar and tie and a scarlet pullover, and his bright yellow hair was neatly arranged into waves like corrugated-iron. It looked as though it had just been marcelled.

'Oke,' he said, balancing himself on his sharp-pointed shoes on the edge of the pavement.

Annie smiled. She pranced along proudly at his side in the direction of the Gaiety. She tried to think of something to say, but she could think of nothing. Charlie kept his eyes on the pavement, a cigarette dangling from his lips.

At the paybox Annie fumbled in her bag. 'It's okay,' Charlie said, 'I'll get it again.' And he bent down to the bowl and said: 'Two sixpennies.'

The Pathé Gazette was showing. Annie was not much interested in soldiers marching and in naval reviews. She looked sideways at Charlie. He was slumped down in his seat, his hands in his pockets. Annie admired his profile in the semi-darkness.

The feature film started. It was a torrid romance. Annie placed her hand on her knee close to Charlie's leg. He made no response for a long time. Annie could not enjoy the film for wondering why not. Then about the end of the film Charlie placed his hand over hers. But he took it away when the lights went up.

They said nothing as they walked to Annie's house. She slipped her hand through his arm, but he never took his hands out of his pockets.

'Well, I'll see you tomorrow,' he said at the door of the tenement. 'Cheerio!'

'Cheerio!' Annie said.

At first Annie kept the bike in the wash-house, but the foreman advised her to keep it elsewhere. 'Ye'd better watch it doesnie get scratched here, lass,' he said. 'If I was you, I'd put it in the garage. It would be safer there.'

But Annie discovered that the bike was not as safe in the garage as it had been in the wash-house under her own eye. The boys in the office and the two louts who looked after the yard were always racing it around the yard. She began to notice marks on the paint, and sometimes when she went to get it she found that the seat had been raised.

'If I was you, I'd tell thae galoots where they got off,' Lizzie said, 'Especially that lazy brute, James. It would be wicer-like if he helped puir Tammy to sweep up the yard instead o' racin' roond and roond.'

But James did not heed Lizzie when she gave him a flighting. 'Awa' and mind yer ain business,' he said.

And he continued to cycle madly around the yard whenever Harry, the foreman, was out of the way, leaving Tammy, a simple-looking youth of about seventeen, to do all the work.

Annie would have brought the bike back into the wash-house, but they got in an extra lot of barrels and there was no room for it. Sometimes she thought that she would be better to leave the bike at home and take the tram to work as she used to do. But although she was now getting twelve-and-sixpence a week she could not afford anything from it for tram-fares. She went to the pictures once a week with Charlie and she always paid herself. Lately, too, they had taken to going to dances, which meant spending one and sixpence or two shillings which she could ill afford.

Apart from her dislike of James for using her bike, she disliked him for his influence on Charlie. They were as thick as thieves. Every night after work they went into the public-house at the end of the street, although already they had drunk all the wine and whisky they could scrounge from the warehouse. 'I'd like to see their insides,' Lizzie said. 'They'll be bonnie and burned!'

Whenever Charlie had too much to drink he talked about 'the capitalists grinding the faces of the poor', and there were always several adjectives describing the capitalists. But he had so great a capacity for drink that it was difficult to tell when he'd had too much. Annie hated to see him at those times, though she was fascinated and could not help listening to what he was saying. She was terrified that he would drink too much at the dances they went to and cause her to feel embarrassed.

One forenoon six or seven weeks after Annie had bought the bicycle, Charlie was in such a state that even the foreman remarked upon it. 'He's awa' oot as fu' as a puggy,' he said to Lizzie. 'And him wi' a load o' stuff on his lorry that's worth thoosands. I hope he's able to deliver it a', and that nothin' happens to him.'

But Charlie was able to deliver all his orders safely at the various pubs and licensed grocers. He returned to the warehouse about five o'clock, and his lorry swung into the yard far too quickly for the amount of space available.

'That yin'll kill somebody yin o' thae days, if he's no' carefu',' said Lizzie, looking out of the wash-house.

'He's needin' taken doon a peg,' Bessie said, wiping her red hands on her packsheet apron and scowling over Lizzie's shoulder at the boastful Charlie as he swung empty boxes and crates from his lorry on to the ground. 'I havenie forgotten aboot what he did to the puir cat.'

This had happened some time before. The cat was a great favourite with everybody in the warehouse except Charlie. It was a good ratter, and when it was about, the girls weren't afraid to plunge their hands into the straw in the crates: they knew there was no danger of rats lurking there when Touser was about.

But one day Charlie had swung his lorry into the yard and headed straight for the cat, which was lying stretched out in the sun. Somebody had noticed and cried a warning. But Charlie had taken no notice, and the wheels had gone right over the animal. And when Lizzie and Bessie had lashed him furiously with their tongues, Charlie had laughed and said: 'The beast had no right to be lying there.'

'He'll get an awfu' drop yin o' thae days,' Bessie muttered now. 'I only hope I'm there when he gets it.'

'Me too,' said Meg.

'Lookit the way he's chuckin' the boxes doon and leavin' them lyin' for puir Tammy to put in their places,' Lizzie said.

'That's a Socialist for ye,' Bessie said.

'Thae kind that talk sae big aboot their socialism are aye the worst,' Lizzie said.

Annie felt that she should champion Charlie, but she could think of nothing to say. She continued to wind pink tissue wrappers around bottles of Lodestar Ruby Wine.

Having thrown off every box and crate, Charlie jumped into the driving-seat and started his lorry. He headed straight for the garage door. 'He'll run into it if he doesnie look oot,' Lizzie said.

But he managed to scrape through. 'That was a near thing,' Lizzie said, turning and picking up a crate of empty bottles.

Just then there was a crash. It was not very loud, but it was loud enough for the sound to be unfamiliar. 'What's that?' Bessie cried.

The four girls ran into the yard. Harry had already run out of the office, and some of the young clerks were following him. They approached the garage door.

Charlie met them. He was grinning broadly. 'It's okay,' he said.

'What was that noise?' Harry said.

'That!' Charlie shrugged. 'That was just that lassie's bike. What did she need to leave it for in the middle o' the garage?'

Numbly Annie stared at the twisted wheels and the broken red frame. She scarcely heard the arguments that went on around her. Dimly she heard Lizzie shriek: 'That's that James goin' and leavin' it lyin' there in the middle o' the floor!' And even more dimly she heard Charlie reply: 'D'ye think I'm lookin' oot for every heap o' scrap-iron that's in my way?'

That night Annie cried herself to sleep. Harry had assured her that she would get a new bike. 'I'll make Charlie and James pay it between them,' he promised her. 'Charlie can rant as much as he likes about the insurance being liable, but I'll see that he pays for it.'

But Annie knew that even if she got another bike it would never be the same. She would always remember Charlie's derisive grin as he looked down at the broken frame, and his scornful words. She knew that something more than her bike had been broken. Nothing would ever be the same again.

THE BIKE was written in the summer of 1939 and was broadcast by the Scottish BBC on 5 August 1939, produced by James Fergusson and read by Jean Taylor Smith. It was published in *I Fell For A Sailor* (Duckworth, 1940). It appeared in *The Ploughing Match*, the second volume of Urquhart's *Collected Stories* (Rupert Hart-Davis, 1968). It was broadcast again in a programme about Fred Urquhart, produced by Gordon Emslie and read by Rose McBain on 23 January 1975, and again as the Morning Story on Radio 4 on 28 August 1979, produced by Mitch Raper and read by Fraser Kerr.

4 *Tomorrow Will Be Beautiful*

RELUCTANTLY EVE rose and prepared to follow her mother and her aunt off the tram-car when it stopped at the barracks. For a moment she thought of continuing to the terminus and going for a walk in the woods at Colinton, but she knew that her mother would kick up a row if she did. She felt listless and tired and she had no heart to push her way through the crowd that was alighting. As a result, her mother and her aunt, who had forged ahead like miniature steam-rollers, were waiting impatiently for her. 'Hurry up, Eve,' her mother cried. 'You'd think you were going to a funeral.'

Already her two young cousins, Albert and Gladys, were inside the gates and gazing inquisitively at the sentry. They stood quite close to him and talked about his uniform in their shrill English voices. He might be an animal in the Zoo for all they care, Eve thought as she passed him, and she took a firm grip of the boy and girl and dragged them after her. She supposed, however, that he was used to people staring at him. He wouldn't need to be self-conscious with all this crowd passing him.

A great many soldiers belonging to the two regiments in the barracks were mingling with the crowds of sightseers in the barracks-square and directing them to the various places of interest. Eve wondered if they really felt as cheerful as they looked, or were they simply obeying orders? This throwing open of the barracks to the public was all a lot of eyewash to make people think what a grand life they had in the army. She wondered how many of the young men she saw in civvies would be foolish enough to join up after they'd been here. She knew that if she'd been a man she wouldn't have thought about it for a moment. She wouldn't have anything to do with soldiers. Lots of girls were attracted by the uniforms and the trained erect carriage, but she wouldn't be such a mug. Give your heart to a man who was little better than a machine, a man who'd have to go at once if there was a war, and spend months, perhaps years of anxious worrying over him—No, sir! Even although you were married to a soldier in peace time you really couldn't call him your own. He was liable to be shifted to another depot at a moment's notice. You could

21

go with him, of course, but what was life in most of these barracks? The soldiers' wives were no better than their men; she wouldn't associate with them. Catch her making eyes at a soldier! She and her friend Ann had had a row about that only the other night.

They were in a café at Portobello when two kilties sat down at the neighbouring table. Ann, at once, did her best to click with them. The soldiers showed that they weren't unwilling; they began to pass facetious remarks specially for the benefit of the two girls. Eve tried to ignore them; she sipped delicately at her iced drink and kept her eyes primly on the table. But although she could ignore the soldiers, she couldn't ignore Ann when she began to giggle helplessly at one of the remarks. Another second and Eve knew that her friend would give an equally facetious retort. So she rose hurriedly, said, 'Come on,' and marched out.

'Here, what's the big idea?' Ann said breathlessly when she joined Eve on the pavement. 'What's the idea of going out like that when we're just starting to have some fun?'

'I didn't want to have anything to do with them,' Eve said.

'But why not?' Ann said, amazed.

'Because they're soldiers.'

'Well, for the luvva Mike!' Ann said. 'They're as nice a pair of boys as we could of picked up in a day's march. It was only for a bit of fun, anyway.'

'I know,' Eve said. 'But you never know who might of seen us with them. There's no good making ourselves cheap. Only common girls go with soldiers. Girls like that Cora Roberts. You wouldn't like to be classed with her, would you?'

'Well—no.' Ann made a face. 'You might of given me a chance to finish my drink, anyway,' she grumbled as they bent their heads against the east wind from the sea and walked towards the car-stop at Willowbrae Road.

They hardly spoke in the tram on the way home. Eve knew that Ann was annoyed and she was annoyed at Ann for being annoyed. But she decided that she'd make up for her seeming stickiness. She'd go to whatever pictures Ann wanted to go to on Saturday. This would probably mean Loretta Young's latest film at the Ritz, and Loretta Young was mud to her. But she'd endure it to make amends.

On Saturday afternoon, however, when she was getting ready to go for Ann, her mother insisted that she accompany her and her aunt and cousins to the 'At Home' at Belhouse Barracks. 'You can help to keep an eye on Albert and Gladys,' she said. 'Your Aunt Lily and I aren't able to keep running after them.'

'But I'm going to the pictures with Ann,' Eve said.

'You can go to the pictures at night,' her mother said. 'Besides, it's not good for you sitting in the pictures on a hot afternoon like this.'

'It aint good for yer in the pictures at any time!' Aunt Lily said, winking at her sister-in-law. 'Yer never know what mischief them young girls'll get into. Ee, my! I wouldn't 'ave been allowed to the pictures alone when I was a girl.'

Eve thought about this as she trudged after them across the barracks-square. Aunt Lily maybe thought she was funny, but you had only to look at the mark made by her corsets under her floral frock stretched so tightly across her big behind to see that it was the funniest thing about her. As if you didn't know that there hadn't been any pictures when she was a girl! She hoped that Ann wouldn't think that she hadn't called for her because of what had happened in the café. And she hoped that her friend wouldn't wait in for her all afternoon. She wished she'd had time to let her know about the visit to the barracks; Ann might have come with them, and then it wouldn't have been so unbearable.

'Programme, lidy?' At the sound of the cheerful cockney voice, Aunt Lily stopped suddenly. 'Ee, my!' she said to the young kilty. ''Oo'd 'ave thought to see an Englishman in the kilt?'

'Not my old lidy anyway,' the soldier said, laughing. 'Coo! She wouldn't 'alf 'ave gone on about it if she'd known.'

'What part of London do yer come from?' Aunt Lily said.

'Camberwell.'

'Camberwell! Ee, my! We come from Camberwell too, We're only in Edinburgh on 'oliday.' Aunt Lily was delighted to find a kindred spirit in this fog of Scottish faces. She and her sister-in-law chatted animatedly to the soldier, but Eve stood sullenly and looked around her. Fancy talking to a person like that! He was a real genuine guttersnipe—anybody with half an eye could see that. It just showed how hard up the Army was for men when Scottish regiments took men like that into their ranks; no decent Scot would join up.

'D'yer want me to show yer around?' the soldier said, and without waiting for an answer he said: 'Come on, follow little 'Erbert an' 'e'll show yer what's what.'

It was very hot. The forenoon had been dull and sultry, but now the sun was shining. It blazed on the white stones that bordered the plots of grass in the square, and Eve had to force her eyes away from them; the glare made her head ache. Her feet were beginning to get sore, too. She wished she'd done what her mother had told her and put on her low-heeled sandals.

'Erbert led them into the barracks and began proudly to point out the billiard-room, the recreation rooms, the gymnasium and all the other places that were open.

'Ain't they nice?' Aunt Lily said. 'Ee, my, but you're comfortable!' She laughed. 'But they tell me that you get every comfort in the Army nowadays; the sergeant comes round tuckin' you up an' everythin'.'

'Ma, can I be a soldier when I grow up?' young Albert said loudly.

'Yes, yer'll be a soldier whether you likes it or not,' 'Erbert said, and he turned and winked with easy familiarity at Eve.

She stared past him. She knew that he was doing his utmost to bring her into the conversation, but she wasn't having any! She began to push her way through the crowd thronging the long wide corridor. God, how they were all staring! What a lot of rubber-necks! All here because it was a free show and determined to get everything possible out of it! And, God, how her feet ached on the hot stone flags. She must get some fresh air. She pushed her way outside. The air was scarcely better there, but there were fewer people, and thankfully she leaned against a corrugated iron hut and shut her eyes for a moment.

But she didn't get peace for long. Her relations and the soldier soon joined her. 'We wondered where you'd got to,' her mother said. 'Whatever made you run off like that?'

'It was so hot in there,' Eve said.

'Coo, yes, it is 'ot,' the soldier said. 'What about summat to drink? I could do with summat myself, I could. What about goin' into the NAAFI and 'avin' some lemonade?'

He indicated the canteen, a huge wooden hut from which came sounds of trays rattling and dishes clinking.

'Ee, my, I could do with summat, too,' Aunt Lily said. But her sister-in-law drew back. She frowned at the other woman, indicating half by whispers and half by dumb show that the soldier was going to pay and that they couldn't allow him to treat so many because he couldn't possibly afford it on his small Army pay. 'No, let's leave it just now,' she said. 'Let's see the stables before we get too tired to move.'

Slowly Eve trailed after them. She would gladly have taken the soldier's offer of lemonade even if it had put her at a disadvantage. The sun had slid again behind a shade of smoky clouds but the air was no cooler.

Everything in the stables was spotless, though Eve would hardly have liked, as her mother said, to take her dinner off the floor. Here, it was, if anything, hotter than elsewhere with the added smell of humid horseflesh and dung. The horses were beautifully groomed: sleek necks slippery as snake's skin and polished rumps gleamed like jewels in the setting of each stall.

There was a small table at one of the doors where soldiers were selling small bags of lump-sugar for visitors to feed to the horses. The proceeds were to go to some charity. A soldier was stationed at every third or fourth stall; most of them were making wisps with straw. 'Erbert stopped beside one of them, a tall young fellow with a tanned face. "Ere, Scotty,' he said. 'I wants yer to meet some friends o' mine.' He turned to Aunt Lily and said: "Im an' me oughter change plices. 'E oughter be wearin' the kilt an' I oughter be in the Artillery.'

Scotty grinned shyly but said nothing. Eve noticed how beautiful and white his teeth were; they were as neat and even as false teeth, but they didn't look as if they were false. Surely not, she thought; he can't be any more than twenty. She liked his strong-looking brown neck and the way his small ears grew on his head, and she wished that he hadn't had on his hat. He's a nice-looking boy even although he's a soldier, she thought.

"Ere, I'd better be goin',' 'Erbert said suddenly. 'I'm supposed to be givin' away programmes, not gassin' to people.'

'Ee, my, I 'ope you won't get yourself into trouble,' Aunt Lily said anxiously.

'Not me! Trust little 'Erbert!' He laughed. 'Well I'd better be goin'. Ta, ta! It's been nice meetin' yer. It's not every day I gets the chance of escortin' such beautiful lidies.'

'Get on with yer!' Aunt Lily said, laughing.

'Righto, I will.'

And he did. But he popped his head around the door to give a farewell cry to Eve: 'Smile, Beautiful, smile! An' give the pore Tommies a treat.'

Eve flushed.

'There you are now!' her mother said triumphantly. 'That's what you get for going about with a face like a flitting!' She turned to Scotty and said: 'She's been sulking all afternoon because I made her come here instead of going to the pictures.'

Scotty smiled. Through her anger at her mother, Eve noticed that it was a sympathetic smile and it cheered her a little. But she could have struck her mother and her aunt. She hated them. If they only knew how foolish they looked in their floral frocks and with the perspiration running down their fat cheeks, streaking the powder dabbed so lavishly on their noses. God, she hoped she would never get fat. Even although she had to diet for ever she'd never get like them. They didn't need to laugh at her.

She was glad when Albert said: 'Ma, can I 'ave some sugar to give to the 'orses?'

'I daresay,' his mother said. 'Though I don't 'old with it. All that sugar ain't good for 'em. Ain't it not?' she said to Scotty.

'I don't know,' he said.

'It makes 'em slaver all over their 'arness,' she said. "Owever——'

She rummaged in her bag for pennies for Albert and Gladys.

They all helped to feed the horses except Eve. She leaned against the wall and gazed at the invisible patterns she was drawing on the floor with the toe of her shoe. 'Don't yer want to feed sugar to the 'orses, Evie?' Aunt Lily cried.

'No,' she said.

The soldier smiled at her and she lowered her eyes. She could feel her eyelids pricking as they sometimes did when she was going to burst into tears. She wanted desperately to feed sugar to the horses; to run her hand down their glossy silken necks. But she didn't want to do it before her mother and her aunt and her giggling cousins. She wanted to be alone when she did it—alone except for the soldier. She glanced covertly at him. He was staring at her, his lips half-open. She walked to the door and looked out.

She could have killed her mother and her Aunt Lily. Why had they to be here? Why couldn't she have come here herself? And why did they giggle and chaff the soldier like that? They were only making themselves look ridiculous. And talking to the horses with silly baby-talk—they were worse than Albert and Gladys!

'We'd better hurry up,' she said. 'We'll miss the Red Indian Display if we don't hurry.'

The Red Indian Display was even more important than the horses to her two cousins. They rushed past Eve, crying: 'Come on, ma, come on!'

'It's about time!' Aunt Lily said, looking down ruefully at the slavers on her floral frock. 'Ee, my, you big brute!' she said, shaking her fist at one of the horses. 'If I'd known yer was goin' to do that I wouldn't 'ave given yer no sugar.'

The Red Indian Display was the main feature of the 'At Home'. Already the crowds were flocking to the field where it was to take place, leaving such lesser attractions as the Shooting Range, the Machine-gun Practice, the Gymnasium Display and the Highland Dancing. Benches had been erected all around the field, but there were so many spectators for this free show that most of them couldn't get seats. Soldiers dressed as cowboys and soldiers dressed as Indians were rushing about trying to get seats for those who couldn't get them for themselves. Eve's mother and aunt were among the lucky ones whom they assisted. Eve stood behind them, wondering if she'd be able to stand for long; her feet were on fire. Before the show started

Albert and Gladys demanded ice-cream, and they got it. Eve refused to have any, but the older women sat and licked cornets self-consciously. Eve could not keep from thinking about the brown-faced soldier, Scotty. . . . She wondered what his name was. And she wished again that her mother and her aunt hadn't been with her in the stables. If only Ann had been with her. She began to feel rather guilty about Ann. Maybe this was how Ann had felt in the café at Portobello. But, no, that had been different. This wasn't the same kind of feeling at all. . . .

It was so hot that she felt suffocated; all those people hemmed in around her were choking her. She hoped she wasn't going to faint; her head was aching and she couldn't follow what they were doing in the centre of the field. All that galloping backwards and forwards; nothing but the legs of horses, and men standing on horses's backs, and men jumping off and on horses. She heard her Aunt Lily exclaim: 'Ee, my, ain't that wonderful!' But she couldn't see what was wonderful; everything was blurred. She looked around desperately for a seat, but there was none. 'I can't stand this any longer,' she said in a low voice to her mother. 'I'll meet you outside the canteen when this show's over.'

Her mother called something after her, but she didn't stop to hear what it was; she struggled through the crowd and got out of the field. She went into the NAAFI hut, but she stopped a few yards inside the doorway.

Leaning against the counter, laughing and talking to two soldiers, were Ann and that Cora Roberts creature. Ann didn't see Eve. Half of her face was hidden by the pie she was guzzling, and above it her eyes looked boldly at one of the soldiers. Between bites she was giggling at what he was saying.

Eve turned quickly and hurried out. The sky was overcast again. She thought that she felt a spot of rain on her cheek as she approached one of the doors of the stable. Suddenly she knew that she was glad she'd seen Ann like that. Now she didn't need to feel guilty about her.

There were no visitors in the stable. Two or three soldiers were lounging at the door farthest from the one she went in at. Scotty was leaning against the post of a stall, plaiting straw. He looked up when he heard the tap of her high heels on the stone floor. He smiled.

'Hello,' he said.

'Hello,' she said. And then after a moment's awkward silence she said: 'I've lost my handkerchief. I wonder if I dropped it here?'

'I don't know,' he said. 'I'll see.'

And he began to look about in the straw in the stalls.

She hadn't been in any of them, and she knew that he knew that. But he searched diligently in every stall. He said occasionally: 'It's not there.' But she said nothing; she watched his strong shoulders stooping and the easy way he shoved the horses aside to let him get into their stalls. At last he straightened himself and he pushed back his hat and scratched his head. (So it *was* black and *it was* curly.)

'I'm afraid it's not here,' he said, smiling.

'It doesn't matter,' she said.

'Are you sure?' he said.

She nodded. She looked at him for a while without speaking. Then she smiled. 'Was I very childish a little while ago?' she asked.

He nodded. They both laughed. 'I couldn't help it,' she said. 'I was mad at *them*.'

'I saw that,' he said.

'D'you think I could feed sugar to the horses now?' she said in a tone very like that of a little girl who has been naughty and who wants now to make amends.

'I think so,' he said, grinning.

She bought some sugar from the soldiers at the door. 'Which one will I give it to?' she said to Scotty.

'Give it to Star,' he said. 'He's a special pal of mine. Aren't you, old boy?' he said, smacking the big grey horse on the flank to make it move over.

Timidly, Eve sidled into the stall. She was surprised at the small amount of space between the polished grey barrel of Star's side and the wood of the stall. Scotty followed her and shoved away Star's eager mouth. 'No, just you wait a minute,' he said. 'Mind your manners!' He showed Eve how to hold the sugar in the palm of her hand. While the horse was nuzzling her palm, she put up her other hand and stroked his neck. 'He's lovely,' she said softly to Scotty.

'He's not a bad old codger,' Scotty said, and he patted the horse. 'It's not every day he gets petted by anybody so nice,' he said. 'There's not much time for petting in the Army.' And he drew his hand down the horse's neck until he touched Eve's fingers, letting his hand lie on top of hers.

She shivered ecstatically and laughed. 'His lips are tickling my palm,' she said.

It had got very dark. The stable seemed to fill with a fine black mist. Suddenly there was a peal of thunder. And then there was the rain.

Star plunged at the noise. The other horses followed his example. 'Steady, there,' Scotty cried. He held the horse's head and shoved Eve into the corner.

'Don't be frightened,' he said, 'He won't hurt you.'

'I'm not frightened,' she said.

Scotty stood between her and the trembling horse. She wondered if she was trembling as much as Star; she could see his fine flesh shaking. But she knew that if she were trembling it was from a different cause.

A crowd of people came running into the stables to shelter. Eve looked anxiously for her relations, and she prayed that they would seek other shelter. The horses were kicking and plunging. The loud voices, the laughing and grumbling were such a change from the quiet peace that had been there that Eve sighed. She shivered.'Cold?' Scotty said. She shook her head, but he put his arm around her. She leaned against him. Her head only reached his shoulder and she had to look up at his face. He was staring through the open door above the heads of the bedraggled sightseers at the falling rain. It fell heavily: silver sword-stabs from the sky, streaking the doorway like a beaded curtain. Eve looked away from it to the rough cloth of Scotty's tunic. Beyond him she could see the little hairs on the horse's neck.

'It can't last long,' Scotty said.

'Does that matter?' she said, smiling up at him.

His fingers clamped firmly around her waist. He held her so tightly that he hurt, but she said nothing. They looked out at the rain in silence.

Presently the sky began to clear, and then the rain lessened and finally stopped. The crowd hurriedly left the stable in case they would miss any of the free show. But Scotty didn't take his arm away from Eve's waist, and the girl made no move. She was content to stand like that for ever, if need be. Her headache had gone and her feet no longer troubled her.

'That's cleared the air,' Scotty said. 'Tomorrow will be beautiful.'

There was a burst of firing. Machine-gun practice had started again. Eve shrank nearer to Scotty. She felt terrified suddenly of what all this meant.

'Will it?' she said.

TOMORROW WILL BE BEAUTIFUL was published in John Lehmann's *New Writing:* New Series, number one, in the autumn of 1938. It was in Fred Urquhart's first collection *I Fell For A Sailor* (Duckworth, 1940) and in *Penguin New Writing*, number 8, edited by John Lehmann, published in July 1941.

5 *Washed in the Blood*

I REMEMBER THAT once I wanted to be saved. When I was a little girl a black Revivalist came to our village and converted a lot of the villagers. He had a tent pitched on the village-green, and every night he stood outside it and cried to everybody to come and be washed in the blood of the lamb. Always he drew a crowd around him; partly because most of them had nothing better to do, and partly because his blackness was strange. We children especially never got tired of gaping at his shiny black face; his strangeness seemed to us something desirable and romantic.

The men who stood and gossiped and smoked every night at the bridge used to laugh when the Nigger came and began his oration, 'Ay, man,' they would cry. 'How many souls have ye saved the day? Has another auld wife got doon on her knees and seen the light?' But the Nigger never took any notice of them. He grinned and stood on top of a box outside his tent, which was plastered with Biblical messages, and he would begin to deliver his message to suffering humanity. And soon the inevitable crowd would gather around him, even the men at the bridge gradually drawing nearer in a sheepish fashion. 'Just in case we miss onythin' guid,' they would remark to each other in excuse.

Only one of them always remained seated on the wall of the bridge, and that was Nessie McEndrick's father. Jamie McEndrick never moved from his seat. He puffed at his clay pipe and spat occasionally into the greenish-brown water far beneath him. He was the village joiner and carpenter, a big stout man with a brosey red face. He always sat still, his blue-striped shirt showing between his unbuttoned waistcoat and the bulging top of his trousers, and when he was very drunk he would cry out things about the Nigger and the Polar. I didn't know what he meant then, but I would know now.

The Polar was Mrs Campbell who cleaned the school and kept lodgers. She was a widow, a huge stout shapeless woman with dirty white hair screwed into a bun on top of her head. She was usually dressed in a dirty whitish-grey overall, and it was this overall that had earned her the name of the Polar. Somebody had seen her bending down one day and had remarked that she looked like a big dirty Polar bear, and the name had stuck.

Besides keeping lodgers and cleaning the school, the Polar had a Cyclists' Rest. There was a crudely-printed notice on a board beside her door: CYCLISTS REST. TEA AND REFRESHMENTS. The Polar was tireless in finding ways to make enough to keep herself and her family. They were a shiftless lot. There was Willie the Polar who was two classes ahead of me at school. He was supposed to be half-daft; though as some people said, 'You would have a job touching the daft bit!' Occasionally the Polar's Soldier came home. He was a fine-looking young man who had served in the Boer War and had elected to remain in the army. He was the only one of the Polar's family about whom I ever heard my mother say a good word. I had a school-girlish crush on him. He was tall and, in my young and inexperienced eyes, romantic-looking. I daresay that if I'd been older I wouldn't have given him a second thought. If I saw him now I'd probably think him common. But then I spent a lot of time thinking about him, and for years I kept a post-card that he once sent me—why God alone knows, because he hardly ever had taken notice of me in the village, and his family and mine were not on what you'd call speaking terms. It was a gaudily coloured view of Salisbury Plain, and on it was written: 'Here on manoeuvres for two weeks. Hope you are well. I am in the pink. Your friend, B. Campbell.' Lastly there was Bella the Polar, a gawky girl in her teens. She was in service, but she was more often at home between jobs than she was employed. She didn't seem able to keep jobs. 'And no wonder!' my mother said: 'Who would keep a slut like that in their kitchen? But what else could you expect with a mother like that?'

My mother never spoke to the Polar, and she would not have dreamed of eating anything out of the Polar's house. I remember that once the Polar made toffee, and Willie the Polar canvassed for orders at the school. Everybody was buying it—out of pity, I suppose, for the Polar's penury—and I wanted to be upsides with everybody else; I hated to be different from the other children. I begged my mother to buy some, but she wouldn't. 'I'll toffee you!' she said. 'I wouldn't eat one mouthful that came out of that woman's house.'

My mother was what was called a bit uppish in the village, and she had few friends. Not that she saw the need to have any. She had her husband and her children to look after, and she was satisfied with doing that. She said that she hadn't any time for Revivalist meetings and nonsense like that.

During the short time he stayed with her, the Nigger was the

Polar's favourite lodger. It was the Polar who first gave us children a row for calling him the Nigger.

'Ye should be ashamed o' yersels,' she said. 'Cryin' decent folk names like that. If I hear ony o' ye callin' him onythin' but Mr Abdul after this, I'll sort ye.'

It was the Polar who learned that Mr Abdul came from Abyssinia. 'It's just ower the hill frae Egypt,' she explained to somebody. 'He says that he's goin' to take oor Willie back wi' him when he goes. Oor Willie's awfu' keen to be a missionary.'

I heard Jamie McEndrick say that the Polar had learned lots of other things about the Nigger besides this, but when I asked my mother what sort of things, she told me not to be inquisitive. 'Bairns should be seen and not heard,' she said.

We children used to crowd around Mr Abdul every night and listen to his exhortations, and it wasn't long until nearly every child in the village was saved. Every one of them wanted to go with him to Abyssinia to be a missionary like Willie the Polar. We were all sure that we would be much better missionaries than him.

Pretty soon everybody was saved except me and my little brother, Archie. We would have been saved too, only our mother wouldn't let us. She forbade us even to go near the mission tent.

I pleaded and argued with her. 'Why can't I be saved?' I asked. 'Everybody else is getting saved but me. Lizzie Macdonald and Bessie Simpson and Nessie McEndrick—everybody in my class is getting saved. Even Murdo Anderson, and you know how wild he is. Why can't I get saved, too?'

'Because you can't, that's all,' my mother would say. 'Now get out of here and don't let me hear any more about it. Away along to Mrs Irving's and get me five pounds of sugar and a bar of yellow soap.'

But nothing that my mother said could damp me. I saw how happy all the other children were after they had been saved, and I wanted to join them in their happiness. They still looked the same as usual, but I knew they couldn't be the same. Inside they must be different. Only something wonderful inside them could make them pray and sing like that inside the tent every night. None of them had ever prayed and sung in the same way in the drab Parish Church. Except Murdo Anderson, and he had always been up to some mischief under the book-board in the Anderson pew in the gallery. All the others, however, had always been quiet and frightened-looking. But here around the Nigger, warmed by his wide grin and ever-spread arms, they leaped and shouted joyfully, frisking like the new-born lambs the Nigger said they were. And the more they frisked and sang the more deeply I wanted to frisk and sing with them. I felt like a pariah, out in the cold.

And so, although my mother had forbidden it, I used to sneak out of the house every night and go down to the green. I hovered about the outskirts of the crowd around the door of the tent, and above their heads and shoulders I could see Mr Abdul's face, grinning and sweating with love and tenderness. The sight of it heartened me and made me forget my fears of being found out. 'Come unto Jesus all ye who labour and are cast down,' he would cry. And under the soothing magic of his voice, impelled by his wild dark eyes, those sedate Scottish ploughmen and villagers, the product of generations of Calvinism, would cry 'Hallelujah!' and get down on their knees, moaning and recounting their sins. And then they would enter the tent: accepted into the bosom of the Lord. They were the Elect, and I wanted passionately to be one of them. I wanted to enter the tent, too, to become part of the mass; to think as they did, to do what they did and to have the same emotions at the same time.

Almost the entire village was soon filled with an air of religious ecstasy, and people were going about calling each other Brother and Sister.

Our household was one of the few that was not saved. My mother rigidly set her lips against it. 'A lot of havers,' she said. 'As if the auld Scottish kirk and the Reverend Mr McIver wasn't guid enough for most o' them.'

The Rev Mr McIver also had something to say about it. He saw his congregation growing smaller and smaller every Sunday. 'Something must be done about it,' he said to my father who was one of the chief elders.

'Ay, but what?' My father began to scratch his head, but he stopped when he remembered that he was speaking to the minister. 'It's no' as if it was a heathen religion he was teachin' them.'

'That's right.' Mr McIver tapped his thin lips with the tips of his soft white fingers. 'It's not as if it were Buddhism or Mohammedanism or any of those new-fangled things . . .'

The Rev Mr McIver began to come to our house often after this, and he and my father would sit and talk in low voices in the front parlour, stopping their conversation whenever anybody went near the door. My mother warned my brother and me that we were not to go in. 'Out ye go and play,' she would say.

This I was always glad to do. And gradually I would play farther and farther away from the house, until when I thought I was far enough out of sight and hearing, I would make for the village-green. And when I got there I would skulk around the outside of the tent, listening to the joyous Hallelujahs and Hosannas that sounded from within. And all the time, although I wanted desperately to creep in, too, I was terrified to do so in case some woman like ourselves who was not saved and who remained faithful to Mr McIver's preaching might tell my mother that I was one of the Nigger's followers. It was galling to remain outside the tent, but much as I wanted to become part of the swaying and singing mass inside, my fear of my mother was stronger than any pleasure I might have obtained from it. And so I remained near the bridge, and I often heard Jamie McEndrick's drunken remarks about the Nigger and the Polar.

Of all the men who had been in the habit of gathering at the bridge after they came out of the pub, Jamie McEndrick alone remained. They said that he was almost the only customer the publican had left; the Nigger had saved the others. But as if to make up for the others' default, Jamie drank more than ever. Many a night my attention wandered between the sounds that came from the tent and the antics and roars of the drunk man. I used to shiver in the darkness, knowing that I should have been home and in bed long before, knowing that I would get a row for being out so late, and yet afraid to move, fascinated by the two rival attractions. Often he nearly fell over the bridge when he got caught in a drunken frenzy of denunciation against Mr Abdul and his prophetic teaching. I began to dislike Jamie very much; I felt that he was an evil man, and I wouldn't have been sorry if he had fallen into the burn. It seemed to my childlike mind that the tent and he represented good and evil, and I passionately wanted the evil to be exterminated, even though it was just in the person of the drunken joiner. I realise now that this was a thought of which Mr Abdul would probably not have approved.

After Mr Abdul had been in the village a few weeks and had converted everybody but a few faithful Auld Kirkers, the Polar started a Sunday School for those children who were saved. I see now that religious fervour alone could not have accounted for this; the Polar always had an eye to money-making. Though what money she could have made out of her Sunday School I cannot imagine.

I urged my mother to allow my brother and me to go. 'Everybody's going to it,' I said. 'All the girls in my class are going. Bessie Simpson and Nessie McEndrick . . .'

'Nessie McEndrick?' my mother said. 'Her father should be ashamed of himself.'

'Can I go?' I pleaded.

'No, you can't go,' she said. 'And that's final.'

There were only a few children remaining at the Parish Church Sunday School, and it seemed a dull place compared with what I heard about the Polar's Sunday School. She held it in her parlour, and the children sang while the Polar pounded hymns on her wheezy old organ. Murdo Anderson boasted to everybody that he had been allowed to play the organ and that Mr Abdul had given him his blessing. 'I'm maybe goin' to Abyssinia to be a missionary, too,' he said. 'I'd be a better missionary than Willie the Polar.' This made me more passionately anxious to go, but no matter what I did to please my mother she would not allow me to go.

Archie wanted to go, too; he was as keen to be saved as I was, but for different reasons. He wanted to go to Abyssinia with Murdo Anderson and Willie the Polar. 'But we'll get rid o'daft Willie quick,' he said. 'I hope a tiger eats him.' He talked a lot about the elephants and lions he was going to shoot. It never seemed to occur to him that being a missionary was something quite different. But this had occurred to me. I wanted to nurse the little black children and pray for their souls; I wanted to pray that they would never be unhappy and outcasts as I was an outcast at that time. I wanted them to bask in the radiance of Mr Abdul's smile and to sing Hosannas with the other children. That I was apart from the others at that moment did not matter; I knew it was only temporary. I knew that soon I would be one of them. I would be saved and I would go with Mr Abdul to Abyssinia to be a missionary. I knew it would be a hard life, a precarious life, and that I might never see my mother and father again. But that did not matter. I would be a missionary and I would do good. Archie, however, though he was keen to be a missionary, too, did not seem to think of the dangers and hardships. Apparently his immediate desire was to go to the Sunday School because he heard from the other boys that the Polar gave them sweeties to eat between hymns.

But our mother said: 'Enough of this nonsense. You're not going one foot. I dare you to step inside that woman's dirty house.'

Finally Archie made the awful suggestion. 'We'll skip our own Sunday School,' he said, 'and we'll go to the Polar's.'

I was horrified, but not as horrified as I should have been. For the same idea had struck me, though I had been too afraid to mention it to Archie.

The following Sunday when we came out of the kirk, we stayed behind as usual in the church-yard, and our parents left us. 'Have you got your halfpennies for the bag?' my mother said, although she knew quite well that we had. But it was a question that she asked every Sunday, a sort of ritual, every bit as important as the actual going to kirk and Sunday School.

We nodded.

'And have ye got a clean hankie, Archie?' she said. 'See that he keeps his nose clean, Thomasina.'

'Yes, mother,' I said.

We stood beside old Sandy Irving's grave and we waited until they were out of sight, my mother's long black skirt sending the dust up over my father's highly-polished black boots and narrow trousers. While we waited, we traced our fingers over the lettering on the new granite stone. *Sacred to the Memory of Alexander Ramsay Irving. Born 3rd July 1820. Died 4th April, 1905.*

'Now,' Archie whispered.

We looked to see that neither the beadle nor the minister were at the kirk door and that none of the small congregation still standing about in groups were watching us; and we ran across the churchyard and climbed the style that led into Ned Purdie's orchard. We skirted through it, watching warily for Ned or his old dog, Snatcher. I was terrified of Snatcher, but I was so anxious to be saved that I would have dared a dozen Snatchers in order to go to the Polar's Sunday School.

We were almost out of the orchard when we heard a bark. 'Come on!' Archie cried, and he grabbed my hand and hauled me after him. I clutched my muff and prayed that I wouldn't let it fall. It was a white ermine muff that I had got from my Aunt Minnie and I was very proud of it because none of the other girls had muffs. The branch of a tree caught my large white leghorn hat and whipped it off my head, but the elastic band under my chin held it. I was so terrified of Snatcher and so intent upon running that I didn't feel any pain when the elastic nipped into my throat. 'Quick, Ina!' Archie gasped. 'Through here.'

We scrambled through the hedge. My long curls that my mother had twisted so patiently into curl-papers the evening before got caught in the hawthorn, but I jerked them loose. My ribbon was dangling; I tore it off in case it would fall. I panted across the field after Archie.

'We're all right now,' he said.

We leaned against the gable of an old stable, breathless with our exertions. 'You should see yourself, Ina,' Archie grinned. 'You aren't half a sight!'

'You're a sight yourself,' I said.

We tidied each other's clothes, then we began to walk sedately towards the Polar's, going the back way and keeping careful watch in case anybody saw us. As we edged round the Polar's house we heard the sound of singing and the pealing of the organ.

'We're late,' I whispered. 'It's started.'

Archie tugged my skirt and whispered: 'Let's look in the window first.'

I held his hand and we peered in the parlour window. I saw Murdo Anderson bawling loudly, a beatific look on his snub-nosed face. The Nigger was playing the organ, and the Polar was standing in the middle of the floor. Her arms were held wide and she lifted them up and down as she led the singing:

'Are you washed? Are you washed? Are you washed in the blood of the lamb?'

I closed my eyes and swayed with the rhythm. This was what I wanted: this being part of a crowd, all feeling the same emotion at the same time. I moved towards the door, eager to get inside and to become even more welded into the mass. I put out my hand for Archie, but he drew back.

He tittered, and then to my horror he began to sway his arms, imitating the Polar. And he twisted his face into a caricature of hers. 'Are you washed . . .?' He couldn't sing for giggling.

I made a dive at him, but he drew back, and then when I clenched my fists, he ran away laughing. I ran after him, but he was faster than I was. I had already run so much and my high black lacing-boots were hurting me so much that I couldn't make up on him. I was furious. He was making a mock of something that I knew to be precious and holy.

I went back to the window, but my tears of rage clouded my vision. I pressed my face against the pane, realising dimly that more than the glass separated me from the joyous crowd inside. I wanted desperately to go inside, but I hadn't the courage to go without Archie. It was galling to remain outside, an outcast.

I sank my teeth into my lips to keep me from crying aloud at the sight of their happy faces. The singing stopped and they left their places and crowded around the Polar. She engulfed as many of them as she could in her outspread arms. I heard cries of 'Tell us a story, Mrs Campbell.' I strained my ears, afraid I would miss anything, and I watched them enviously. Mr Abdul was sitting at the organ, smiling at them all, his hands lying loosely on the keys. I ached to stand beside him, to have him put his hand in blessing on my head. And I wished passionately that I could become clean and saint-like like him and go with him when he went back to Abyssinia.

'Tell us a story, Mrs Campbell!' The cry came from all corners of the room, and the Polar smiled and nodded at them. I pressed myself against the window, trying to warm myself from her love through the dirty glass. I wished that her arm was around me as it was around Nessie McEndrick.

The Polar closed her eyes and held her face up to the ceiling as if praying for divine guidance. The children watched eagerly, their eyes wide with expectation.

'The Lord Jesus was a carpenter,' she cried. 'He was the son of a carpenter, and he became a carpenter himself, just like—just like little Nessie McEndrick's father . . .'

I stood back horrified. I remembered the things that I had heard Jamie McEndrick say at the bridge. And slowly I turned and went home. I no longer wanted to be saved. And I've never wanted to be saved since.

WASHED IN THE BLOOD was written in the summer of 1940 and published in Denys Kilham Roberts's *Penguin Parade*, number 10, in January 1944. It appeared in Urquhart's second collection of stories *The Clouds are Big With Mercy* (William Maclellan, 1946) and was in *The Dying Stallion*, the first volume of his *Collected Stories* (Rupert Hart-Davis, 1967). It was broadcast on BBC Scotland on 19 March 1970, read by Joan Fitzpatrick and produced by Stewart Conn.

6 *The Dying Stallion*

THE STALLION WAS in one field, the two mares in another; an empty field separated them. The stallion stood in the corner beside the gate, his neck out-stretched, his tail held high. The mares bunched in the corner nearest him, whinnying enticingly. Suddenly the stallion reared and, wheeling quickly, he set off at a gallop round the field. In the middle he stopped, reared again, then set off at full gallop towards the gate. He leaped . . .

Old William Petrie of Duncraggie Mains was standing at the door of his potato store. His sons-in-law, Dick Jeffreys and Bill Johnston, were examining his Arran Pilot seed, discussing it, comparing it unfavourably with their own. Petrie was not listening. The two young men did this every Saturday afternoon. He was staring at a puddle in the middle of the close.

'Here's trouble!' he cried when the three horses came galloping around the corner of the steading. He rushed into the middle of the close, trying to stop them. But they swerved and galloped down past the silo. The old man shouted and began to run after them. Men appeared from odd corners, following him. But his sons-in-law did not exert themselves; they ambled after the old man, grinning at each other, still talking about the quality of their Arran Pilots.

By the time they reached the corner of the field beside the silo the stallion and the two mares had been cornered. Old Petrie and the first horseman were putting a halter on the stallion. 'Ay, ye've had a run the day, laddie,' the old man said, patting the beast's satiny black neck. 'There now, there,' he muttered soothingly as the animal plunged with excitement when the mares were led away. 'We canna have this. Ye canna go wi' yer own mother!'

'What're the bandages on his legs for?' Dick said, straddling with his hands in the pockets of his tight khaki breeches, eyeing the stallion.

'His hocks were a bittie weak,' the old man said. 'So the vet put them on yesterday. They werena that weak that ye couldna leap that gate, though, were they, ye rascal?' He laughed, slapping the beast's neck.

'Ye wouldna like to ride him across to the stable, Dick?' he said, thinking how well his huge young son-in-law would look on the big horse.

But Dick laughed and said: 'No, no, Mr Petrie, I wouldna trust myself on his back. I dinna like the look o' that brute. Horses are just beasts I have no use for. Ye ken that fine.'

'Come on then, laddie,' Petrie said, stroking the stallion's nose and leading him away. 'Young men arenie what they were in ma young days. I wouldna hae needed a second invitation to back a fine strappin' cratur' like yersel'. But young men arenie what they were . . .'

The old man stayed for a while in the loose box, helping the first horseman to rub down the stallion. Apart from the fact that he was sweating a lot, the stallion seemed none the worse for his adventure. The old man was in no hurry to go into the house. He knew that his two unmarried daughters and their married sisters would be screaming at each other all over the house. After a while one of his grandchildren came out to tell him to come in for his tea.

They were half-way through the tea when the maid came to tell the old man that the first horseman wanted to see him in the kitchen. 'He's nae pleased wi' the looks o' the staig,' she said.

Petrie made to rise, but a chorus from his daughters pushed him down. 'Finish your tea in peace,' they shrieked. 'Your horse can wait.'

'That's the beauty o' tractors,' Dick said, shoving a huge lump of cake into his grinning mouth. 'If they do break down they dinna need instant attention. Ye'll have to get tractors, Mr Petrie. I dinna see why ye winna put yer horses awa'. Great big smelly brutes, I canna be doin' wi' them.'

Petrie never answered, though Bill helped Dick in baiting him. He gulped down his tea, and as soon as it was polite he rose. Dick and Bill rose, too, pushing back their chairs noisily, grinning at each other. 'We'd better go and help the old man to mourn, laddie,' Dick said, putting his arm round Bill's shoulder and drawing him to the door.

The stallion was lying on his back, rolling about on the floor of his loose box. He held his legs stiffly in the air, and every now and then he would stretch out his neck, biting in the region of his belly, trying to bite the bandages that bound his hind legs. The four men stood and watched him. 'I dinna like the looks o' him at all, Wullie,' the first horseman said to Petrie. 'I doot he's hurt himsel' someway when he jumpit that gate.'

'Ay, he's dyin', I doot,' the old man said. 'I never saw a horse in such a bad way.'

'Havers,' Dick said. 'It's just wind that's botherin' him. Listen to him fartin'. He's just got a pain in the guts.' He seized old Petrie's stick and poked the stallion in the belly. 'Up, man!' he roared. 'Get up ye lazy swine! Up! Up!' He whacked the stallion across the belly and the haunches. 'Up, ye lazy devil, up!'

The stallion made an effort to rise, but fell back, snorting with exhaustion. His huge body writhed about among the straw and dung, his hide glistening with sweat. His eyes rolled wildly; his neck curved like a snake as he tried to reach his hind legs.

Old Petrie went towards him, speaking softly. 'What ails ye, laddie? Have ye hurt yersel', man? Come on then, up ye get, laddie, Up ye get, like a good boy.'

Dick pulled him back roughly. 'D'ye want to get hurt, Mr Petrie?' he shouted. He reached out with the stick, careful not to get within reach of the stallion's floundering legs, and he whacked the beast across the belly again. 'Get up, ye big lazy swine!' he roared. 'Get up when ye're bid. Up! Up!' And he slashed the beast across the genitals.

'Ay, I thought that would make ye rise,' he said triumphantly when the horse nickered with pain and with a supreme effort staggered to his feet. 'There's nothin' like kennin' the right place to hit a beast—or a man, for that matter!' he laughed, nudging Bill.

The horse stood shaking his head. His body was trembling. He began to move towards the men—for sympathy, old Petrie knew— lifting his hind legs high. He stretched out his nose towards them. Dick stepped back, lifting the stick threateningly. 'Get away, ye nasty brute, get away!'

But old Petrie reached out and stroked the beast's nose. 'Poor laddie,' he muttered. 'There's somethin' far wrong wi' ye, man.' He patted his neck, sliding his hand soothingly up and down the withers. 'There, laddie, there, ye'll soon be all right again.'

'Awa' in and phone the vet, Bill,' he said.

'There's no need,' Dick said. 'Ye'll just be wasting yer siller. Cut the bandages off his legs. That's what's wrong wi' him. They're too tight. See he's aye bitin' at them. It's that and a sore guts that's wrong wi' him. See, there he is, fartin' again.'

'Go and phone for the vet, Bill,' old Petrie said again.

He stood, stroking the horse about the head and neck, speaking softly to him, while Dick told the first horseman in a loud voice what he considered was wrong with the animal. He stood well back from it, one hand in his breeches pocket, the other caressing his bottom. Every time the horse moved towards him he shooed it away, shouting: 'Get away, ye nasty brute!'

The vet arrived in about half an hour and took off the bandages. 'Though it's not them that's hurting him,' he said. 'I don't know what it is, but we'll give him a shot to quieten him.'

Holding the stallion's head while the vet pushed the needle into him, the old man was surprised that the horse did not give a plunge. 'Poor laddie,' he said softly. 'Ye're worn out.'

The vet said he'd come back in an hour or two to see how things were. 'But frankly I don't like the look of him, Mr Petrie,' he said. 'I don't think he'll last till morning.'

Bill and Dick went into the house to play cards with another brother-in-law who had just arrived. The old man, feeling that he could no longer bear to see the horse's pain, went into the stable and sat there in the darkness. He felt comforted by the sounds the other horses made, moving and champing in their stalls. He knew that his three hefty sons-in-law would be playing three-handed bridge in front of the fire while all around them their wives and sisters-in-law would be shrieking to each other about food and Women's Guild meetings and about how few eggs their hens were laying. The wireless would be on full blast, but nobody would be listening to it. And the children would be screaming and running out and in, banging doors. And every now and then Dick would yell: 'Get to hell out of here, the whole lot of you.' Everybody, including the children, would think this a great joke.

About ten o'clock the vet came back and examined the stallion again. 'He's ruptured himself when he leapt that gate,' he said.

The old man stood in the corner of the loose box, watching the horse walking round and round in a circle. He was thinking of his son who had been killed at Dunkirk, and who was the only one in the family who had tastes like his own. Dimly he was aware that Bill and Dick and his other son-in-law, James, had come in. They stood, hunched in their greatcoats, keeping well back from the circling horse. The vet stood in the middle, watching it. The animal moved slowly, like a dream horse in a circus, lifting his legs stiffly. Nobody spoke. The only sounds in the place were the deep breathing of the horse and the heavy slow pounding of his hoofs. Even in his dejection there was something magnificent about him. He completely dwarfed the three hefty young men who stood staring compassionless at him.

The vet began to explain to them what was wrong with the horse. 'I doubt he's finished,' he said. 'He'll never be any use again.'

The old man sat down, crouching in misery on the lid of the corn-bin, not listening to what the vet was saying. He felt numb and finished. He watched the horse unseeingly as it circled more and more slowly round the loose box, head drooping, once-proud haunches caving in, tail hanging slackly. The glossy hide was beginning to lose lustre. The large dark eyes were growing dim and pathetic. The old man wanted to stretch out his hands and touch the animal, willing to give all his own dying vigour to revive it, but he was afraid of the ridicule of the young men. As if wakening from a dream, he heard Dick address him. He tried to rouse himself when the young man shouted his name. He shook his head, straightening his shoulders. 'Ay?' he said.

'Ye'd better cut him,' Dick said, 'and yoke him to a cart.'

THE DYING STALLION was written in January 1944 and published in September by Robert Herring in *Life & Letters Today*. It was then published in the March–April 1946 issue of Whit Burnett's *Story* (USA). It was included in Urquhart's *Selected Stories* (Maurice Fridberg's Hour Glass Library, 1946) and then was the title story of the first volume of his *Collected Stories* (Rupert Hart-Davis, 1967).

7 The Moley was a Diddler

THE MOLEY WAS the champion diddler in the countryside. He said this with great pride to young Mrs Lindsay on the first day he came to Mill of Sponden to catch moles. Mrs Lindsay was rather taken aback; she was a city girl, newly married to the farmer, and she had never heard anybody in the town being quite so frank about their shortcomings. Besides, she thought, the Moley looked disrespectful enough without blowing about it. He was a short broadset man with a weather-beaten face and a bushy black-and-grey beard. A greasy flat bonnet sat straightly on top of his bald head, seeming to be held up by the flaps of his large red blue-veined ears. He wore an old raincoat, fastened at the neck by a large safety pin; it was pressed out like a balloon-barrage by his enormous stomach.

'But how do you manage to do it?' Mrs Lindsay said politely.

'Well, I diddles and I diddles,' he said proudly. 'I'm aye diddlin' everywhere I goes. I diddles all the time I'm workin'. Everybody for miles around kens the Diddlin' Moley. Whenever they hear anybody diddlin' they cock up their lugs and say, "Here comes the Moley!"'

Mrs Lindsay was more mystified than ever. But enlightenment crept into her face when the Moley said:

'Look, I'll diddle for ye right now!' And he began to make weird sounds: 'Da de da da de da da de da diduddyo!'

'Dae ye ken fut tune that is?' he asked at the end.

Mrs Lindsay shook her head. The Moley hawked and spat triumphantly. 'You toon lassies! Ye dinna ken the guid auld tunes when ye hear them. That was *The Weddin' o' McGinnis and His Cross-Eyed Pet.*'

'A real guid auld tune,' he said. 'Many a diddlin' competition have I won wi' diddlin' that. I diddled it at ma ain weddin', and I mind the wife was real affronted at me. "Ye'd think it was me ye was meanin'," she says. "What'll fowk think?" But I tellt her never to mind what fowk thought. Ye'll nae get verra far in this world if ye're aye botherin' yersel' about what fowk are thinkin'.'

'However,' he said. 'the wife's gotten ower it. She's real prood o' me and ma diddlin'. And so is the laddie. He's in the sodgers, and he

44

tells a'body he meets about his father, the Diddlin' Moley. Him and his mother are real proud o' me. And well they might be! I've won every diddlin' competition for miles around for the last thirty years. If that's nae a record I'll eat ma bunnet!'

Mrs Lindsay said she was sure it must be a record; she had no wish to see the Moley attempting to eat his bonnet; the sight of it nearly made her sick.

'How many moles have you caught today?' she said.

'Just a dozen,' he said. 'Just a dozen. Moles, like the fowk, are nae fut they used tae be in ma young days. They're gettin' fly, too! I'll nae get much for this lot, I dinna think.'

He dived into the 'poacher's pocket' of his waterproof and took out two or three dead moles. Mrs Lindsay shuddered when she saw them lying so still and helpless in his huge grimy palm, their piteous pink paws stuck up in the air as if trying to shield their tiny faces from the outer world. She could not help shivering; they were so rat-like. For years she had wanted a mole fur coat. She had wanted to rub her cheek against the soft fur. But now she thought of it with horror. It would be like having rats running up and down her spine . . .

'How do you catch them?' she said, turning away.

'Well, it's like this,' he said, taking a small bottle out of his waistcoat pocket. 'I takes a wee droppie o' this strychinine and I puts it on a worm. Then I walks along between the mounds where the moleys ha'e their holes, and I presses down ma foot and says till masel', "Just there!" And I takes ma stick and presses it down, and puts the worm in the hole. And that's how I catches them,' he said.

'Well, well,' he said. 'I maun awa' hame and see Mother and get ma tatties! I'll be seein' ye the morn!'

And away he went, diddling to himself. Mrs Lindsay stood and looked after him for a few minutes, then she went inside to make her husband's tea.

The Moley was at Mill of Sponden for several days, going about the fields, pacing between the mole-hills, pressing down his stick with determination and putting his poisoned worms in the holes he made. Every night he would stop at the back-door of the farmhouse and proudly show young Mrs Lindsay his day's catch. And every night he told her stories about his wife and his son and the Diddling competitions he'd won. Mrs Lindsay looked forward to a gossip with him every night, though she did not like him to show her the dead moles. 'Ah, but moles are nae what they used to be,' he said every night when he put them back in his pocket. 'And neither are fowk.'

'Even diddlers,' he said one night. 'Man, lassie, I was at a diddlin' competition last night and I wouldna ha'e seen ane o' the other diddlers in ma road. I went hame last night soakit through after bein' oot after the moleys a' day, and I says til ma wife, "Well, I maun awa' to Clovey to diddle at the competition there." She says, "Ye're daft, man, to ging oot on such a night." But I didna mind ava. I just jumpit on ma bike and cycled the fifteen mile to Clovey, and when I got intil the hall I had a bit look round me and when I saw whae a' was there I just leaned back and says till masel', "The prize is mine."'

'And was it?' Mrs Lindsay said.

The Moley snorted. 'Need ye ask, lassie, need ye ask! Of course, it was mine. Whae else in the countryside can diddle as well as me?'

He shook his head. 'Ah, but a prize isna everythin'. When I came hame the wife was sleepin', so I didna see her to tell her about it till this mornin', and afore I was up the Post had been wi' a letter to say that the laddie had been taken prisoner.'

'Oh, isn't that dreadful,' Mrs Lindsay said.

'Ay.' He hawked and spat. 'The wife's real put out about it. She's awfa fond of the laddie.'

Mrs Lindsay stood, undecided about what to say. Words of sympathy seemed so inadequate. 'Just a minute,' she said.

She rushed into the kitchen and opened the oven-door.

The cake she had spent all afternoon baking specially for her husband's tea was just ready. She took it out tenderly and placed it on her last piece of grease-proof paper. Then she put it in a box and wrapped it up carefully. 'Take that home to your wife,' she said to the Moley. 'And tell her not to worry too much. The war can't last for ever.'

'Thank ye, thank ye,' he said. 'Ye're a fine lassie. Mother'll be awfa pleased wi' this. I maun diddle ye a tune for bein' sae kind.'

While he diddled *A Pair O' Nicky Tams*, Mrs Lindsay leaned against the door, her eyes clouded, thinking of the mother who had just lost her son. Of course, he would come back to her . . . it wasn't as if he'd been killed like so many other women's sons . . . But when and in what shape would he come back?

After the Moley had gone away, diddling, with the parcel in his 'poacher's pocket' beside the moles, Mrs Lindsay still leaned against the door, thinking . . .

She was still there when her husband came in from the steading at lousing-time. 'Well, well, lass!' he said cheerily. 'What are ye standin' there for, lookin' like a dyin' duck in a thunderstorm? Come on awa' inside and let's ha'e oor tea. I've been lookin' forrit a' afternoon to that cake ye've been bakin'.'

Mrs Lindsay sighed. 'I'm sorry, dear, but . . .'

Her husband laughed, 'Dinna tell me ye've burned it! Oh, lassie, lassie! Ye will try yer hand at makin' cakes!'

'No, it's not that,' she said. 'I gave it to the Moley. His son has just been made a prisoner, and I gave him the cake to take home for his wife.'

'His son taken prisoner!' Lindsay began to laugh. 'Oh, lassie, lassie! I wonder what it is that the Moley has got about him that diddles a' the weemen-fowk? His wife! He's nae married, ye gowk! He bides a' by himsel' in a wee bothy doon by the Guthrie Water. He's the biggest diddler in the whole countryside . . .'

THE MOLEY WAS A DIDDLER was published in *Tribune* on 13 November 1942 and then in Urquhart's *Selected Stories* (Maurice Fridberg's Hour Glass Library, 1946). It was broadcast by the BBC on 21 July 1950, read by A M Shinnie.

8 *Beautiful Music*

LIZZIE, THE MAID at the Barns of Dallow, was skirling as she washed the tea dishes. Mrs Moyes, reading Virginia Woolf in the sitting-room, could hear her tuneless voice accompanying the rattle of the china along the long stone passage. And she smiled at Lizzie's choice of song. 'Every night should be filled with beautiful music. The stars should be shining on high . . .'

'It's a night made for love,' she hummed, turning a page. 'All in favour say Ay!'

'All in favour say Ay!' Lizzie shrilled triumphantly as her fingers, like rationed red sausages, swirled through the soapy water and brought out the last saucer. She pulled the plug and leaned on the window-sill, looking dreamily out at the court. She was a hefty girl of seventeen with a wall eye. Her dirty overall was stretched across her broad hips; her bare legs were splashed with dried dung. Her wide mouth slid up over her big yellow teeth when she saw young Chae Niven come out of the barn and go to the pump. She watched the short golden hairs glistening on his sun-reddened neck as he bent down to take a drink. And she sighed and reached for the dish-towel. She'd tried nae handy to get Chae to take her to the pictures, but he aye went with the other loons. She'd heard that he was after the maid at the Mains, though she'd never seen him with her. And until she had she wasn't going to give up hope.

It was lousing-time. The men were coming in from the fields. Old Ake clattered into the dairy beside the kitchen with his milk-pail. 'Ay, ay, Lizzie!' he cried. 'Ye're busy!'

'Ay, ay,' she said.

'For the picters the nicht?'

'Ay fairly.'

'Ha'e ye got somebody to sleeve ye the noo?'

Lizzie grinned and said 'Ay, ay,' though she would be going only with Bella Annandale, the maid from the next farm. But it wouldn't do to tell old Ake that. He was a right coarse old tink, Ake, and you weren't safe with him. It needed a real coarse quaen like Maggie Jane Cowie to settle his hash. Now if only Chae had been a bit more like him . . .

'Oh, Lizzie!' Mrs Moyes ran along the passage, her pretty young face aglow with excitement. 'There's two officers in the sitting-room wondering if we could billet some soldiers for the night. Have you seen Ian—er—Mr Moyes—anywhere?'

'I saw him ging intil the byre a while syne,' Lizzie said.

And she scurried quickly in search of the farmer, eager to get inside again to get a bit keek at the officers. As soon as she had told Mr Moyes she ran inside, pulling off her hair-net and patting her hair into place. Although she could hear him already coming in the back-door she opened the sitting-room door and said: 'He'll be here the now.'

They were nice like loons. The one with the red face and the wee fair moustache looked a real lad. She wondered if he would be staying in the house. 'Oh, every night should be filled with beautiful music,' she sang loudly, beginning hurriedly to prepare the mash for the hens.

She was taking the pailful of mash outside when Mrs Moyes came along to tell her that fifty soldiers would be arriving about ten o'clock. 'Fifty!' Lizzie's grip tightened on the handle of the pail. 'Yes, and four officers,' Mrs Moyes said. 'They'll be billeted in the house. We'd better prepare beds for them.'

'Then I'd better bide at hame the nicht,' Lizzie said. 'I can take ma nicht oot some other time.'

'But I thought you wanted to go to the pictures?'

'Och, I can easy ging some other nicht,' Lizzie said.

'But I can manage fine,' Mrs Moyes said. 'If you help me with the beds before you go and leave out the tea-things. They'll only need a cup of tea and some biscuits. Maybe I could get Maggie Jane to come in and help me,' she added.

'No, I'll bide,' Lizzie said, and before Mrs Moyes could say any more she went away to feed the hens, skirling joyously. The idea! Wanting to get that glaikit Maggie Jane in to help her! A lot of help she'd be. Standing at the back-door chaffing the sodgers more nor likely! No, no, she was for none of that!

The rest of the evening passed in a flurry of excitement. Some of the farm-hands cleaned out the loft and took up straw for the soldiers. Mrs Moyes and Lizzie made beds ready for the officers. Lizzie went about in a daze, her imagination at the gallop. She saw her room being besieged by officers. All the situations she had seen on the films or read about were jumbled together. Her imagination could hardly cope with the prospect. There were fights outside her door. The one with the wee fair moustache had just battered his way in and was putting his arms around her when the door burst open. The wee fairmoustached one dived under the bed, and drawing her nightgown around her, Lizzie turned to find an even more handsome officer advancing to claim her . . .

'Lizzie!'

She gave her head a shake. 'Ay, ay, Mrs Moyes, I'll be there the now!'

As soon as she could find time Lizzie dressed as if she were going to the pictures. She put on her pale blue print frock and little blue ankle-socks and she tied a blue scarf around her head. Mrs Moyes could say what she liked! After all, it was her night off, wasn't it? She tossed her head indignantly and told Mrs Moyes exactly what she thought of her. After trying to get her to go to the pictures! Wanting her out of the road more nor likely so that she'd have a better chance herself.

After looking in the mirror she kept in the drawer of the kitchen table Lizzie went to the back-door and leaned against the jamb. It was half-past nine.

Chae Niven cycled around the corner of the byre. 'Ay there, Lizzie!' he cried, jumping off his bike.

'Ay, ay,' Lizzie said.

Chae leaned on the handlebars, ready for a news. But Lizzie stared past him, looking anxiously down the loan. 'Here they come!' she cried.

'Oh, ay, the sodgers.' Chae looked round in an uninterested way at the fawn-coloured lorries that were beginning to appear between gaps in the trees. 'We'll ha'e plenty o' company the nicht.'

He took a stub of cigarette out of his waistcoat pocket and lit it. 'Ye werena at the picters the nicht?'

'No.' Lizzie craned her neck as the first lorry jolted into the steading. A soldier jumped out and walked backwards, directing the driver into a corner of the court. Other soldiers jumped out before the lorry had got settled. Another lorry roared round the corner, and another. Soon the place was ashrill with the roaring of engines and the shouting of men in khaki. Lizzie never looked at Chae: she gaped at the soldiers. 'There's plenty for ye to pick frae, Lizzie!' Chae grinned. 'Maybe ye'll get an officer! They tell me there are some gey lads amongst them.'

Lizzie did not heed him. She watched a car swerve round the corner and stop. Some officers jumped out and began to give orders. Lizzie saw the one with the small fair moustache point at the house and walk towards her. She pulled nervously at the curls at her ear.

'Good evening.' The officer saluted.

Lizzie flushed and grinned coyly. 'Good evening,' Mrs Moyes' voice said behind her. 'You've arrived!'

'Lizzie,' she said, 'you might run and tell the cattleman that the soldiers are here. Has he got the loft ready yet?'

When Lizzie came back the officers were in the sitting-room and the door was shut. She could hear the sound of their voices and Mrs Moyes' high almost hysterical laughter. She sighed and loitered about the passage for a few minutes. Then she went to the back-door and watched the soldiers. But most of them were too busy to notice her. They bustled about with kit, carrying blankets up to the loft and making meals on their oil-stoves. One or two of them grinned and waved, but none of them came over to talk to her. She saw that Chae had nosed his bicycle in amongst the lorries and was peering over the shoulder of a soldier who was tinkering with one of the engines. She went over beside him. 'What's wrong, Chae?' she asked.

'Don't know,' he grunted, without looking at her.

Lizzie twisted one foot self-consciously and looked about her, but although many of the soldiers nodded at her none of them spoke.

'Lizzie! Lizzie!'

Mrs Moyes was standing in the back-door. 'Get some tea ready for the officers,' she said. 'They're all tired and want to go to their beds.'

Lizzie was spreading pancakes with butter when a soldier looked round the back-door. 'Any idea where I could get a wash, kid?' he asked in a high Cockney voice.

Lizzie bustled before him into the wash-house. 'In here,' she cried, her high heels tapping on the stone floor. 'You're sure it's no bother?' the soldier said diffidently.

'Nae bother ava,' she said, leaning against the wall and watching him roll up the sleeves of his khaki shirt. She looked admiringly at his firm brown arms. He grinned sheepishly and began to roll down the collar of his shirt. ''Aven't 'ad a decent wash for days,' he said. 'Been on this bloomin' manoover four days naow.'

''Ello there, Clinky!' Two soldiers stood in the doorway, grinning. 'Gettin off with the dames already? You'll 'ave to watch 'im, sister.'E's a bad lad this!'

'Do not trust 'im, gentul maiden!' one sang in an exaggerated falsetto. ''E's a bad lad, gentul maiden, though 'is 'air is snowy white!'

'Nothin' white abaht that, is there?' The other soldier leaned over and pulled down Clinky's shirt, showing the thick dark hair on his chest. 'Regular nest 'e's got there, eh sister?'

'Aw shuttup!' Clinky's sunburned face grew brick-red with embarrassment.

'LIZZIE! Are you there, Lizzie!'

'Ay, ay,' Lizzie called.

She scowled sulkily and put the cups and saucers on a tray, but she perked up as she went along the passage. The officers were better than the men any day! They wore swankier uniforms and had better manners. It would be real fine if she could land an officer.

But the officers were all so busy talking to Mr Moyes, who was asking them what they thought of Russia, that none of them looked at Lizzie when she put down the tray. She was pulling out the small gate-legged table from the corner when Mrs Moyes stopped her. 'I'll do that, Lizzie. It's all right, I can manage.'

When Lizzie went back to the wash-houe it was crowded with soldiers. Clinky and the other two had gone. Seeing her in the doorway there were grins and winks, and remarks were addressed to her, but there were too many there for her to say much. One after the other they went out. The last to go said 'Cheerio' in a shy way.

'Cheerio,' Lizzie said.

She walked to the outer door and leaned against it, pressing her plump shoulder into the jamb. She folded her arms and looked about expectantly, but none of the soldiers took any notice of her beyond nodding or saying *Hello* if they passed near her. A young soldier with his tunic unbuttoned, showing his singlet and brown chest, was sitting in the driving-seat of the truck parked nearest the door. He was reading a paper-covered book held on the steering-wheel. Lizzie coughed, but he did not look up. She pretended not to be interested in him; she leaned the back of her head against the door and looked up at the sky. He was a fine like loon; not as good-looking as Chae maybe, but a real fine loon for all that. She shifted her position until the jamb was between her shoulders, arching her back so that her big breasts stood out, and crossing her feet. Then when she thought that her pose was picturesque enough she coughed again. But there was no sign from the soldier. Lizzie glanced at him and saw that he was still reading intently. She began to hum *Every Night Should be Filled With Beautiful Music*. But still there was no response. Determined to keep at it, Lizzie began to sing the words, at first in a low voice, then as she gained confidence more loudly . . . 'The stars should be shining one high . . . It's a night made for love . . .' The soldier looked up from his book and grinned, but before Lizzie could smile back at him he looked down and went on reading.

Lizzie braced her back against the jamb. Her position was becoming a bit of a strain, but she was determined to keep at it. She closed her eyes and went on singing. The soldier went on reading. Then suddenly he awoke to the fact that liquid golden music was streaming across the farm-yard, its haunting refrains borne on the still night air. He looked at the girl. Her face was transfigured with ecstasy. A beautiful girl. Stylishly dressed. A girl any man could fall in love with. 'Hello,' he called softly. The singing went on for a few seconds, then Lizzie smiled. And at her smile he smiled back and leaned over, opening the door of the truck. 'Hello!' he said again, leaping out and striding towards her. Vitality oozed from him as he stood beside her. Radiant masculine vitality. He murmured something that she could not catch, something that she did not need to catch. And he put his hand on her arm. 'Where have you been all my life?' he whispered, putting his arm around her and drawing her against him.

'Lizzie!'

'LIZZIE!'

"Ay, ay,' Lizzie took her shoulders away from the jamb and wriggled them. The soldier was still in the truck, reading his book. He did not even look up as she went away. A strong smell of cow-urine was coming from the open door of the byre.

After she had washed the dishes Lizzie read *The Red Letter*. But she did not find any of the stories interesting at all. They didn't thrill her as they usually did. She couldn't give he complete attention to them. She kept jumping up and going to the door. But all the soldiers were in the trucks. It was getting dark, and cigarettes shone out of the darkness of the waggons, and there was a murmur of voices and occasional laughter. When she went to shut up the hens at eleven o'clock Lizzie took the long way round the yard, looking into the backs of the trucks. But most of the soldiers were lying down. Only one or two of them noticed her and said: 'Good night.'

Disconsolately Lizzie shut up the hens and went to her small attic. She undressed slowly and got into bed, listening all the time for strange sounds. But there was only the noise of the ducks settling down for the night and the faraway drone of a plane, and Mr Moyes shouting to his wife to come to bed. Lizzie lay flat on her back with her arms pressed tightly across her chest, her fingers clasping her shoulder-blades beneath her. She thought of the man who would come to her. He was Chae and He was the officer with the small fair moustache and He was Clinky and He was any man . . . But she saw only the blankness of the ceiling above her and felt only the weight of the quilt lying heavily upon her. And desperately in anger she flung it off the bed. There were no furtive footsteps on the landing outside her door, no cautious hand on the door-knob, no voice whispering: 'Are you there, darling? Can I come in?' But for a long time she lay expectantly, listening . . .'

She was awakened by a shouting and a banging of doors. 'Hurry up, Laurie, you lazy bugger! You can't lie there for ever. Come on, Struthers!'

Lizzie sat up with a jerk, thinking she had slept in. But it was still dark. It was only half-past one on the luminous dial of the alarm-clock.

What was wrong?

For a moment she thought that her suitors had met in the passage and were fighting it out. Then she realised that it was the Germans. It was the Invasion at last! That's why the soldiers were here! The officer lads had known all the time and had come to defend the farm. They hadn't wanted to frighten Mrs Moyes and her, so that's why they had said nothing . . . They'd be besieged! Maybe for weeks. Heavens above, and there wasn't enough meat in the house . . .

Wishing that she had a swanky dressing-gown like Mrs Moyes, she pulled her coat over her shoulders and ran outside. In the hall Mrs Moyes was standing among two or three of the young officers. Mr Moyes, in his pyjamas and dressing-gown, was speaking to another at the door, holding it behind him for the black-out. 'It's really terrible,' Mrs Moyes was saying.

'Yes, it's a damned nuisance—if you'll pardon me saying so,' the young officer with the fair moustache said. 'But it's all in the day's work as the scavenger said to the elephant!' He laughed. 'Did you see the film that crack was in? Damned fine flick. She's a damned fine actress that Aline M'Mahon.'

'No, I didn't see it,' Mrs Moyes said.

'Oh, it's an old flick. Must be years since I saw it. Oh yes, it's years. But I always remember that crack.'

'We haven't much chance to go to the flicks here,' Mrs Moyes said.

'No! Damned hard luck. Well, we'll have to go. Many thanks again for all you've done for us.'

Huddled in the corner, Lizzie realised that it wasn't the Invasion after all. The soldiers were leaving. She tried to smile, but even if she had been able the officers would never have noticed; they were all so busy clicking their heels and saluting Mrs Moyes. The noise of trucks and cars being started sounded worse to her ears than the booming of guns.

'Poor souls!' Mrs Moyes said. 'Fancy being called out at this time of night. After thinking they had got safely settled down. Some of them were saying that they hadn't slept for three nights. But I suppose they've got to expect that when they're on manoeuvres. It's all in the day's work as that chappie said.'

She yawned and began to go upstairs. 'Poor souls, too!'

'It was an awfa sook,' Lizzie said to Bella Annandale the following

Saturday night when they were standing in the queue for the pictures. 'I was fair lookin' forrit to them bidin' for days. Damn their headquarters for callin' them oot at that time o' nicht.'

Bella shrugged. 'Och, ye're daft to bother yersel' aboot them, Lizzie. There are Poles comin'.'

'Poles!'

"Ay, ay,' Bella said. 'Either Poleys or Dutchies, I'm nae sure which. Foreign sodgers, onyway. They're comin' on manoeuvres too. We had them at the Mill this forenune, speirin' if they could get billeted. Ye should ha'e seen them, Lizzie! Ane o' them was a big fat ane wi' a monocle. A' dressed up nae handy wi' top boots and spurs. He wasn't bad-looking ava. A nae bad loon, I thocht, and sae did Mrs McWilliams.'

'Really,' Lizzie said.

Bella nodded and went on to give more details. Lizzie's eyes were wide with interest, and she could hardly wait for the pictures to go in; she was eager to get back to the Barns to see if any Polish soldiers were to be billeted there. She could not pay attention to the programme, and as soon as the show ended she jumped on her bike. 'What ails ye at comin' to the Chipper the nicht?' Bella cried in astonishment. 'Ye're nae aye in such a hurry to ging hame!'

Lizzie cycled as fast as she could back to Dallow, but when she got there the house was in darkness. Mr and Mrs Moyes were in bed. Lizzie shut the back-door behind her and sighed as she went up the backstairs. She would just have to content herself until tomorrow morning.

But they were preparing the dinner before Mrs Moyes said casually: 'By the way, Lizzie, there'll be some Polish soldiers coming here at the end of the week for a night.'

'Oh, will there?' Lizzie said.

"Ay,' said Mrs Moyes. 'I'll have to polish up my Polish!' She gave a hysterical laugh. 'Though I doubt all the Polish I know is the Polish for "I love you!" You'll have to learn that, Lizzie!'

Lizzie giggled and looked apprehensive.

'It's *Cocham cibie*,' Mrs Moyes said. 'Ko-ham-sib-yeah! I wonder what Mr Moyes would say if I said that to the officers! You'll have to practise it, Lizzie, and say it to the soldiers when they come!'

'Oh, I couldna say that!' Lizzie giggled and hung her head coyly against her shoulder. 'I just couldna ha'e the nerve!'

But at odd times during the following week Mrs Moyes often heard Lizzie, when the girl thought she was alone, going about the kitchen repeating the phrase. 'Ko-ham-sib-yeah!' she would say slowly and distinctly. And then she would giggle hysterically, thinking of the hordes of handsome Polish officers who would click their heels and bow courteously before seducing her. It would be beautiful music to hear them murmuring love in Polish . . .

The coming of the Polish soldiers caused far greater excitement than the coming of the British soldiers. They arrived at the Barns of Dallow about three o'clock in the afternoon. Clouds of dust heralded the approach of their lorries and Bren-carriers as they roared up the loan. Immediately most of the cottar women found that they had to take a walk up to the steading about something. They brought their prams and their children, and they stood in groups and gazed at the soldiers. And Lizzie, who was standing at the back-door talking to Maggie Jane Cowie, wished that she could become as quickly acquainted with the Poles as the children, who were running about amongst the lorries. She wished that Maggie Jane wasn't with her, for Maggie Jane was looking even tougher and more slatternly than usual. But at the same time she was glad of her company; she felt bolder and more able to grin and call greetings to the men.

'Dae ye see the ane wi' the beard?' Maggie Jane exclaimed. 'Well I nivir! Whae'll he be, dae ye think?'

'Mrs Moyes says he's the padre,' Lizzie said. 'A minister, ye ken.'

'Goad Almichty!' Maggie Jane said, shaking her head. 'I nivir saw such a big black beard. It would make a real fine nest for a craw!'

She giggled and nudged Lizzie. 'Dae ye see auld Mrs Geekie takin' a bit keek at the sodgers? She's been joukin' oot and in her hoose nae handy!'

'Ay, ay,' Lizzie sniffed disdainfully. 'Thinkin' she'll get a Pole at her age!'

Maggie Jane was inclined to linger and gossip about Mrs Geekie's shortcomings, but Lizzie had a lot of work to do. All afternoon she was nearly rushed off her feet, making beds and shake-downs ready. For when the officers saw the rooms they were to have they asked if others could share them with them. 'Three can sleep here, oh yes! And what is in this room?' They opened a door. 'Oh, that's a sun-parlour,' Mrs Moyes said. 'Nobody could sleep there. It hasn't a bed and the windows were blown out in the winter. Ian's always been going to put them in, but he never seems to have had time.' But the officers said, oh yes, they could sleep there. 'Veree comfortable after hard ground!'

Late in the afternoon Lizzie ran out to the barn for fresh straw for the hens. The farm was just hotching with khaki-dressed men with the little red tab on their shoulders. Everywhere she looked Lizzie saw yet another that she fancied. If only she could get them all! She was shouldering her bundle of straw when three of them came through the barn-door. They stood aside to let her pass, and she smiled at them, wondering if maybe now . . .

One of them said something. Lizzie gaped and for a second she did not realise what the man had said. It was: 'Can yiz tell iz where we'll get ony wa'er?'

He laughed at the expression on her face. 'Did yiz think we wiz Poles?' he said. 'No bloody fear. Us boys are H.L.I. There are ten o' us wi' thae Poles.'

That evening Harriet Moyes ran along to the kitchen for more tea cups. She was nearly off her head rushing about after the Poles! Really, it was all terribly funny! Instead of there being five officers in the house as expected there seemed to be nearer fifteen. New ones were arriving every minute. Ian and she just looked at each other whenever another one stalked into the hall, thinking that here was still another to whom they'd need to talk slowly and distinctly or on whom they could try their French. Lizzie had really been very funny. It was a lovely story to tell to their friends. She had overheard Ian talking to the Major and she had come awestruck to Harriet and said: 'I didna ken that Mr Moyes spoke Polish!' Polish or French—it was all one to Lizzie! Either of them was an accomplishment far beyond her dreams—if Lizzie had any dreams behind the blankness of that wall eye.

A soldier was sitting beside the Esse Cooker. Lizzie was leaning against the table, humming *Every Night Should Be Filled With Beautiful Music*. When she saw Mrs Moyes she pretended to be very busy, spreading sandwiches. Harriet smiled, thinking that surely Lizzie could have done better for herself out of all these soldiers; for he was small and stunted, with a wizened worldly face. She nodded to him and, spreading out her hands, she said: 'You . . . are . . . having. . . a . . . heat . . . yes?'

'Ay,' he said with a pronounced Glasgow accent.

Her face twitching with suppressed laughter, Harriet went back to the sitting-room to tell Ian; thinking that it was a pity that Lizzie had never taken the chance to air her Polish! The odds were that she'd never get another chance now.

BEAUTIFUL MUSIC was written in August 1941. It was published in *Scottish Art and Letters*, edited by R. Crombie Saunders, in July 1944, and then in Urquhart's *Selected Stories* (Maurice Fridberg's Hour Glass Library, 1946). It was included in *The Dying Stallion*, volume one of his *Collected Stories* (Rupert Hart-Davis, 1967).

9 *The Red Stot*

ONE OF THE STOTS was choking. The loon heard it as he was wheeling the heavy barrow-load of turnips out of the neep shed, across the muddy ruts in the snow. He sniffed up the drip at the end of his snub nose. It was just after eight o'clock on a February morning and it was still so dark that when he went into it he could not see the rear of the large cattle-shed. He put down the barrow, sighing from the effort of pushing it up the short slope that led on to the path beside the troughs. A few feet below him the cattle were snorting and slobbering at the turnips in the first two troughs. Their heads were shoved under the wooden rails. 'Goutyebrute!'. the loon cried as a turnip was sent hurtling in front of the barrow. He heaved it back into the trough, then he hurled the barrow along to the third trough. He put it down with another sigh of exhaustion, pushing back the imitation airman's helmet that he wore, showing his closely-cropped, blind-fair hair. Beads of sweat were trickling down his brow. he could feel it running coldly down his chest and back, aggravating the tickliness of his woollen semmit. He scratched himself.

He made a tremendous effort and tilted over the barrow, shooting the turnips with a squelching rumble into the trough. There was a scamper, and heads were shoved under the railing. The cattle dunched each other, their mouths groping greedily for the turnips. The loon staggered another few yards and emptied the other half of the load into the fourth trough. 'Another four barryfu',' he muttered.

This was the sort of work that made you wish you were back at the school. Auld Stormont was the coarsest dominie in the Howe o' the Mearns, but you'd rather get strappit twice a day than attend til thae store cattle. You were right fed up with them and you'd be glad when you saw their hint ends on the way to the Mart.

He was picking up the empty barrow when he heard the wheezing and hoasting again above the crunching of the other cattle. He peered over one of the straw-racks. 'It's that reid ane,' he muttered. 'Chokit again!'

A red stot with a white diamond-shaped mark on its forehead had backed out of the struggling mass and retreated into the centre of the shed. It was standing, head held high, front legs braced among the straw- and dung-littered muck, and its hind legs shoved forward under it. Thick ropes of white saliva were hanging from its mouth. And it heaved its sides and stretched its neck as if it were in a death-throes. 'Goutyebastard!' the loon cried. 'That's what ye get for gutsin'. See!'

The stot opened its mouth wide and lowered its head, stretching and retching. But still it could not get the piece of turnip out of its thrapple. It heaved for a few more seconds, then it charged again into the crowd around the troughs, butting its way into the centre of one; where it shoved away the others, not bothering about the turnips until the other stots had gone to the neighbouring troughs. Then it grabbed a huge turnip in its mouth, shaking it vigorously. The loon swore and wheeled the barrow back to the neep shed.

By the time he had given the cattle four barrow-loads of turnips, and two of potatoes the loon was completely exhausted. He was wheeling away the barrow when he noticed a brindled stot with a gentle face standing in the centre of the shed. It had been shoved away from the troughs. 'Ye stupid hoor!' he called. 'If ye dinna push yer way in ye'll never get onythin' in this world!'

What a difference it was from that red one! The red stot was more bother than the rest of them put together. It was aye choking. Just now it was trying to keep the others away from the seventh trough which was still almost full of neeps and tatties. It was butting those on one side and lashing out with its hind legs at those on the other.

The loon shook his head, wondering why they did not join together and give it a dunt out of the way. There was plenty of meat for them all. He began to hash the biggest neeps that were left in the first trough. Hearing the clatter of the iron on the stone the cattle rushed away from the turnips they were gnawing in order to get the slices that fell whitely from the hasher. They crowded in so that the loon could not get room to lift the hasher up and down, so he moved to the next trough. But the cattle rushed to it, grunting and paiching in their anxiety to get the best slices. They swallowed greedily, throwing up their heads and stretching their necks to the full. The loon held his face away from their slobbering, fawn-coloured muzzles, slimy with saliva, and their great walloping tongues. 'Keep yer stinkin' breaths oot o' ma face, damn ye!' he cried.

The red stot had been choking again in the middle of the shed. But although the froth was still clogging its mouth, it came charging in again, sending the other stots hurtling away from the troughs. It seized a huge turnip the loon was trying to hash and pulled it away from him. The loon was so angry that he struck the stot across the muzzle with the hasher. 'Take that, ye hoor o' hell!'

Thankfully he flung the hasher back into the neep shed and went into the barn. As he pushed open the large sliding-doors he noticed suddenly that it was light. The sun hadn't risen yet over the snow-covered Mearns hills, but its first rays were shining behind a thin mass of cloud. The rest of the sky was a pale heliotrope. Only this peculiarly shaped mass of cloud was vividly coloured. It was like one of yon birds in the book the dominie had. Flamingoes they were called. Queer-like birds that bed in Egypt or one of those places. . . .

He was dragging bunches of straw and putting them in the racks when he heard somebody say: 'Ay, ay, loon ye're sortin' them again!'

A tall, bandy-legged man, wearing dirty khaki breeches, was slouching along the narrow path. He had a high-coloured face, and he hadn't shaved for several days. A shapeless cap was stuck jauntily on the side of his head. He stood on the edge of one of the troughs, shoving back the cattle's heads while he looked over the railing at them. 'Ane o' yer stots is chokit, man,' he said.

'Ay,' the loon said.

'Dae ye hash yer neeps?'

'Ay,' the loon said.

'I widna if I were you, boy. That's what makes them choke. Thae three-cornered edges that the hasher makes stick in their guzzles.'

'But the grieve tellt me to hash them,' the loon said.

'Thae cattle ha'e got teeth, boy! What's their teeth for? Dinna you bother aboot the gaffer. I ken mair aboot cattle-beasts than he kens or's ever likely to ken.'

He was repeating this with greater emphasis when the farmer came into the shed and cried: 'Are ye there, cattler?'

The cattler shambled quickly towards him. The loon hurried back into the barn for more straw. He worked so quickly that soon he was almost breathless with exhaustion. He stopped only when the farmer cried: 'Here, loon, seek the grieve if he can gi'e ye a stick. And tell him I want to see him.'

When the loon came back with the grieve, the farmer said: 'Thae beasts 'll ha'e to go to the Mart this mornin'.'

'But I thocht they werena to ging for three weeks yet,' the grieve said.

'Ay, but I got a Ministry o' Food order wi' this mornin's post. It seems the Army needs food.'

'Ye can take the loon wi' ye,' the farmer said to the cattleman. 'Ging ower there, loon, and dinna let them into the steading.'

The loon stood at the opening between the barn and the potato-shed, holding his stick in readiness, while the grieve opened the gate of the cattle-shed. The cattler went inside. The cattle came out slowly. They blinked and mooed, lowering their heads and sniffing at the tractor-ruts in the snow. One or two of them leaped skittishly, but most of them seemed disinclined to leave the shed. But as the cattler prodded some, they forced the others out. 'Come on, man, come on!' the cattler shouted irritably to the last beast inside. The loon heard the whacks of the stick, then the red stot galloped out. Immediately it sent the others into a flurry of activity. They ran here and there, butting each other and leaping on each other's backs, mooing and tossing their heels in the air. The loon had to keep on the alert, waving his stick frantically at those that tried to get past him. Beside him the cattleman's dog yapped, rushing at the most forward stots and snapping at them.

'A' richt, gaffer!' the farmer cried.

The grieve stood away from the end of the loan and let the beasts get past him. Then he scrambled over a fence and ran across a field, ploughing his way through the snow. 'Awa' wi' the grieve, loon!' the farmer cried.

The loon followed the grieve. He could see the cattle running down the road, followed by the cattler and his dog. The grieve was making for an open gate, but before he could reach it, the foremost cattle had come into the field. They waved their sticks and shouted, and after some skirmishing the beasts went back on to the road. 'Now, loon,' said the grieve. 'Awa' doon the field and get oot in front o' them. Just ging at a walkin' pace.'

The loon scampered down the field, the snow sucking at his Wellingtons as if it would drag them off his feet. Just ging at a walking pace! He was running as fast as he could, but he saw the cattle getting farther and farther away from him. The cattler was shouting on the road behind him, but except for an oath here and there he could not make out what the man was crying. He tried to run faster, but the more he tried the more the snow sucked at his boots, making him stumble and slither. He almost cried with relief when he saw the cattle stopping at a straw-soo about a quarter of a mile down the loan. And so he stopped running. And when he had recovered his breath a little he climbed the fence. He wiped the sweat off his face with his checked scarf while waiting for the cattler.

'Ay, loon,' the cattler said. 'They're awa' at a richt rate. They're het wi' bein' in sae long, but they'll soon cool doon.'

'I hope so,' the loon said. 'They're nae the only anes that's het.'

The cattler began to fill his pipe, rubbing and squeezing the Irish Roll between his large dirt-engrained palms.

'Will we nae better hurry up?' the loon asked tentatively. 'They'll ha'e a' that stray eaten.'

'Ach, what's a' yer chase?' The cattler laughed. 'They'll nae dae muckle damage.'

And right enough the cattle had done no damage. One or two had pulled a few strands of straw out of the soo, but most of them were too busy galloping round and round it to bother about anything else. A few shouts from the cattler, some waving of sticks and some yapping from the dog, and soon they were back on the road. Their gallop had cooled them down a bit, and they walked quietly. The cattler went in front of them. The loon walked behind, one hand in the pocket of his blue dungarees, the other swinging his stick. Now that he'd got his breath back he'd rather be doing this than spreading dung or pulling neeps. It was even better than dressing tatties, and dressing tatties wasn't so bad sometimes; it was warm in the potato-shed, and there was aye a lot of speak among the tattie dressers, and a lot of laughing and chaff.

Most of the snow had disappeared off the road, but there had been frost earlier in the morning and that made it slippery. They had safely passed all the open gates, so the cattler came back to walk beside the loon. Sometimes one of the cattle would slither on its haunches but it aye got up quickly when the cattler yelled at it or prodded it under the tail. The sun was shining brightly now and it glittered on the snow-laden branches of some fir-trees. The loon thought they looked like yon tinsel-covered trees you saw on cards at Christmas.

'There's mair cattle comin' doon that road,' the cattler said. 'We'd better get a move on and get in front o' them.'

The loon heard men shouting and a dog yapping behind the snow-covered hedges, and when they were passing the end of the road he saw them. The cattler waved his stick and shouted a greeting. 'They're a gey mangy bunch o' stots, thae,' he said.

As they approached Auchencairn several other herds came on to the main road and there was some difficulty in keeping them separated. The cattler walked in front of the lot from Dallow, and the loon and the dog followed them. The loon felt that the herd behind was pressing in on him, and he was relieved when they came to the Auction Mart.

Soon the stots were penned in a large shed. It was full of local farmers and cattlemen, and the atmosphere was thick with tobacco-smoke and the breath of the cattle. The farmers walked about, greeting each other and looking at the cattle. The loon heard one man say when he stopped before the Dallow lot: 'This is a fine bunch. They surely havena been rationed.' His companion said: 'Ay, but ha'e ye seen mine? They're ootside in the pens. A' Silage fed. Come on oot and see them.'

'Silage!' The cattler snorted contemptuously. 'I dinna haud wi' that stuff at a'. It's nae fit for beasts.'

The loon did not listen. He was wondering when the cattler intended to start back for Dallow; he was beginning to feel hungry. It must now be about eleven, he judged. It would take him and the cattler all their time if they were to get back to Dallow before lousing-time at half-past eleven.

But the cattler walked about, looking critically at the other cattle and speaking to cattlemen from neighbouring farms. The loon leaned against a pen, making patterns with his stick on the sawdust-covered floor. The air was getting thicker and thicker. You couldn't see much farther than three yards. Beyond that the men and the beasts were indistinct and then lost.

The loon yawned, wishing he was eating his dinner. His mother had promised to make bannocks this forenoon. They would go fine with the tattie-soup, left over from yesterday. He looked up when somebody said: 'Hello, John!'

He had noticed a girl going about among all the men, a sheaf of papers in her hand, taking note of all the cattle that came in. He saw now that it was Elspeth Dickson who had been in his class at school. He hadn't recognised her in her swanky pale blue pixie-cap and brown coat with the fur collar.

'Ay, ay,' he said, giving his head a slight jerk to the side.

She leaned against the railing beside him. 'I hear you're fee-ed at Dallow,' she said.

'Ay,' he said.

'Like it?' she said.

'Ay, it' a' richt,' he said. 'D'you like this job?'

'Ay, it's all right,' she said.

She twirled her pencil in a strand of dark hair that fell across her cheek. The loon had never noticed before how pretty she was. It must be that pixie-cap and that coat. She looked right grown-up like. He wished he hadn't been dressed the way he was. Although he was usually very proud of his working-clothes, he wished that he was wearing his new long-trousered blue serge Sunday suit.

'It's always a job,' Elspeth said.

'Ay,' he said.

He wondered what he could say to her. They had never got on very well at school; they had aye been fighting. He drew some more patterns with his stick.

Elspeth flattened herself against the pen when a man pushing a trolley stopped in front of them. 'Thae anes next,' the man said, taking some iron-lettered brands from the trolley and dipping them in yellow paint. He opened the gate and began to stamp the cattle's haunches with the iron. 'Twenty-eight to fifty-two, that's Dallow, isn't it?' he asked Elspeth.

'Yes,' she said, looking at her bunch of papers. 'Poor things,' she said to the loon. 'They dinna ken what's comin' to them. You know I'm fair scunnert wi' beef now. I canna eat it for thinkin' about thae cattle and where the beef comes from.'

'Ach, dinna be daft,' the loon said, grinning.

But he looked at the gentle-faced brindled stot hemmed in the corner. And he turned away quickly. 'Dinna be soft,' he said to Elspeth. 'That's what beasts are for, aren't they?'

She looked at them pityingly. The loon leaned his elbows on the top rail and tried to look at them in the professional way the cattler looked at them. The red stot was bucking about in the middle of the pen, clearing a place for itself with heels and lowered head. It charged into the corner where the brindled stot cowered and leaped upon it.

The loon did not look at Elspeth; he drew some more patterns in the sawdust. He was glad when he saw the cattler approaching. He readjusted the strap of his helmet under his chin.

'This beats a',' the cattler said, pushing back his cap with disgust. 'That reid ane's been rejected, loon. We'll ha'e to take him back.'

'God!' the loon said.

'Well, cheerio!' Elspeth said, moving off. 'I'll be seein' you,'

'Ay ay,' the loon said, glancing at her, then watching the cattler go amongst the cattle to drive out the red stot. The loon hit it a crack on the rump. 'Get on, ye beast!' he cried.

'What's a' yer chase, loon?' the cattler said when they had driven the stot into the street. 'Jist bide here a meenit till I ging intil this shoppie for fags.'

The stot was snuffling at the gate of old Mrs Morrison's house. The loon yawned and leaned against the railings, wishing the cattler would hurry up. He was hungry, even if the cattler wasn't. And he was wondering what would happen about this troublesome beast. Would he still have to sort it? Or would it be put in the cattler's charge?

'Hoy!'

The cattler had come out of the shop. He rushed past the loon, waving his stick. His bandy legs curveted on the slippery pavement. But he was too late. The red stot had pushed open Mrs Morrison's gate and was already half-way up the path. Hearing the cattler's yell, it lurched forward and lumbered into the porch.

'Hell, what are we to dae noo?'

The stot was nuzzling the inner multi-coloured glass door. 'If ye dinna watch it'll ging richt through the glass,' said the cattler. 'What way did ye nae keep an eye on it, loon?'

'Here, man!' he called softly. 'Here, man? Guid lad!'

But the stot stood still, its hindquarters sticking out of the porch with massive disdain. The loon felt like giving them a crack with his stick, but he remembered old Mrs Morrison's face and what he had heard about her nippy tongue. 'If it moves at a', it'll break that glass and then there'll be hell to pay,' the cattler mutterd anxiously. 'What way did ye nae keep an eye on it, loon?'

He chirruped and smacked his lips enticingly, but the beast did not move. He put out his hand and touched it cautiously, but the stot gave such a lurch that the cattler jumped back. 'Christ!' he muttered. 'Ye've been a nuisance ever sin' we got ye. Are ye goin' on to be a worse nuisance, ye ill-gettit hoor?'

Suddenly the loon had an inspiration. He sidled past the stot and pulled the bell. Surely to God the sight of Mrs Morrison's face would make the stot step back!

But when Mrs Morrison opened the door it was she who started back. And the stot, as if hypnotised, advanced a few feet into the hall. Then, its bowels contracting with fear at the woman's yell, it raised its tail.

'God knows what the boss'll say when he hears,' the cattler kept saying as they drove the stot homewards. 'Mrs Morrison kicked up a hell o' a fuss, but she'll be sure to kick up an even bigger ane wi' him. As if we could help it. . . .'

The loon said nothing. He pushed his hands farther into his trousers-pockets, completely miserable. He wondered what his mother would say if he got the sack. She had been so pleased when he got fee-ed at Dallow. His wage meant so much to them. . . .

'Dammit, snaw again!' the cattler exclaimed suddenly. 'There was ower reid a sky this mornin' for ma taste.'

What had looked like a thin mist creeping down from the hills, flattening out the land so that soon you thought you were walking on a wee bit plateau and that soon you'd come to the edge and fall over into the mist, now turned out to be a small fine snow. You only knew it was snow because the drops stung your face like blunt needles. And already you saw that the bits of reddish clay showing beneath the last fall were growing paler and paler pink as the drops fell on them like icing sugar.

The red stot lumbered from side to side, its head bent against the stinging flakes. Its back and rump were soon covered with the fine white powder, but before the covering got time to thicken the steam from the stot's heaving sides condensed it.

The cattler began to sing an old bothy song, *Macfarlane o' the Sprots o' Burniebosie.* 'Oh, I dinna like Macfarlane,' he roared, hitting the stot a hard smack, making it scamper for a few yards. 'It's awfa, but it's true . . . His lugs would cast a shadow ower a sax-foot gate. . .'

'His legs like guttapercka, ilka step his knees gang ki—nack!' the loon joined in, swinging his stick and walloping blindly in the direction of the dark shape in front. 'Macfarlane o' the Sprots o' Burniebosie!'

The snow fell faster and faster, and the flakes grew bigger. Soon they could see only a few yards in front of them. The going got more and more difficult. But on they struggled into the whiteness leading to Dallow, following the dark shape of the lumbering red stot.

THE RED STOT was written in 1941, but was not published until it appeared in Fred Urquhart's collection *The Year of the Short Corn* (Methuen, 1949).

10 The Prisoners

FOR THE FIRST TWO or three days Mary did not come into contact much with the prisoners. She saw them working in the fields or going about the steading, but she could not bring herself to go near them. She felt ashamed. She was ashamed because they were herded together in that camp over there behind barbed wire and put on a lorry like cattle every day and brought here to the farm to work. And she was ashamed because of Will. Some of the prisoners perhaps had been farmers in Italy, used to walking about as Will walked about, giving orders. She tried to imagine how he would have felt had he been unlucky enough to be a soldier and taken prisoner. Could he have stood docile and uncomplaining as they had to stand while strangers jabbered about him in Italian, sizing him up and talking about his points as if he were a horse? Could he have sweated and strained while another man stood by with his hands in his pockets? She felt that it was disloyal to him to think that, but she could not help it. If only he were a bit more sensitive; if only he had enough imagination to think *There but for the grace of God go I. . . .* She wished that he would stay inside, that he would not stride about amongst them like that, head and shoulders above them, pushing his way through them as if they were cattle or slaves. It was like the old Roman days you read about in the novels of Naomi Mitchison . . . only now the Romans were the slaves. . . .

She realised that she was being unfair to Will. He really did not look down upon the prisoners—he couldn't help being so tall. He wasn't like lots of farmers, looking on the prisoners merely as cheap labour. Actually he had been very good to them. He had had the barn swept out and tidied up for them to sit in at dinner-time, and seats had been put in and a fireplace built. And he gave them as much milk and potatoes as they wanted to supplement the rations they brought with them. They needed that, of course. Will was wise enough to see that they couldn't be expected to do a hard day's work in his fields on the rations the Government allowed them.

But she was being nasty again. Why should you be so nasty? she asked herself. If you weren't in love with Will, if you didn't adore him,

I could see the force of it. But you know fine that you worship him. You know that you'd let him walk over the top of you. . . .

And by God he would walk over the top of you, too, if you gave him the chance. He walks over the top of you often enough and you not asking for it.

It was just his manner. He couldn't help looking so sulky and dour. It was just the way he was made. Even with his own men he hardly ever unbent. She knew that it was a certain shyness, an unsureness, that made him like that. He was aggressive because he was really at sea within himself. All the psychology books said that. He was still a little boy playing at being a man. And like a little boy he could be so charming when he liked. He needed only to look at her and all the hard things she had been thinking about him were swept away.

There were sixteen prisoners. They all looked very young, little more than boys; the average age would be twenty-two. At first they all looked alike: just small dark figures in a chocolate-magenta coloured uniform with a blue circle sewn on the back of the tunic and on one leg of the trousers. But after a few days she began to know individuals as she knew the other men who worked on the farm. There was the very short, broad-shouldered youth who came to the back door every day at dinner-time for boiling water for their coffee, and there was the tall one with the forage-cap pulled far down over his eyes, who was always singing and who gave pennies to the children about the farm. She heard from the maid that his name was Luigi. 'That means Willie in Scotch,' Bella said. 'He tellt Geordie that.'

Most of them had been captured at Tobruk or Benghazi. 'They dinna like the Australians ava,' Bella said. 'They stole their watches and their rings. They even cut off their fingers if they couldna haul the rings off. Fancy onybody doin' that! Oh, they're wild, cruel devils, thae Australians. And they tore up their photographs.'

'Surely not, Bella!' Mary said.

'Ay, they did that,' Bella said, nodding her head solemnly. 'Luigi tellt Geordie that. They tore his photo o' his wife. I ca' it a disgust for onybody to dae that—even though they are Italians.'

'But one can hardly blame all the Australians for something that was done by one or two ruffians,' Mary said. 'After all, there are rough elements in all armies. In the British as well as in the German or the Australian.'

'I dinna believe that ony o' *oor* boys would dae things like that,' Bella said.

'There's no knowing what men 'll do when they get together and get out of hand,' Mary said.

'Och, maybe some men. But ye could nivir imagine the likes o'

Geordie—or Mr Murray—doin' things like that even to Italians,' Bella said.

'No, I can't imagine Geordie being so cruel,' Mary said.

Once or twice Mary saw Geordie standing with the gang he was in charge of, talking, while they leaned on their spades, listening and laughing. 'Whether Geordie's speaking Italian to them or whether they're understanding his Mearns tongue, I don't know!' Mary said to her husband. 'But he certainly lays off plenty to them!'

Will laughed. 'Geordie's nae speakin' Italian whatever he's speakin'! He's been teachin' them a grand lot of auld Scots words beginning with F and B. It's awfa funny. I heard Geordie say to one yesterday, "Mussolini no effing good." But the lad was quick; he laughed and said, "Churchill no effing good."'

Will roared and laughed at the remembrance, slapping his thigh like a schoolboy. Mary could not help smiling. After two years of marriage she was still in awe of her huge husband; more afraid of him than in love with him. But at times like this, when his eternal boyishness showed, she felt almost maternal and protecting towards him. Perhaps it was this maternal feeling that had made her leave her teaching and marry him; it must have been that. What else could have made a woman of her education come and bury herself on a farm, even a farm as large as this? Sometimes when she was feeling bitter and angry against him, remembering the things she had given up when she married him, she wished that his boyishness would assert itself oftener; it gave him that charm that never failed to win her round. But unfortunately his other side, the dictatorial, patri- archal, father of his people side, was almost always on the ascendant.

Often she made up her mind to have a row with him, but as soon as she saw him she could not say all the things she had rehearsed. When he wasn't there, when he went away as he so often did without saying where he was going or when he would be back she would rage and say to herself all the things she was going to tell him when he came back. But as soon as she saw him she could not bring herself to say anything. She knew that it would have been hopeless, anyway. He would just have laughed. Or—what was worse—he would just have ignored her, treating her like a child. Or he might have lost his temper so much that he would not have listened, no matter how reasonable her complaints might have been. He would listen to nobody. 'I will not be dictated to by you or by anybody else,' he had once said to her. It was the same when any of the men complained about anything. It was not that he bullered and swore like so many of his farmer neighbours. Their men knew what to expect from them, and they swore back, knowing that the next day they could speak to them as if nothing had happened. But Will Murray was different. His word was law. He was the Big White Chief. He had been used to getting his own way ever since he was a child, and like a child when he first hears the word 'No', he could not understand. As a child he had been a bully—Mary knew that indirectly from the stories his mother and sisters had told her about his childhood. He was still a bully. He loved to pinch her or slap her bottom, and he would laugh delightedly when she made to pinch or slap him back. But she did not do that often, because she always came off worst. 'I'm like Churchill, I'm still a schoolboy,' he said once to her. 'Only I'm not as fond of fighting as he is.'

But usually his sadism was much more subtle than his boisterous pinching and slapping. He kept her guessing about things; she never knew where she was with him. She could not imagine what he was thinking. He never told her anything. And like every other woman she wanted to know the ins and outs of things; she wanted him to confide in her, to ask her opinion about things. But he never did that. He never spoke about his business. He could be going to build a new byre or sack the whole lot of his men—it was all the same; she would never have known from the expression on his face. 'The Sphinx!' she sometimes said to him. 'The Sphinx! I bet it would be more communicative than you!' But he just smiled—that slow, mocking smile that made her furious. She wanted then to slap his smooth, plump cheeks. To make *some* impression on him. . . .

It had been like that about the Italians. She had not known that he was getting prisoner-of-war labour until the morning the Italians came and she saw them going about the steading. And when she asked him how they were shaping as workers he merely said: 'The grieve thinks they're all right.'

Mary tried to speak to those who came to the back door, but she found that they knew only a few words of English. So she tried them in French. But her *'Parlez-vous français?'* elicited no response beyond a shrug and a smile. She realised then that most of them belonged to the peasant class. Like Geordie and the other men on the farm who would also have stared uncomprehendingly if they had been prisoners in Italy and somebody had said: *'Parlez-vous français?'*

They had one weary-looking guard with them. 'A damned nuisance,' Will said. 'He's no bloody good at all. He does nothing. He's never with them. He spends all his time in the dairy, putting off the land girls' time. I must see what can be done about him. I don't see why they send him at all.'

'But if one of them should try to escape?' Will's mother said anxiously.

'They'll nae try to escape. Where could they go? And what would they try to escape for, anyway? They've got plenty of freedom about here. They get to move about as they like. They get a loan of the men's bicycles and cycle up and down. I even saw one of them playing with the guard's rifle and steel helmet yesterday.'

'But surely that isn't safe?' Mrs Murray said. 'I mean, they might be quite desperate characters for all we know. And after all, they're our enemies. I don't think it's right to give them such freedom at all.'

'Dinna be daft, mother!' Will said. 'They're all quite harmless, and they all look happy enough. What would they want to escape for? They're better here than in that camp behind barbed wire. They're better here than in Libya. I bet they're all glad to be out of the war. No, no, they'll nae try to escape. They all look quite happy.'

'Maybe they *look* happy,' Mary said. 'But that isn't quite the same thing.'

'Ach, there's nothing coming over them,' Will said. 'They get leave to wander about as they please. They're as free as you or me.'

'I wonder,' Mary said. 'Bella tells me that that Luigi one has a wife and a baby that he's never seen.'

'Now, Mary, you're just getting sentimental about them,' Mrs Murray said. 'It's a great mistake. Remember that they're our enemies.'

Often Mary felt that next to throttling Will she would have liked to throttle his mother. Indeed she would have preferred to throttle his mother. For, after all, his mother had none of Will's endearing points. She was a small thin woman with an eager face. She was always rushing about after Will—rushing after him as she had rushed for the last twenty-five years. She was so eager to please him. She had spoiled him so much, ran after him and waited on him hand and foot, that she had quite spoilt him for any other woman. Even yet when he had a wife who was in her way as eager to please, to make a footstool of herself, Mrs Murray could not refrain from rushing about, jumping at his slightest command. Will would just come in, slump down in his chair, and both women were on their toes. 'Bring me my cigarettes from the office, Mary,' he would say, and before Mary had time to move, Mrs Murray would be away for them, half-running. 'There you are, dear,' she would say brightly, and she would look at Mary as much as to say: See now, you're far too slow. What my boy needs is somebody who'll anticipate his every wish.

Mrs Murray was very concerned about the guard lounging about. 'If he's not needed to watch the Italians,' she said, 'he could at least do some work himself. I think it's scandalous. Why can't he bring his mending with him or something like that?'

'Dinna be daft, mother!' Will winked at Mary.

'I'm not being daft at all,' Mrs Murray said. 'It's scandalous. The Commandant at the Prison Camp had the cheek to ask the ladies of the Women's Guild if they'd do the men's darning and mending for them.'

'The prisoners?' Mary said.

'No, the guards.' Mrs Murray shuffled about on her chair like an indignant hen on eggs. 'I think it's perfect cheek! He wants to send fifty or sixty parcels to the Guild every week after they come back from the laundry.'

'Well, well, it'll give the Guild wifies something to do,' Will said. 'They're all that keen to poke their noses into other folk's business, anyway. This'll be a grand chance for them.'

'I think it's scandalous,' Mrs Murray said. 'The ladies have all got plenty of other war work as it is. And almost all these men have got wives of their own. What's to hinder them sending their mending home? For that matter, what's to hinder them doingtheir own mending? I'm sure all these poor sailors and the lads in the Middle East do their own mending. These men at the Camp have nothing else to do. Guarding a puckle poor Italians!'

'Who might try to escape!' Will grinned.

'The guard who comes here could easily bring his mending with him instead of lounging about, putting off the girls' time,' Mrs Murray said.

'And get the girls to do it!' Will said. 'Or maybe you'd like to do it for him?'

'Don't try to be funny, Will. I'm perfectly serious. There's nothing to hinder the man doing his darning while he's sitting out there in the barn. It would give him something to occupy his attention.'

'What about the prisoners?' Mary said. 'Who's going to do *their* mending, poor things?'

'Ach, they've nothing to mend,' Will said.

'Now, don't you get sentimental about them, Mary,' her mother-in-law said. 'I'm as sorry as you are for them, and all that, but remember they're our enemies!'

But Mary could not help feeling a little bit sentimental about the Italians. Even in their captivity there was something romantic about them. They sang, and when they spoke or shouted to each other, their voices had a lilt. They brought an exotic note into the drab life of the farm. You felt that they should be going about with gold rings in their ears, that there should be bright sunshine and laughter and a full ripe moon and love. . . . She felt a fellow-feeling with them, she told herself. For after all, she was as much a prisoner as they were. A prisoner bound by her love and fear of Will.

Every day about lousing-time she began to stand near the sitting-room window, waiting to see the tractors bringing them up from the fields. But she could not watch them as she would have liked. She remained tense, ready to move away quickly from the window at the first sounds of her mother-in-law coming into the room. That was the only good thing about Mrs Murray—she gave you good warning of her approach! Although a small body, she made a tremendous noise, banging down her heels and singing as she rushed about. A sign of her good temper, she said. 'I've always been sunny and on the go,' she would say. 'Nobody has ever been able to say that I sulked or wasn't full of beans! I'm sure I don't know where Will gets his silence and moodiness from.' She infuriated Mary with her brightness—especially in the mornings when she came downstairs to breakfast, singing, and insisting upon chattering all through the meal. Mary and Will would sit and eat, never answering her, staring at the tablecloth or out of the window. And their silence would in its turn infuriate Mrs Murray, so that after a few remarks about some people having got out of bed on their wrong sides and about their unsociableness the morning meal usually ended in either a quarrel or in repressed tempers—Mary and her mother-in-law brushing past each other in the passages, each of them looking at something over the other's shoulders.

Mary was standing like this at the window one forenoon when Will came into the room silently and came up behind her. 'Well, are you watching our Italians?' he said, pressing his forefingers under her armpits.

Mary shifted uneasily. She felt dwarfed and insecure when Will stood like that behind her; he was so huge and solid. She felt that sometime without warning he might reach out and crush her.

'Yes,' she said. 'But I must away and see about the hot water for their coffee.'

It was a new one who came for the water today. A tall youngster Mary had not seen before. 'Excuse me, madame, you speak French, yes?' he said, smiling and handing her the pail. '*Les autres me dit que vous le parlez.*'

Mary blushed. '*Mais . . . oui. . . .*'

He grinned. '*Ah, bien!*' And he began to speak rapidly in French. Mary could catch only a word here and there, but she was able to make out the sense of what he was saying. He wanted to have conversations with her everyday. He would speak in English and she would speak in French.

He came close to her, looking down at her almost flirtatiously. 'I speak good English, too. Yes!'

'*Oui*' Mary said. She spoke slowly in her pedantic schoolmistress French that she would be delighted to speak with him, but not *à ce moment*; she had work to do. Perhaps she would see him at night before he went back to the camp?

'*Ah, mais oui, mais oui,*' he said, and he drew himself up and clicked his heels, bowing to her as he backed out of the kitchen.

Mary went back to the sitting-room, smiling. Of course, he was too charming—like all Southern people—and he was probably a rogue into the bargain. Still, she liked it: all this heel-clicking, these half-bows from the waist. The Polish soldiers they'd had for the harvest last year had also had it, but with them she had felt it was just put on. There was a coldness about them, a superiority, that she did not feel with the Italians. Of course, the Poles were a free people; maybe they had every right to be arrogant—whereas these Italians were prisoners. But this one was more like a Pole than the others; none of them had that heel-clicking and half-bowing; they were more like children, warm and natural and gay.

Mary opened the sitting-room window as wide as it would open. It was the first sunny day they'd had for several days, and the Italians were taking full advantage of it. Some of them had brought out their dinner and were sitting around the barn-door. The tall French-speaking youth was in the centre, speaking and gesticulating to those around him.

Mary opened the gramophone. 'What are you going to do?' Will asked.

'I'm going to put on some records. Italians like music.'

Mrs Murray sniffed. 'Pampering them, that's what it is. I bet nobody does all these things for our own poor boys in Italy or Germany. My word, they'll be made to work and slave. They won't get fires built for them in barns and coffee boiled for them and gramophones put on at dinner-time. . . . Really, Mary, I whiles think you're not wise.'

Will winked at his wife. 'It's only the auld wife! Never let on you hear her!' he said. 'But see and dinna put on any of your highbrow dirt. None of your Beethoven and Bach! Give them something cheerful.'

'But Beethoven's quite cheerful,' Mary said, putting on the *Emperor Concerto*. 'What could be more cheerful than that? It's like a parade. You can imagine you see horses prancing and nodding their heads and trumpets blowing and flags flying and people cheering. . . .'

'See here,' Will said, searching among the pile of records. 'Here's something more like the thing. *The Muckin' o' Geordie's Byre.* 'That'll make them cock up their lugs! I hear that Geordie has been trying to teach them it, anyway.'

But Mary did not take the record. 'Don't be daft, Will,' she said, and she selected Elisabeth Schumann singing *Batti, Batti, O Bel Masetto* to put on after Beethoven.

'It's just pure nonsense,' Mrs Murray said. 'It's scandalous, pampering them like this. Remember they're our enemies. I'll never forget that it was the Italians who first used poison-gas against the poor defenceless Abyssinians. Really, what between having to do the darning and the mending for their guards and letting them cycle about the steading as they like and play with the guard's rifle. . . . This country 'll soon be run by Italians! And it's people like you and Will that encourage it. All your silly Socialist nonsense. . . .'

'Is the dinner near ready, Mary?' Will cut into his mother's chattering.

They were sitting at dinner when the telephone rang. Will was away for a long time in the office, answering it. 'Who was it, dear?' Mrs Murray said when he came back.

'A man,' he said, shovelling his food quickly into his mouth and not looking up from his plate.

'I knew it must be a man,' Mrs Murray said, trying to be arch. 'I hoped it would be a man, anyway. Mary would have something to say if it had been a woman, wouldn't you, dear?'

Mary looked at her plate, too. She would have liked to have struck Mrs Murray. Did you ever see such a fool! Not even after all these years did she know when to hold her tongue. No wonder Will was so silent. He must have been driven into this silence in self-defence. His mother's inane questions would drive anybody daft.

'Who was it , dear?' Mrs Murray said again.

Will heaved himself round and put his empty plate on the sideboard behind him. 'It was Mr Johnston of the Prison Camp,' he said. 'He phoned to tell me that our Italians are to be cut down to ten on Monday. Now, are you satisfied! What about shouting for the rest of the dinner, Mary?'

Throughout the remainder of the dinner Mrs Murray chattered angrily about the injustice of cutting down the number of their prisoners to ten. 'After Will taking them all this week when he wasn't really needing them! And then next week when the harvest's starting and we're needing them—to be cut down! It's not fair at all. If I were you, Will, I'd complain to the Executive Committee. You have the biggest farm around here. Surely you need more labour than any of your neighbours? I think it's scandalous!'

Will ate his pudding as quickly as possible, then he rose and went out in the middle of his mother's chattering. Mary would have liked to have risen and followed him, but she knew that if she did, Mrs Murray would take offence. So she sat silently and let the old woman air her grievances.

I babble, babble, babble . . . just like Tennyson's Brook. No wonder Will was moody and queer sometimes—after putting up with this for twenty-five years. Mary did her best to protect him from his mother's possessiveness and nagging. She knew that she was possessive about him, too, but not in the same stupid way, she hoped. She realised that he was a man and that he had all a man's outside interests. But his mother still thought of him as a little boy. It was undoubtedly Mrs Murray with her endless stupidities who was the cause of so much of his childishness. Mrs Murray always boasted that she had never thwarted him in any way—and see the result! A pocket dictator! She said, too, that she had always tried to get his confidence—and again see the result! This secretiveness that would drive anybody crazy. Once in a moment of expansion Will himself had blamed his mother for his secretiveness. 'When I was a loon she was aye wanting to know where I'd been or what I'd been doing, and so I got into the habit of telling her as little as possible.' Mary had always remembered this, and so she never questioned him—or if she did she was more furious at herself for asking than she was at him for not answering— and she never nagged at him in the way his mother did when he would not answer.

He was sitting listening to the one o'clock news when she went into the sitting-room. 'We'll have to pick the ten best of our sixteen Tallies,' he said. 'I'll tell the grieve to get their names and we'll send a list back with them to the Camp. After training them and getting them into our ways it would be a pity to send them to somebody else—especially if we got some duds.'

That afternoon Mary went on her bicycle round some of the neighbouring farms to collect for the Red Cross. She returned home at lousing-time. Some of the Italians were speaking to Geordie's two children. The French-speaking youth was down on his hunkers, with his arms round one of them, laughing and talking in a mixture of Italian and English. He sprang up when he saw Mary, clicking his heels and bowing. *'J'aime les enfants,'* he said, smiling. *'J'aime tous les gens.'*

Mary leaned against her bike, smiling from him to the children. 'I like children, too,' she said. 'And I also like all people.

'You do not like this war?' he said, beginning to speak so rapidly in French that she could not follow every word, although she understood the gist of what he was saying. 'It is horrible and useless. Our leader is swollen up with ambition. I do not like our leader. Me—I would not go to the war. I had to be taken. I hate war. I am not Fascisti. I hate Fascisti. I had to run away from the police. I am not well known—but still I had to run away in my own country. I shall not go back to Italy after the war.'

'*Après la guerre . . .*' she said slowly.

He shrugged. 'It must finish some time. In 1944 I think. It must finish then. Then I go to America. I have friends there. Rich friends. They will help me. I shall not go back to Italy.'

'But your family?' she said.

He smiled sadly. 'They must come to America, too. I shall not go back to Italy.' He took a pocket-book from his tunic and opened it, taking out some photographs. 'This is my mother and my sister-in-law. And this is my fiancée,' he said, handing her another.

'*Très jolie,*' Mary said.

It was not a very good photograph of a very ordinary-looking Italian girl. Mary was disappointed. He was a good-looking youth and deserved better. '*Elle est très jolie,*' she said, handing it back. 'The Australians did not get this!'

He sighed. 'No, but—they got other things. Oh, madame, how I hate this war! How glad I am to be here, away from it. This work'— he waved his hand around—'I am not used to it, but I am not afraid of it. It is better to work. Work helps you to forget. In South Africa I was a prisoner for six months and all that time I did nothing. In the camp we just slept. It is not good. Our muscles, they got soft. Our brains—they got soft, too! No, it is very bad. But now here we are in Scotland. We can work. We are not behind barbed wire all the time. Soon when we are able we will be able to work very good.'

'Farm work is hard,' Mary said. 'To those who are not used to it.'

'Ah, but I am not afraid of work, madame. I only say that we are not fit yet for it.'

All the time he was speaking and gesticulating with a purely Southern charm of manner Mary kept telling herself that he was a fraud. He was too plausible, too charming. Watch yourself, she said, don't let yourself be tricked. He's going to ask for something, sure as fate.

'*Apres la guerre,*' he said, 'I shall not go back to Italy. I shall go to America. But I shall need a good friend in this country to help me. You madame—you will be my friend?'

'*Oui, oui,*' she said, unable to explain that, of course, she would be

willing to help him in any way, but with reservations. Who knew
where either he or she would be after the war?

He smiled happily and took a piece of paper from his notebook. 'My
name,' he said, writing it down. 'Mario Belavito. Compagnina, Sicily.
After the war you will write to me there. Yes?'

She nodded, thinking that 'after the war' was such a long way
away that it was quite safe to promise anything.

'Your name?' he said, handing her a piece of paper. 'Write,
please.'

She wrote 'Mrs Mary Murray, The Braes of Lunan, Auchencairn,
Scotland.' Handing it back to him and watching him put it in his
pocket-book beside his photographs, she felt her face go fiery and then
go cold. She knew she'd done something foolish. All sorts of ideas
rushed through her imagination. If anybody saw that slip of paper!
After all, he was a prisoner. An enemy. Suppose anything happened
to him at the camp and he was searched? How did he come to have
her name and address? They'd never believe that she'd given it to him
in a purely friendly way. She might be arrested as a spy. In any case,
what would Will think? The prisoner might show it to any of the
men. They'd say she was carrying on with him. . . .

'Excuse me, I must go,' she said quickly. 'My husband will be in for
his tea soon.'

All evening Mary kept thinking about that scrap of paper. It was
'trading' with the enemy . . . wasn't there a law about it? Heavens, if
the man got caught with it on him? What a fine speak for the folk of
the Howe o' the Mearns! It was a good job that man, Grassic Gibbon,
who wrote the books about the Mearns folk and who was so disliked
by them because of it, was dead, or what a story he'd have made of it!
Should she tell Will? Or should she wait and ask the Italian for the
paper back tomorrow? If the Italian came back tomorrow. . . .
Heavens, what if he didn't. . . .

She was so worried that she had nightmares about it, waking at
last in a sweat because she was standing in the dock with both
Churchill and Mrs Murray scowling down from the bench at her.

The next day Will said: 'There's a Tally here that speaks English and
French.'

"I know,' Mary said. 'I've been speaking to him.'

'The grieve says he's no bloody good,' Will said. 'He talks too
much. We don't want him back.'

'Oh, but Will!' she cried. 'The poor thing—he was so pleased to get

somewhere where somebody understood him. You can surely find
something for him to do.'

'There's nothing he can do,' Will said. 'Except talk! We don't want
him back.'

He put on his cap and went out. Mary sighed. The poor devil of an
Italian—just when he had come to some place where somebody
understood him—somebody of his own kind—for obviously he was
not a peasant like the others—to be driven away because he was not
a good worker. And why should Will be allowed to judge, anyway,
whether a man was a good worker or not? He was as strong as two
men himself—though he would not have lifted a finger to help a man
of half his strength and size lift anything too heavy for him.'And why
should I?' he would have said if he'd been tackled about it. 'I'm paying him to work, amn't I? If he can't manage it, then it's his look out.'

Mary seethed with rage, and she seethed more because she had
nobody she could talk to about it. She knew that it was hopeless to
mention it to Mrs Murray. She felt like speaking to Bella, but was
terrified lest in some way it came back to Will's mother.

About four o'clock that afternoon Will came in and said: 'Mary,
you might get in that boy that speaks English. He's got a list of the ten
best Tallies. You copy it out and we'll send it to the Camp with them
tonight.'

'But he'll want his name on it, too,' she said. 'I don't like . . .'

'Och, we can easy make out another list and keep his name off it,'
Will laughed. 'We'll send it in an envelope!'

Mary did not like the job, but she went to the field where the
Italians were working. The tall one smiled and drew himself up
straight when he saw her coming. *'Pouvez-vous venir avec moi?* she
said. And she added, smiling: *'S'il vous plaît?'*

He spoke rapidly to the Italian sergeant who was in charge of the
squad. The sergeant nodded to Mary, then he started to come with
them. All the way to the house she spoke in French, and the tall
prisoner translated it into Italian to the sergeant.

She sat down at the kitchen-table and dipped her pen in the ink. 'I
will write down the names,' she said slowly in French. 'Will you read
them out to me, please?'

He leaned over her and she shifted uneasily. All the time she was
writing she was acutely aware of the little black hairs on his brown
forearms. 'ANTONINI,' he spelled, 'GIOVANNI. English? John! French,
Jean!'

The sergeant stood back a little frowning. He looked enquiringly
from Mary to the tall prisoner when they spoke. Every now and then
Belavito spoke quickly to him in Italian, and occasionally they

laughed. Mary felt embarrassed and very defenceless. She wished desperately that Will were there. Even Mrs Murray would have been a comfort. . . .

'*Je vous donnerai . . .* the list,' Mary said slowly, '*quand vous avez fini le . . .*' She snapped her fingers. 'Work, work, work! What's the French for work?'

'Ah, *quand nous avons fini le travail!*' Belavito grinned.

Then he drew himself up, clicking his heels. 'Monday—you and me—we will speak more, yes?'

She nodded, feeling sick at her deception. God, how she hated Will for making her do this!

He saluted. 'Good-e-night.'

'Good night,' she said.

She waited for the sergeant to follow him out, but he stood still. Mary glanced at the clock and saw that it was almost five o'clock, time for them to go. The sergeant took the two slips of paper which had to be signed every night from his pocket.

Mary was panic-stricken. She knew that he was waiting for the list of names. 'Excuse me!' she cried. She rushed outside for Will. He was standing with his hands in his pockets, watching the cattlemen branding numbers on the horns of some cows; making no attempt to help them. 'Look!' she cried. 'I've made out a list of names and that boy's name's on it. He insisted that I put it on. I was going to write out the list again, but the sergeant's standing, waiting.'

Will laughed. 'What are you worrying about? I'll soon settle things.'

'What's the lad's name?' he said, following her in. She pointed it out on the list. 'Mario Belavito,' he said, writing it in his note-book. He whistled cheerfully as he signed the slips for the sergeant. 'Good night, sir!' he said in his hearty way, handing back the slips and the list.

The sergeant saluted and went.

Will picked up the telephone. 'Is that the Prisoner of War Camp? That you, Mr Johnston? Well, I've made out a list of the names of the prisoners that I want back. But there's one man's name on it that I don't want. What's his name again, Mary? Belavito—Mario Belavito. Don't send him back at any price! What's that? Oh, my wife put his name on the list to please him. You know what women are, Mr Johnston! Right, you'll see that he doesn't get sent back. Yes, send anybody else you like—but not him!'

All evening Mary had thought about the poor Italian and the way they had tricked him about the the list of names. Every time she looked at Will she hated him. He was so callous, so cruel, so unimaginative. . . . What in God's name had made her marry a man like this?

Wearily she rose, her mind numb with all the thought and venom that had been spinning through it since the afternoon. 'Eleven o'clock,' she said. 'I'm going to bed.'

'Right, dear, I'll be up in a few minutes,' Will said.

She was opening the sitting-room door when he spoke. 'You know,' he said, looking past her, 'I've been thinking a lot about that poor bugger of an Italian all night—you know the one I mean? The one we told the camp not to send back. The one who spoke French, but who's no bloody good. He must have thought he was on velvet when he came here and got you to talk to. It's a pity but . . . Well, I suppose war's war and work's work, and that's an end of it.'

THE PRISONERS was partly written in September–November 1942, laid aside, then finished on 13–14 July 1944. It was published in *The Year of the Short Corn* (Methuen, 1949) and in *The Ploughing Match*, the second volume of the author's *Collected Stories* (Rupert Hart-Davis, 1968).

11 *Alicky's Watch*

ALEXANDER'S WATCH stopped on the morning of his mother's funeral. The watch had belonged to his grandfather and had been given to Alexander on his seventh birthday two years before. It had a large tarnished metal case and he could scarcely see the face through the smoky celluloid front, but Alexander treasured it. He carried it everywhere, and whenever anybody mentioned the time Alexander would take out the watch, look at it, shake his head with the senile seriousness of some old man he had seen, and say: 'Ay, man, but is that the time already?'

And now the watch had stopped. The lesser tragedy assumed proportions which had not been implicit in the greater one. His mother's death seemed far away now because it had been followed by such a period of hustle and bustle: for the past three days the tiny house had been crowded with people coming and going. There had been visits from the undertakers, visits to the drapers for mourning-bands and black neckties. There had been an unwonted silence with muttered 'sshs' whenever he or James spoke too loudly. And there had been continual genteel bickering between his two grandmothers, each of them determined to uphold the dignity of death in the house, but each of them equally determined to have her own way in the arrangements for the funeral.

The funeral was a mere incident after all that had gone before. The stopping of the watch was the real tragedy. At two o'clock when the cars arrived. Alexander still had not got over it. He kept his hand in his pocket, fingering it all through the short service conducted in the parlour while slitherings and muffled knocks signified that the coffin was being carried out to the hearse. And he was still clutching it with a small, sweaty hand when he took his seat in the first car between his father and his Uncle Jimmy.

His mother was to be buried at her birthplace, a small mining village sixteen miles out from Edinburgh. His father and his maternal grandmother, Granny Peebles, had had a lot of argument about this. His father had wanted his mother to be cremated, but Granny Peebles had said: 'But we have the ground, Sandy! We have the ground all ready waiting at Bethniebrig. It would be a pity not to use it. There's plenty of room on top of her father for poor Alice. And there'll still be enough room left for me—God help me!—when I'm ready to follow them.'

'But the expense, Mrs Peebles, the expense,' his father had said. 'It'll cost a lot to take a funeral all that distance, for mind you we'll have a lot o' carriages, there's such a crowd o' us.'

'It winna be ony mair expensive than payin' for cremation,' Granny Peebles had retorted. 'I dinna hold wi' this cremation, onywye, it's ungodly. And besides the ground's there waiting.'

The argument had gone back and forth, but in the end Mrs Peebles had won. Though it was still rankling in his father's mind when he took his seat in the front mourning-car. 'It's a long way, Jimmy,' he said to his brother. 'It's a long way to take the poor lass. She'd ha'e been better, I'm thinkin', to have gone up to Warriston Crematorium.'

'Ay, but Mrs Peebles had her mind made up aboot that,' Uncle Jimmy said. 'She's a tartar, Mrs Peebles, when it comes to layin' doon the law.'

Although Alexander was so preoccupied with his stopped watch he wondered, as he had so often wondered in the past, why his father and his Uncle Jimmy called her Mrs Peebles when they called Granny Matheson 'Mother'. But he did not dare ask.

' "We have the ground at Bethniebrig, Sandy," ' mimicked Uncle Jimmy. ' "And if we have the ground we must use it. There'll still be room left for me when my time comes." The auld limmer, I notice there was no word aboot there bein' room for you when *your* time comes, m'man!'

Alexander's father did not answer. He sat musing in his new-found dignity of widowerhood; his back was already bowed with the responsibility of being father and mother to two small boys. He was only thirty-one.

All the way to Bethniebrig Cemetery Alexander kept his hand in his pocket, clasping the watch. During the burial service, where he was conscious of being watched and afterwards when both he and James were wept over and kissed by many strange women, he did not dare touch his treasure. But on the return journey he took the watch from his pocket and sat with it on his knee. His father was safely in the first car with Mr Ogilvie, the minister, and his mother's uncles, Andrew and Pat. Alexander knew that neither his Uncle Jimmy nor his Uncle Jimmy's chum, Ernie, would mind if he sat with the watch in his hand.

'Is it terrible bad broken, Alicky?' asked James, who was sitting between Ernie and his mother's cousin, Arthur.

'Ay,' Alexander said.

'Never mind, laddie, ye can aye get a new watch, but ye cannie get a new—'

Ernie's observation ended with a yelp of pain. Uncle Jimmy grinned and said: 'Sorry, I didnie notice your leg was in my way!'

The cars were going quicker now than they had gone on the way to the cemetery. Alicky did not look out of the windows; he tinkered with his watch, winding and rewinding it, holding it up to his ear to see if there was any effect.

'Will it never go again, Alicky?' James said.

'Here, you leave Alicky alone and watch the rabbits,' Ernie said, pulling James on his knee. 'My God, look at them! All thae white tails bobbin' aboot! Wish I had a rifle here, I'd soon take a pot-shot at them.'

'Wish we had a pack o' cards,' said Auntie Liz's young man, Matthew. 'We could have a fine wee game o' Solo.'

'I've got my pack in my pocket,' Ernie said, raking for them. 'What aboot it, lads?'

'Well——' Uncle Jimmy looked at Cousin Arthur; then he shook his head. 'No, I dinnie think this is either the time or the place.'

'Whatever you say, pal!' Ernie gave all his attention to James, shooting imaginary rabbits, crooking his finger and making popping sounds with his tongue against the roof of his mouth.

The tram-lines appeared, then the huge villas at Newington. The funeral cars had to slow down when Clerk Street and the busier thoroughfare started. James pressed his nose against the window to gaze at the New Victoria which had enormous posters billing 'a mammoth Western spectacle'.

'Jings, but I'd like to go to that,' he said. 'Wouldn't you, Alicky?'

But Alicky did not look out at the rearing horses and the Red Indians in full chase. He put his watch to his ear and shook it violently for the fiftieth time.

'I doubt it's no good, lad,' Uncle Jimmy said. 'It's a gey auld watch, ye ken. It's seen its days and generation.'

The blinds were up when they got back, and the table was laid for high tea. Granny Matheson and Granny Peebles were buzzing around, carrying plates of cakes and tea-pots. Auntie Liz took the men's coats and hats and piled them on the bed in the back bedroom. Alicky noticed that the front room where the coffin had been was still shut. There was a constrained air about everybody as they stood about in the parlour. They rubbed their hands and spoke about the weather. It was only when Granny Matheson cried: 'Sit in now and get your tea,' that they began to return to normal.

'Will you sit here, Mr Ogilvie, beside me?' she said. 'Uncle Andrew, you 'll sit here beside Liz, and Uncle Pat over there.'

'Sandy, you'll sit here beside me,' Granny Peebles called from the other end of the table. 'And Uncle George'll sit next to Cousin Peggy, and Arthur, you can sit—'

'Arthur's to sit beside Ernie,' Granny Matheson cut in. 'Now, I think that's us all settled, so will you pour the tea at your end, m'dear?'

'I think we'd better wait for Mr Ogilvie,' Granny Peebles said stiffly. And she inclined her head towards the minister, smoothing the black silk of her bosom genteelly.

Alicky and James had been relegated to a small table, which they were glad was nearer to their Granny Matheson's end of the large table. They bowed their heads with everyone else when Mr Oglivie started to pray, but after the first few solemn seconds Alicky allowed himself to keek from under his eyelashes at the dainties on the sideboard. He was sidling his hand into his pocket to feel his watch when Tiddler, the cat, sprang on to the sideboard and nosed a large plate of boiled ham. Alicky squirmed in horror, wondering whether it would be politic to draw attention to the cat and risk being called 'a wicked ungodly wee boy for not payin' attention to what the minister's sayin' about yer puir mammy,' or whether it would be better to ignore it. But Mr Ogilvie saved the situation. He stopped in the middle of a sentence and said calmly in his non-praying voice: 'Mrs Peebles, I see that the cat's up at the boiled ham. Hadn't we better do something about it?'

After tea the minister left, whisky and some bottles of beer were produced for the men, and port wine for the ladies. The company thawed even more. Large, jovial Uncle Pat, whose red face was streaming with sweat, unbuttoned his waistcoat, saying: 'I canna help it, Georgina, if I dinna loosen my westkit I'll burst the buttons. Ye shouldna gi'e fowk sae much to eat!'

'I'm glad you tucked in, and enjoyed yourself,' Granny Peebles said, nodding her head regally.

'Mr Ogilvie's a nice man,' Granny Matheson said, taking a cigarette from Uncle Jimmy. 'But he kind o' cramps yer style, doesn't he? I mean it's no' like havin' one o' yer own in the room. Ye've aye got to be on yer p's and q's wi' him, mindin' he's a minister.'

'Ye havenie tellt us who was all at the cemetery,' she said, blowing a vast cloud of smoke in the air and wafting it off with a plump arm. 'Was there a lot o' Bethniebrig folk there?'

'Ay, there was a good puckle,' Uncle Pat said. 'I saw auld Alec Whitten and young Tam Forbes and——'

'Oh ay, they fair turned out in force,' Uncle Jimmy said.

'And why shouldn't they?' Granny Peebles said. 'After all, our family's had connections with Bethniebrig for generations. I'm glad they didnie forget to pay their respects to puir Alice.' And she dabbed her eyes with a small handkerchief, which had never been shaken out of the fold.

'I must say it's a damned cauld draughty cemetery yon,' Uncle Andrew said. 'I was right glad when Mr Ogilvie stopped haverin' and we got down to business. I was thinkin' I'd likely catch my death o' cauld if he yapped on much longer.'

'Uncle Pat near got his death o' cold, too,' Uncle Jimmy grinned. 'Didn't ye, auld yin?'

'Ay, ay, lad, I near did that!' Uncle Pat guffawed. 'I laid my tile hat ahint a gravestone at the beginnin' o' the service and when it was ower I didna know where it was. Faith, we had a job findin' it.'

'Ay, we had a right search!' Uncle Jimmy said.

'It's a pity headstones havenie knobs on them for hats,' Auntie Liz said.

'Really, Lizzie Matheson!' cried Granny Peebles.

Auntie Liz and the younger women began to clear the table, but Alexander noticed that Auntie Liz did not go so often to the scullery as the others. She stood with dirty plates in her hands, listening to the men who had gathered around the fire. Unce Pat had his feet up on the fender, his large thighs spread wide apart. 'It's a while since we were all gathered together like this,' he remarked, finishing his whisky and placing the glass with an ostentatious clatter on the mantelpiece. 'I think the last time was puir Willie's funeral two years syne.'

'Ay, it's a funny thing but it's aye funerals we seem to meet at,' Uncle Andrew said.

'Well, well, there's nothin' sae bad that hasna got some guid in it,' Uncle Pat said. 'Yes, Sandy lad, I'll take another wee nippie, thank ye!' And he watched his nephew with a benign expression as another dram was poured for him. 'Well, here's your guid health again, Georgina! I'm needin' this, I can tell ye, for it was a cauld journey doon this mornin' frae Aberdeen, and it was a damned sight caulder standin' in that cemetery.'

Alexander squeezed his way behind the sofa into the corner beside the whatnot. Looking to see that he was unnoticed, he drew the watch cautiously from his pocket and tinkered with it. As the room filled with tobacco smoke the talk and laughter got louder.

'Who was yon wi' the long brown moth-eaten coat?' Uncle Jimmy said. 'He came up and shook hands wi' me after the service. I didnie ken him from Adam, but I said howdyedo. God, if he doesnie drink he should take doon his sign!'

'Och, thon cauld wind would make anybody's nose red,' Matthew said.

'Ay, and who was yon hard case in the green bowler?' Ernie said.

'Ach, there was dozens there in bowlers,' Uncle Jimmy said.

'Ah, but this was a *green* bowler!'

Uncle Jimmy guffawed. 'That reminds me o' the bar about the old lady and the minister. Have ye heard it?'

Alexander prised open the case of the watch, then he took a pin from a small box on the whatnot and inserted it delicately into the works. There was loud laughter, and Ernie shouted above the others: 'Ay, but have ye heard the one about—?'

'What are ye doin', Alicky?' James whispered, leaning over the back of the sofa.

'Shut up,' Alexander said in a low voice, bending over the watch and poking gently at the tiny wheels.

'I dinnie see why women can't go to funerals, too,' Auntie Liz said. 'You men ha'e all the fun.'

'Lizzie Matheson!' Granny Peebles cried. 'What a like thing to say! I thought ye were going to help your mother wash the dishes?'

It was going! Alicky could hardly believe his eyes. The small wheels were turning—turning slowly, but they were turning. He held the watch to his ear, and a slow smile of pleasure came over his face.

'What are you two doing there behind the sofa?'

Alexander and James jumped guiltily. 'I've got my watch to go!' Alicky cried to his father. 'Listen!'

'Alexander Matheson, have you nothing better to do than tinker wi' an auld watch?' Granny Peebles said. 'I'm surprised at ye,' she said as she swept out.

Abashed, Alicky huddled down behind the sofa. James climbed over and sat beside him. They listened to the men telling stories and laughing, but when the room darkened and the voices got even louder the two little boys yawned. They whispered together. 'Go on, you ask him,' James pleaded. 'You're the auldest!'

James went on whispering. Beer bottles were emptied, the laughter and the family reminiscences got wilder. And presently, plucking up courage, Alexander went to his father and said: 'Can James and I go to the pictures?'

There was a short silence.

'Alexander Matheson,' his father cried. 'Alexander Matheson, you

should be ashamed o' yersel' sayin' that and your puir mother no'
cauld in her grave.'

'Och, let the kids go, Sandy,' Uncle Jimmy said. 'It's no' much fun
for them here.'

'We're no' here for fun,' Alexander's father said, but his voice
trailed away indecisively.

'You go and put the case to your granny, lad, and see what she
says,' Uncle Jimmy said. He watched the two boys go to the door,
then looking round to see that Mrs Peebles was still out of the room,
he said: 'Your Granny Matheson.'

Five minutes later, after a small lecture, Granny Matheson gave
them the entrance money to the cinema. 'Now remember two things,'
she said, showing them out. 'Don't run, and be sure and keep your
bonnets on.'

'Okay,' Alicky said.

They walked sedately to the end of the street. Alicky could feel the
watch ticking feebly in his pocket, and his fingers caressed the metal
case. When they got to the corner they looked round, then they
whipped off their bonnets, stuffed them in their pockets, and ran as
quickly as they could to the cinema.

ALICKY'S WATCH was written in November 1948 and published in *The
Listener* in August 1949. It was in the collection *The Last Sister* (Methuen,
1950) and in *The Ploughing Match*, the second volume of Urquhart's *Collected
Stories* (Rupert Hart-Davis, 1968). It was broadcast as Radio 4's Morning
Story on 31 July 1979, produced by Match Raper and read by Fraser Kerr. It
has appeared in many anthologies, the most recent of which is *The Wild Ride
and other Scottish Stories* chosen by Gordon Jarvie (Viking Kestrel, 1986).

12 *Win Was Wild*

THE TOOTHLESS OLD trout in the green coat at the end of the bar was knocking back her stout. She was talking at the man next her. He was leaning on the bar, staring at the array of bottles, not paying any attention. But as she drank she became more and more vehement, catching his arm and saying: 'Now listen 'ere, 'Arold, it's the gospel truth, strike me if it ain't.' Her face had become almost the same colour as her dirty cherry-coloured toque which she kept pushing back, showing that she had almost no hair.

'I 'ad only gone to the Ladies,' she said. 'As sure as I put up me 'and to the living God I was only away two minutes, but when I comes back some dirty sod 'ad swiped me beer.'

'Go on, Rosie,' the man said.

'I'm tellin' yer,' she said.

The publican was standing beside the fire, talking to a few men customers. Their laughter at some joke reverberated through the pub.

A small, mousy woman wearing a long black coat mooched morosely through the door and put some money down at the end of the counter. She wore a black felt hat that drooped over her face so that only the tip of her long nose was seen. There was a drip at the end of it.

Rosie went on talking at Harold, then she leaned round him and shouted along the bar:

''Ello, Win, 'ow are yer?'

'Bloomin' well,' Win muttered.

She stared at the money on the counter, her hand hovering a few inches above it. She stood perfectly still, not looking in the direction of the publican and his cronies.

'Well, I ain't been 'ome yet,' Rosie called to her. And she sat back with such a self-satisfied air that she almost fell off her stool.

Win sniffed up the drip at the end of her nose.

'No, I was in two pubs after I left you,' Rosie said. She hit Harold a playful punch on the arm. 'You should 'ave seen me, 'Arold, when I comes out of the Dog and Duck. Coo, but the fresh air took me breath away! But I wasn't born yesterday. I steadied meself whiles I looked in

Atkinson's winder at the new fashions. Lovely silk blouses they was,
too. Could be doin' with one of 'em.'

The publican and the men by the fire hobbled and shook at
another joke.

'Other winder 'ad dresses with the "new look",' Rosie said.
'Should've seen 'em, 'Arold. Skirts down almost to yer ankles. Silly, I
calls it. Don't you Win? But then, Win always 'as the new look,
'aven't yer, gal?'

She giggled hysterically and nudged Harold, leaning past him to
look at Win. But Win was looking from her money to the fire where
the publican was still unheedful of her, and seeing that she was not to
be baited, Rosie went on talking at Harold.

Win continued to stare morosely at her money. After a few
minutes she picked it up and shuffled out quietly.

'Nobody would believe me when I said me beer 'ad been swiped,'
Rosie said. 'I could 'ave sworn meself black in the face, but not one
sod would believe me.'

She looked along the bar and said: 'Coo, Win's gone! She picked up
'er money and went out.'

''As she?' Harold looked beerily along the bar. 'So she 'as.'

'Picked it up and gone,' Rosie shook her head so firmly that her
toque fell over both eyes. 'I asked 'er 'ow she was and she said,
"Bloomin' well," and then she picked up 'er money and sloped.'

'Frank!' she called to the publican. 'I'll 'ave another stout if yer
don't mind.'

'I'll be with yer in a minute, Rosie gal,' he shouted, and he went on
with the story he was telling.

'Win did look wild, didn't she?' Rosie said to Harold. 'She's gone.
Did yer see the way she picked up 'er money and went?'

'Win's been in, Frank', she said as the publican poured her stout.
'She laid down 'er money and then she picked it up and went.'

'I never see 'er,' he said.

'Yes, she's been said. 'Come in and put down 'er
money on the counter and stood and waited for yer to stop tellin' yer
dirty yarns. "'Ow are yer, gal?" I shouts to 'er. "Bloomin' wild," she
says. Didn't she, 'Arold?'

''S right,' Harold said into his pint of mild and bitter.

'What's she got to be wild about?' Frank said.

'Dunno,' Rosie said, taking another drink. 'But she were wild. She
told me. I says, "'Ow are yer, Win?" and she cries, "Bloomin' wild,"
and then she planked down 'er money on the counter and shouts, "I
want service."'

''S right,' Harold muttered.

'I never see 'er,' Frank said.

'Well, she's been and gone.' Rosie took another drink and laughed ribaldly. 'You should've seen 'er, Frank. The way she comes in 'ere and bangs down 'er money and shouts, "I want service." Coo, Win is a caution!'

"S not like Win,' Frank said. 'What cause 'as she got to behave like that? I'll have to speak to her about it. Can't have 'er comin' in 'ere and creatin' such a disturbance. 'S bad for trade.'

"S right,' Harold said.

Rosie was enlarging upon Win's shortcomings when three bulky farm labourers came in. After he had served them with their pints, Frank saw that Win was standing silently behind them. She shuffled forward, put her money on the counter and said: 'The usual, Frank, please.'

"Ere, what's this I've been 'earin' about yer?' Frank said, leaning both hands on the counter and leaning over to her. 'Wot yer mean comin' in 'ere and shoutin' "I want service" the way you done. Couldn't yer see I was busy?'

'I never,' Win said.

'Oh, yes you did,' Frank said. 'Rosie and 'Arold seen yer. They 'eard wot yer said. I ain't goin' to 'ave it, see?'

'But I never,' Win said. 'I been out to the Ladies.'

Rosie gave a rabelaisian cackle. 'Coo, wot a tale! You ain't never been to the Ladies in your life all the time I known yer. You was in an 'uff, gal, because nobody took no notice of yer.'

'I wasn't in no' uff,' Win said.

'Now Win, don't yer go and get yer dander up,' Frank said. 'I won't 'ave such goins-on. This is a quiet, respectable 'ouse and I won't 'ave no disturbances from anybody like you. Wot call 'ad yer to be wild, anyway? Rosie 'ere asks yer civil-like 'ow you was, and you cries, "Bloody well wild," and then yer shouts, "I want some bloody service 'ere," and yer bangs yer money on the counter and then because nobody was takin' no notice of yer, me bein' busy with me other customers, yer picks up yer money and flounces out as though yer 'ad a couple of wild cats fightin' under yer skirts.'

'I never,' Win said.

She sniffed up the drip at the end of her nose. 'I been to the Ladies.'

'Now don't let me catch yer behavin' like that in 'ere again,' Frank admonished, drawing her a half-pint of mild. 'If yer does I'll 'ave to ask yer to take yer custom elsewhere.'

'But——' Win said.

'That's enough,' Frank said majestically, and he swept up her money and flung it in the till. 'Not another word about it, or I warn yer—out yer go and yer don't come back.'

'Whatever you say, Frank,' Win muttered, and she lifted her glass and crept guiltily to her usual seat beside the pin-table. After a furtive look around at their accusing eyes, she dipped her long nose into the glass and was silent.

Rosie watched her with a patronising air, then she turned to Harold and gave him such a regal nod that her toque again fell forward over her eyes.

WIN WAS WILD was written on 11–14 February 1948 and published in Spring 1949 in *Our Time* edited by Randall Swingler and Edgell Rickword. It was in Urquhart's *The Last Sister* (Methuen, 1950) and in *The Ploughing Match*, volume two of his *Collected Stories* (Rupert Hart-Davis, 1968).

13 *The Last Sister*

FOR OVER TWENTY YEARS Hutcheon the grieve's daughters, one after the other, had been maids at the Mill of Burnhill. First there had been Mary, who had come as a gawky child of fourteen. She was there six years, and by the time she had left to get married she had her sister Sarah well trained to take her place. In her turn Sarah left to get married, but Bella stepped into her shoes. And then after Bella came Nell and Nanny and Jean and Agnes. Mrs Crichton, the farmer's wife, had always hoped that Agnes would not follow her sisters, but after seven years Agnes decided to get married, too. And now Norma, the last sister, had come to be maid.

Mrs Crichton had often wondered what she would do after the 'last' sister. Who would she get so well trained, so dependable? For she had needed to train only the first sister. The following sisters had been trained by the sister immediately in front of her. As children each of them had had the run of the house and had seen how things were done and knew everything long before it was her turn to pack her kist and bring it from the grieve's cottage and cart it up the narrow wooden stairs to the small room above the scullery.

Mrs Crichton had had misgivings about Norma ever since she was a small, snottery-nosed child peering fearfully in the back door. Mrs Hutcheon had been well into middle-age when she'd had her, and there was a space of nine years between her and Agnes. Norma's birth had been a surprise to everybody, even to Mrs Hutcheon herself. At the time, Bella, the third sister, was maid in the farm-house, and Mrs Crichton had said: 'And what'll yer mother be callin' this one, I wonder? I doubt she'll have run out o' names by this time!' But Mrs Hutcheon, who had become an inveterate film fan since the building of a cinema in Auchencairn, had christened the child after her favourite actress. A most unsuitable name, Mrs Crichton had thought that day she had gone to see the baby for the first time, and she had had misgivings even then when Mrs Hutcheon grinned up at her and said: 'This ane 'll be a maidie some time, I hope. The last sister. . . .'

All through Norma's childhood Mrs Crichton had thought about this, wondering if the day would ever come when she would have the sleekit little brat as a domestic. For Norma was sleekit. There was no other word for it. The other sisters, whatever their various and individual faults, were honest and above-board. But Norma was underhand and a thief. Knowing this, Mrs Crichton had done her utmost to keep Agnes from marrying. She had successfully put a spoke in the wheel of all the maid's suitors, and for a long time she had thought she had managed, but Joe McIntyre had been stronger than all Mrs Crichton's hints and warnings, and after seven years Agnes had handed in her notice. 'I dinna ken what we're to do,' Mrs Crichton lamented to her husband. 'I've priggit and priggit wi' her, but no matter what I say she'll nae bide.'

'Well, well, if the lassie wants to up tail and get married we canna do anythin' about it,' Mr Crichton said. 'We maun make the best o' it, wife.'

Mrs Crichton sighed. She knew that the best would have to be Norma. Even though other maids had been available, she knew that she could not go past the last of Hutcheon's daughters. Norma was nineteen now, and she had been in several jobs already. She had been maid to young Mrs Moyes of the Barns of Dallow, but she had stayed there only a term. She had told people that the work was too heavy and that Mrs Moyes expected too much, but there was a rumour that Mrs Moyes had missed too many pairs of silk stockings and other articles. Then Norma had joined the A.T.S., but she had been put out of that. She said it was because of a weak heart, but different stories went round the countryside, 'If she'd said because o' a weak head,' Mrs Stormont, one of the cottar women said, 'begod, I'd ha'e believed that quick enough!'

For, added to her other faults, Norma was simple. She was quite a pretty girl but she had a vacant look. She was always giggling and putting up her hand to her mouth. And she was a dirty slut. She never bothered to tidy herself, except when she went to Auchencairn to the pictures. In the house she shambled about all day in her dust-cap and a huge pair of felt slippers. At eleven o'clock at night she would be found crouching in front of the dying kitchen fire, still wearing her dust-cap, writing letters.

She wrote and received a lot of letters. 'Norma's fan mail,' Mr Crichton called them. 'Who the hell does she get to write to?' he often asked his wife.

'Oh, she's got dozens of boy friends. God knows where she gets them all.' Mrs Crichton puffed with exasperation. 'I whiles wish some o' them would come here and see her sittin' like a craw nancy in front o' that fire. I wonder if they'd be sae keen on writin' to her then?'

Norma's amours were a continual source of interest not only to Mrs Crichton but to many others on the farm. Norma could not keep from telling everybody and asking their opinion about the merits of this swain or that. This infuriated Mrs Crichton and she said: 'The quaen's a feckless jade. It's a wonder to me that the lads put up wi' her. I ken if I was a lad I widna be havin' my name bandied about like that by her or any other glaikit limmer.'

But Norma had no sense. 'Tammy doon at the Mains is after me noo,' Mrs Crichton heard her say one morning to two of the cottar women, who were waiting for milk at the byre door. 'I wonder what I should dae? I'm nae terrible keen on him, but . . . he's a nice kind of childe. . . .'

'Has he speired ye yet, Norma?' asked Mrs Stormont.

'No, nae yet,' Norma giggled. 'But he's goin' to. I ken by the way he carries on.'

'Mercy, quaen, ye'd think ye'd had a lot o' experience,' Mrs Dickie said, winking at Mrs Stormont.

'Well, so I ha'e!' Norma giggled again.

'What aboot yon soldier laddie you met last week at the dance?' Mrs Stormont said. 'I thought you were keen on him.'

'Och, him!' Norma gave her head a toss. 'I'm for nae mair ado wi' him. He was tryin' to set me off against Biddy Smith at the Mains, and I'm for nane o' that.'

'Well, what aboot the sailor ye were goin' to get engaged to?'

'I dinna ken.' Norma put her hand up coyly to her weak mouth. 'He's a bit ower serious for me.'

'But they're better to be serious than the other way,' Mrs Dickie said.

'Och, I dinna ken,' Norma tittered.

'I dinna ken what to make o' that maidie, John,' Mrs Crichton said to her husband that evening. 'She's really nae wice. There she was standin' gawpin' and gigglin' while thae two cottar wifies took a loan o' her. I fairly had to bawl at her to make her shift. She was leanin' against the byre door as though fire widna lift her.'

'I wish fire would lift her in the mornins,' Mr Crichton grumbled. 'She's that damned slow. She widna run even though a mole was howkin' it's way up her arse.'

'Really, John! There's nae need to be sae vulgar aboot it,' Mrs Crichton said. She clicked her knitting-needles viciously. 'I'm fair worried aboot her. She's the last sister, mind. I dinna ken what we're to do for a maidie if she gings.'

'I whiles think she'd be better to ging,' Crichton said, puffing his pipe moodily. 'The other Hutcheon lassies were nae bother ava. But this ane! I dinna ken what's come ower the young lassies nowadays. They have respect for neither man nor beast. This mornin' when I asked that limmer, Norma, why ma breakfast wasna ready in time she had the cheek to say: "Well, why do ye nae come and boil the bloody kettle yersel'?" '

'Agnes would never have said that,' he said morosely.

'None o' them would ha'e said it,' his wife said. 'They kenned better than talk like that to their betters. I canna see why Agnes had to go and get married after a' thae years.'

'Well, well, I suppose the lassie felt the urge like everybody else,' Mr Crichton said, switching on the wireless.

'I never thought she was the marryin' kind,' Mrs Crichton said. 'If I had kenned she was for leavin' I would ha'e lookit for another maidie long syne; I widna ha'e put up wi' that Norma and her daft capers.'

Her needles clicked irritably in time with Oscar Rabin and his band. 'It would be awfa to have to train a new maidie after all thae years,' she said. 'And she'd be sure to follow the rest and get married afore long.'

'Ach, there's time enough to worry aboot that when Norma ups and gives notice,' Mr Crichton said.

But despite all her boy friends, Norma never seemed to get any nearer to matrimony. Mrs Crichton soon lost count of her sweethearts. there were always letters from new ones. 'Ye canna blame the lads for stoppin' writin' to her,' Mrs Crichton said. 'That slow, soft way she has o' speakin' would drive ony man to drink. And that face o' hers—faith, I ken it's bonnie enough, but it's got as much expression as a cow's hint end.'

'A cow's hint end has often more,' Mr Crichton said.

When she wasn't crouched in front of the fire, writing letters, Norma would spread all her photographs on the large kitchen table and pore over them. She wrote to all her favourite male film stars, enclosing postage for their photographs; and she had photos of all her boy friends. 'I dinna ken which is worse,' Mrs Crichton lamented. 'Whether it's waur to see her moonin' like a sick cow over thae photos or whether it's better to see her wi' that writing-pad on her knee. Every time I see her gettin' it out, I feel like screamin'. I only wish she was as keen on scrubbin' as she is on writin'. Ye should see the blethers she writes, too!'

Norma was not content with writing the letters; she had to show them to somebody else before she sent them off. And Mrs Crichton was usually that somebody. Night after night Norma would insist upon reading over what she had written. 'Now do ye think that's all right?' she would say. 'If I say that, do you think he'll ken what I mean? Or do ye think I should say this?'

'As if it mattered what she said!' Mrs Crichton said to her husband or whoever else would listen to her. 'She just gets an answer frae them once or twice, and then they stop writin'. Not that Norma seems to care. She's got new fowk to write to by that time. Faith, it beats me what the men see in her. They've never seen her in that dust-cap or else the game would be up.'

But apparently Norma did not think this. Slatternly dressed though she was at all hours of the day, she was continually going out of her way to ogle any man. She waved and shouted out of the windows to the farm-hands, and they were always chaffing her. If she had not been so exasperated, Mrs Crichton would have been amused at all the trouble Norma took. She would slither frantically in her large slippers from the front room where she was making the bed to the stair-window to lean out and shout: 'Ay, there, Wullie!' or 'Ay, ay, Geordie, what a cauld mornin'!'

Most of the farm-hands were safely married, so nothing was thought of their harmless chaffing of Norma. But things took a different turn when three hefty young Irish labourers came to the Mill of Burnhill at the May term. By this time Norma had been with the Crichtons for a year, and Mrs Crichton's fears about her leaving them had died down. She realised that there was nothing in Norma's letters and photographs, and so she worried more about her other faults, which were many. And she worried especially about her habit of petty pilfering.

But the coming of the Irishmen restarted all the old fears about Norma being the last sister. The Irishmen were bachelors, or said they were, and they lived in the bothy at the back of the steading. This bothy had been a stable, but some years ago Mr Crichton had converted it into a dwelling-house for his unmarried men. A regular pig-sty of a place at the best of times, it rapidly became worse by the time the Irishmen had been in it for a few weeks. Every time she passed the open door, Mrs Crichton's nose wrinkled with disgust, and she complained bitterly to her husband. 'Can ye nae make them clean it up, John?' she said. 'It's a fair scunner. I'm sure they could easy take a brush to the floor and gi'e the windows a bit dicht now and then.'

'It's nane o' my business, wife,' he said. 'I pay them for workin' in my fields. They can live like pigs for all I care, so long as they do their work.'

'If ye're sae keen on cleanliness,' he said. 'Why do ye nae send that limmer Norma ower wi' a brush and pail? She could easy gi'e the place a bit red up.'

'Ay, and maybe get red up hersel' into the bargain,' Mrs Crichton said. 'No, no, she's nae settin' foot inside that bothy. If she ever does, I'll have to know the reason why. I widna trust thae Irish loons as far as I could throw them. And I certainly widna trust Norma wi' them.'

'I widna trust Norma wi' anything,' she added.

The bothy-lads gave Mrs Crichton a sad time of it. They borrowed her towels and crockery, they demanded sheets and blankets, and they calmly proceeded either to break or dirty them all. 'My guid bath-towels that I got frae yer sister, Bess, for our Silver Wedding!' she lamented. 'My faith, ye should see the colour o' them now! I was past that bothy this afternoon and there they were, lyin' at the door, draped a' ower the auld horse-trough, and the colour o' a dirty kitchen grate. When I think that I've kept them bye a' thae years in the cupboard to let thae filthy Irishers make them look like dish-cloots. . . . .'

The Irishmen did not care what they said or did, because they had no fixed roots in the neighbourhood. Knowing they were transient, they went to great lengths in larking with the local girls, and simple Norma was easy bait for them. Every night when they came to the back door to collect their cans of milk Norma nearly broke her neck rushing to greet them.

'Sure now, you're the loveliest girl this side of the Shannon, Norma me darlin',' one of them was saying one evening when Mrs Crichton came into the scullery.

'Och, now, Paddy McShane, ye're just kiddin' me,' Norma giggled.

'Kiddin' ye, is it!' Paddy made a mournful face. 'Sure now, you would be knowin' me better than that, surely. It's destroyed I am entirely for the love of ye.'

'Well, destroy yourself quick and get awa' hame out o' here,' Mrs Crichton cut in. 'Takin' a rise out o' a decent girl! Ye should be ashamed o' yerself.'

Paddy glowered, but he said nothing. He had already felt the rough edge of Mrs Crichton's tongue. He was a tall, loose-limbed blond youth, and he might have been termed handsome except that he shambled rather than walked, and he was always dirty.

'Come now, Norma, get on wi' the tatties and stop standin' there like a sick heifer,' Mrs Crichton ordered.

'Isn't Paddy McShane a smasher,' Norma said, picking up a knife and starting to peel a potato in a desultory fashion. 'I could go for that fella in a big way.'

'If ye do, I'll go for you in an even bigger way,' Mrs Crichton snapped. 'Wi' Mr Crichton's big walking-stick!'

As the weeks went past Mrs Crichton sensed rather than saw that an intimacy had sprung up between Paddy and Norma. Try though she did, she could never catch them together, unless in the most innocent way, and so she could not pin them down to anything. And then one night she found Paddy in the kitchen. And not only Paddy. The other two bothy louts were standing in the doorway, and they grinned uneasily and backed outside when they saw her. But Paddy held his ground. He shifted his thighs lazily from their half-seat on the table and said: 'Good evening to ye, Mrs Crichton, we were after askin' Norma here if we could be gettin' the use of a couple more pots. Sure now, the last ones ye gave us are so full of holes that they can be holdin' nothing in them.'

'So it's pots you want now, is it?' cried Mrs Crichton. 'I thought that a tink like yourself would be able to mend the ones ye've got. Do ye think I keep an ironmongery here to be supplying ye all the time for nothing?'

After they had gone with two old pots that Mrs Crichton had used to boil her hens' meat in, she turned on Norma and said: 'If those stinkin' tinks set one foot inside this kitchen again, Norma Hutcheon, I'll give ye such a flytin' that your ears 'll ring for weeks afterwards.'

'I didna ask them in,' Norma whined. 'I'm nae keen on their company. I'd rather be on my lone wi' the cat than listen to their daft Irish tongues.'

But a few nights later Mrs Crichton found Paddy in the kitchen again. And then she knew what everybody else on the farm but herself had known for weeks. Paddy and Norma were courting. 'Ay, the Irish loon is sleevin' Norma,' Mr Crichton said when tackled. 'I hear tell that they're gettin' marriet in the spring.'

'And who told ye that?' Mrs Crichton cried.

'Geordie the cattler. He heard tell from one o' the other Irish childes.'

'Geordie the cattler should mind his own business,' Mrs Crichton snapped. 'Startin' up a rumour like that! Before we ken where we are that glaikit limmer will be givin' in her notice.'

'And what'll I do then?' she wailed.

She determined to put a spoke in Norma's wheel in exactly the same way as she had tried with Agnes. And to do this she attempted to enlist the aid of Mrs Hutcheon and of Agnes herself. If they had not lived so far away, she would have tried to get the sympathy and help of the other sisters, too. In fact, she did think of going the twenty-three miles to Inverbervie to visit Bella, but she couldn't persuade Mr Crichton to drive her there.

Mrs Hutcheon was not much help. 'Och, I dinna see what the

harm there is in it,' she said. 'If Norma wants to ha'e the loon let her ha'e him. We've a' got to get mairriet sometime.'

'But he's a filthy orra tink,' Mrs Crichton cried. 'Ye widna want your daughter to marry a pig o' an Irisher would ye? Have ye seen the stir him and the others ha'e that bothy in? The stink would knock ye doon a mile away.'

'That'll nae worry Norma ava,' Mrs Hutcheon said placidly.

'Faith, I know that,' Mrs Crichton said. 'She and that Irish tink are a well-met pair. I dinna ken how decent fowk like yersel' and Hutcheon ever managed to ha'e such a gormless goose. And surely you and he widna want a Papish for a son-in-law?'

'Och, me and Hutcheon widna worry ower much aboot that,' said Mrs Hutcheon. 'We're nae what ye might ca' kirk-goers ourselves.'

'Ay, I ken that,' Mrs Crichton said.

She did not get any more sympathy when she called upon Agnes. That young woman still remembered Mrs Crichton's campaign to prevent her marrying her own Joe. She said: 'I doot the best thing ye can dae, Mrs Crichton, is to start lookin' for another maidie. I hear that wee Jessie Stormont 'll be leavin' the school soon. If I wis you, I'd put in a word for her.'

'Ay, and ha'e that mother o' hers aye sittin' in ma kitchen, drinkin' tea and gossipin'!' Mrs Crichton cried. 'No, no, before it comes to that I'll apply to an agency.'

But she did not need to do that, because a few days later something happened to stop the intimacy between Norma and Paddy.

For months Mrs Crichton had been pestering her husband to build a fence near the back door so that it would keep her hens from straying into the kitchen and leaving their dropppings on the floor. He had remained stolidly impervious to her cajolings and pleadings, and she had reconciled herself more or less to being bothered by the hens in the same way as she had reconciled herself to the idiosyncrasies of Norma. And then one morning the bothy-lads appeared with a tractor-load of wood and, directed by Mr Crichton with a measuring-tape, they started to hammer posts into the ground.

'Mercy on us!' Mrs Crichton cried. 'Dinna tell me this is to be my fence at last!'

Norma giggled and leaned over her shoulder to watch. 'Don't fence me in!' she sang, waving to Paddy. 'Let me ride through the open country that I lu-uve! Don't *fence* me in. . . .'

'You ride up to the front bedroom and get that bed made,' Mrs Crichton ordered. 'Or I'll give ye boots and saddles where ye'll feel them the most!'

Though she was glad to get her fence at last, Mrs Crichton

wondered, as the day wore on, whether it was worth all the bother. Norma did scarcely any work. She leaned out of the kitchen window, shouting and giggling at the men, and whenever possible she would be outside, leaning against a post, hugging her breasts, gawping and ogling. By late afternoon Mrs Crichton was exasperated almost beyond words. And when from an upstairs window she saw Norma take out tea to them she prepared to give battle.

'I'll warm that quaen's ears for her,' she muttered hastening down to the kitchen, lips pressed tightly. And she folded her arms and stood at the window, waiting until Norma would return with the tray and empty cups; for she was determined not to upbraid her before the men, knowing that her own reputation and not Norma's would be the one to suffer.

Norma sat on a barrow while the bothy-lads drank the tea. They had started to paint the fence with tar, otherwise she would probably have leaned against it.

'Sure now, and that was grand tea, Norma me darlin',' Paddy said, handing her his empty cup. 'Now, off about your business, girl, while we're after gettin' on with the good work.'

He picked up his brush and belaboured the virgin palings. Norma stood, hugging the tray against her waist.

'Och, what's a' the hurry?' she pouted. 'I've nothin' else to do. I'll just bide here and watch ye slappin' on the tar.'

'Sure and if you do, it's over yourself we might be tempted to slap it,' Paddy grinned.

'I'd like to see ye try,' she giggled.

'Would ye now!' he said, and he winked at the others.

'Ay, would I!' Norma tossed her head, confident of her own invulnerability. 'Ye'd never hear the end o' it, Paddy McShane, if one drop o' that tar went on me.'

Paddy laughed and dipped his brush into the tar-pot again. 'Ye never know what might be comin' over you, me darlin',' he said. 'We might not be after stoppin' at tar. We might put a few feathers, too, to make ye upsides with the other ould hens.'

'Just you dare!' Norma giggled.

Mrs Crichton, straining her ears at the window, could not hear what one of the other bothy-lads said, but she heard the roar of laughter. And then she saw Paddy flip his brush playfully at the maid.

There was a scream of rage from Norma. 'Look what ye've done, ye filthy brute! Look at my clean overall!'

'Clean! It was never clean, me darlin',' Paddy laughed again. 'Sure now, and you wouldn't be after tellin' us a bare-faced lie, would ye?'

The youngest bothy-lad guffawed, and emboldened by Paddy's example, he flipped his brush at Norma. And then in a second they were all flipping their brushes at her, and she rushed screaming into the house.

Mrs Crichton was so overjoyed that she did not give Norma the row she had intended; instead she sympathised with her over 'thae filthy Irish tinks.' And that night when Norma spread her photographs and writing-pad over the kitchen table, she smirked with satisfaction. She was glad to see them again. There was no need to worry any longer about the last sister leaving. A Hutcheon had aye been maid at the Mill of Burnhill and a Hutcheon would go on being a maid there. Photographs and all!

A week later Norma announced that she was going to marry a Pole.

Mrs Crichton was preparing to make jam. 'A Pole!' she said, pouring sugar into the jelly-pan. 'What Pole's this?'

'Och, it's a fella I met at a dance a while syne,' Norma said. 'I'd forgotten all aboot him, but he turned up at the pictures last night, and he askit me to marry him. I might as well.'

'Norma Hutcheon, are ye in yer right senses?' Mrs Crichton cried. 'Do you mean to stand there and tell me in cold blood that you're goin' to marry *a Pole?*'

'Ay, and what for no?' Norma said. 'He's a smashin' fella.'

'A Pole!' Mrs Crichton cried. 'A Pole! Goad Almighty, quaen, ye winna be able to understand what he's talkin' aboot.'

'Ach, I ken fine what he's talkin' aboot,' Norma said. 'And onywye, we widna aye be talkin'.' And she sniggered lewdly.

All morning Mrs Crichton argued with her while they made the jam, but Norma said her mind was made up. 'I'm for leavin',' she said.

'And when may I ask is the great event to take place?' Mrs Crichton said, thinking that perhaps sarcasm might work where all other methods had failed.

'Well, Alexei wants me to marry him next week,' Norma said.

'Next week!' Mrs Crichton almost spilled the jam she was pouring into glass jars. 'Next week! But ye winna be able to get marriet by that time. It's ower short notice. What am I to do? Who's to help me here in this big hoose on my lone? Who's to help me wi' Mr Crichton?'

'I dinna ken,' Norma said. 'And what's more, I dinna care.'

'But the ceremony 'll be in Polish,' Mrs Crichton said. 'Ye'll nae be able to understand one word o' it. Not one word.'

'I dinna care,' Norma said. 'I'm for marryin' him, and it would take more than you to stop me, ye interferin' auld bitch.'

There was a long silence.

Mrs Crichton replaced the jelly-pan on the range. 'Norma Hutcheon,' she said slowly, 'I've put up wi' a lot for your father's and mother's sakes and for the sakes o' yer sisters—nice lassies—decent quaens every one o' them—but I winna stand any more o' yer impiddence. Ging upstairs and pack yer kist. You leave this house this very night.'

'Even if I've to do without a maidie,' she said, turning her back.

Half an hour later Norma pranced downstairs, dressed in her Sunday clothes. 'I'll awa' and get ane o' the tractor boys to lift my kist,' she said. 'I'm damned if I'm humphin' it along to our house.'

Mrs Crichton did not answer. She was stirring another panful of jam. And other things had been stirring in her mind during the time Norma had been upstairs. Already Mrs Crichton had counted and recounted the rows of jars of newly made jam. She was sure that two were missing.

She watched Norma mince in her too-high heels across the steading, walking in a roundabout way to avoid the tractor-wheel ruts. Then she pressed her lips together and went upstairs to Norma's room.

The maid's trunk stood in the middle of the floor. Mrs Crichton gave a quick look out of the window before she tried the handle of the trunk. It was unlocked. She lifted the lid.

The missing two pots of jam were standing on top of the clothes.

Mrs Crichton bared her upper teeth for a second, then she tore off the paper-coverings and lifted the jars upside down so that the jam fell in a thick sticky mass over the entire contents of the trunk. Then she replaced the lid and went downstairs.

THE LAST SISTER was written in February 1949 and published as the title story of Fred Urquhart's sixth collection by Methuen in 1950. It appeared in Canada in *Northern Review* of December–January 1951–2, and it was in *The Dying Stallion*, the first volume of his *Collected Stories* (Rupert Hart-Davis, 1967).

14 The Ploughing Match

FOR YEARS ANNIE DEY'S greatest ambition had been to have a ploughing match at the Mains of Balfrithans. For years while she struggled with Robert Dey's fecklessness, urging him on, she had this at the back of her mind. Once when she was a girl on her father's farm, the Barns of Kethnot, there had been a ploughing match, and she well remembered the horses with their manes and tails beribboned and the ploughmen childes in their best clothes and the gentry who had come to judge and look. It was there that she'd first seen Robert Dey. He was twenty and she was sixteen. She had made up her mind then that some day this would happen on her own farm.

And now there was to be a ploughing match at the Mains of Balfrithans. But it was not to be the ploughing match of which Annie Dey had dreamed.

For Annie Dey was bedridden. She had been in bed for over six months. A stroke, the doctor mannie called it. But whatever it was, it was a right scunner, and she could move neither hand nor foot— except one arm a wee bit, enough to feed herself and to hold a pencil and write what she was wanting to say on a pad.. For the shock had taken her voice as well as the power of her limbs.

And that was really the sorest blow to Annie Dey's pride. She that had aye had a tongue on her that would clip cloots to be lying here speechless! It was a judgement, folk said. She knew because Hannah the maid, had reported it to her. And the old woman writhed as she thought of what the grieve and the ploughman childes must say out there in the tractor-shed: 'Only an act o' God would make the auld bitch hold her tongue!'

Annie Dey no longer slept well at nights, and on the morning of the ploughing match she was awake long before the old grandfather clock in the hall struck six. She lay, propped on her pillows, watching the grey light of morning filter through the old-fashioned lace curtains. . . . Since her stroke she had been removed to a room on the ground floor. For handiness, Rose said.

Today was the day she had dreamed about for the last fifty years. Ay, today. . . . But it would not be such a day as she'd pictured. There

104

would be no horses with beribboned manes and tails. No, there would be nothing but tractors—nasty smelling things that were aye backfiring and that ate up gallons and gallons of petrol and paraffin. And Robert Dey was no longer here to be the upstanding billy amongst them all; poor Robert had been under the sod in Auchencairn kirkyard for full ten years. No, their son, Neil, him that was getting a bit too big for his boots, folk said, would lord it over the ploughing match.

Ay, faith, Annie Dey thought, Neillie will lord it all right. Him with his corduroy breeks and expensive tweed jacket and his cap cocked on the side of his head. Those corduroy breeks that nobody but ploughmen would wear in the old days but that seemed to be worn now by students and all kinds of queer billies. In fact, decent childes like ploughmen wouldn't wear them now, saying they were worn only by the gentry. Faith, how ideas and things changed. . . . Ay, Neillie'll lord it nae handy. And so will that ill-gettit quaen of a wife of his, Rose with her polite Edinburgh voice that sends a shiver down a decent body's spine. . . . And Rose would be queening it at the match as she'd 'aye intended she would queen it herself.

The old woman sucked in her lower lip, clamping down her hard gum on it. She looked at her set of false teeth in the tumbler beside the bed, as she closed her eyes in pain. to be beholden to other folk to get them put in her mouth. . . .

She heard sounds showing that Hannah, the maid, was raking out the Esse Cooker in the kitchen. And for the thousandth time the old woman wished she had the use of her speech. She pulled the writing-pad towards her and wrote: 'Six is the time for getting up in this house and not half-past. See and mind that in future or it's down the road you'll go bag and baggage.'

She poked this towards Hannah when the girl brought her a cup of tea. The maid read it, and an angry flush mottled her cheeks. She tore off the sheet and crumpled it in her large red hands.

'Seven o'clock is the time I was told when young Mrs Dey fee-ed me,' she cried. 'So you can put that in your pipe and smoke it, you auld limmer!'

Annie Dey's black eyes glared angrily, but the girl, knowing that the old woman was at her mercy and that Annie Dey also knew it, went on:

'You'd better keep a civil tongue in your head—or maybe I should say a civil hand on your pencil—for where would ye be, I'd like to know, if it wasna for the likes o' me?'

The old woman stared over the girl's shoulder. She snapped her fingers weakly. But it was several minutes before Hannah handed back the writing-pad. The old woman wrote:

'Draw these curtains as far back as you can get them, and bring me the spying-glasses.'

'Now, what would ye be wantin' them for?' Hannah cried. 'They'll nae help ye to see the ploughin' match any better. And forbye, it's far too early yet. I'll bring them later on when I get time. I've the breakfast to get first.'

Annie Dey lifted the cup slowly to her mouth. Her hand shook and she spilt some tea over her chin and her shrunken bosom.

'Ach, that'll mean a clean nightie for ye,' Hannah cried. 'More o' my time wasted! I dinna see for why they dinna get a nurse for ye. Ye'd need a nurse to be aye waitin' on ye hand and foot. I'm sure ye could well afford it.'

'The pink silk nightdress', the old woman wrote.

'Pink silk!' the girl jeered. 'Set ye up, ye prideful auld limmer! And what would you be wantin' with yer pink silk nightie the day! I'm sure none o' the visitors will be comin' in to see you. It's the match they're comin' for, not to see an auld done jade that should be pushin' up the daisies.'

After the girl had gone, banging the door and clattering along the passage like a cart-horse, Annie Dey wondered for the hundredth time if she should complain to Neil about the treatment the maid gave her. But for the hundredth time she decided against it. Hannah was not everything that could be desired, but Hannah was better than some girls could have been. Better the devil you know than the devil you don't know, the old woman thought. She knew that Hannah wouldn't dare to go too far in her tormenting, for Hannah was afraid that one of these days the old woman would recover the use of her speech and limbs; and jobs, even jobs like being a maid on a farm like this, were not all that easy to come by for girls like herself: girls who were coarse and untrained. And besides, Hannah was not really as cruel as she made out; she might complain and be rude, but she aye did what was wanted in the long run. And Hannah was aye willing to come when she rang her bell. She could ring until she was black in the face for all the notice Neil or his wife sometimes took.

Sure enough the spy-glasses were on the tray when Hannah brought her breakfast, but neither she nor the old woman took any notice of them. 'I hope yer egg's soft enough boiled,' the girl said. 'I was standin' over it, watchin' to see that I didna give it more than three minutes, when that coarse tink, the grieve, came bawlin' at the back door. I tellt him to wait a minute, but do ye think he would wait! That man has nae patience ava. I gave him a guid piece o' ma mind, I can tell ye. He wanted to see the maister about some ploy for the ploughin' match, but I just tellt him Mr and Mrs Dey were still in their bed.'

As she ate the egg, trying unsuccessfully to keep the yolk from running down her chin, the old woman reflected bitterly that even on an important morning like this Neil could not rise early. You'd have thought he'd be up betimes to attend to everything. But not him! Lying there beside that thin, jimpit quaen of a wife, while his grieve and men strove and got things ready. Now if only Robert had been here . . . or she had been able herself . . . For she'd aye been able to see to things better than Robert. Poor Robert, he'd never been able to manage. A bonnie-like mess the farm would have been in if it had been left to him. It was she who had striven to make it a success, she who had worked herself to the bone, harrying on the men, planning and striving. . . . And to what end? That Neil should reap the benefit. That Neil should take over, and in a few short months do away with everything she had accomplished. For Neillie had no use for old things. He had done away with the horses she'd been so proud of, the horses she'd reared and gotten prizes for at shows. And in their place he had installed tractors.

Tractors and machinery. . . . Grain elevators and milking-machines and a lot of new-fangled dirt like that. . . . That was all Neillie thought about. They were his gods. 'Man, they're quicker,' he often said. 'Machinery does away with a lot of useless labour.'

The old woman picked angrily at the fringe of the bedcover with her one unpalsied hand. Laziness! That was what was at the root of Neil's liking for machinery. Laziness! He wanted to get things done as quickly as possible so that he could spend the evening playing cards or daffing with his glaikit wife. Or talking into the early hours of morning to other farmer-billies about Massey-Harrises and potato-diggers, talking so much and so late that he couldn't get up in the mornings at a decent hour like his father and grandfather before him. It was just sheer luck that the farm was paying better now than it had ever done. Neil pointed proudly to his tractors and said it was them and all his modern ideas that were making this possible, but the old woman liked to think that she knew better.

Ay, farming was not what it had been. And neither were farmers' wives. That was nine o'clock striking, and there was no sign of Rose. She'd still be lying beside Neil, warm in their bed, leaving that trollop Hannah to trauchle on as she liked. It was high time she was up and seeing about her preparations for the day. For she was be having a big lunch party for the important folk coming to the match. . . .

Annie Dey closed her eyes, trying to shut out the thoughts that came crowding upon her. She pressed down her lids tightly, fighting against the disappointment and the tears. . . .

She put the spy-glasses to her eyes, but they were far too heavy for her weak arm, and she could not adjust the sights properly. She was mouthing silent curses when Rose rushed in with a gay: 'Good morning, Mother, and how did you sleep last night?'

Annie was glad she wasn't able to give an answer and that none was expected of her. Her daughter-in-law's false brightness was a never-healing sore.

Rose fancied herself as a nurse, and she plumped up the old woman's pillows and fussed around her. Annie Dey glowered, for she'd been perfectly comfortable the way Hannah had left her. Whatever Hannah's faults, and clumsy trollop though she was, she aye made a body far more comfortable than Rose could do.

'Were you getting ready to watch the match?' Rose said, taking the spy-glasses. 'Look, I'll get them properly sighted for you.'

You forget that your sight and my sight are two entirely different things, the old woman said to herself. A thing like that would never enter your empty senseless head.

She took the glasses from Rose and mouthed her thanks. Nothing but a blur met her vision as she placed them to her eyes. But she held them there all the time her daughter-in-law was in the room, holding them as a barrier against Rose's chatter.

'It's going to be fine, I think,' Rose said. 'I hope it keeps up, for I don't want folk to be bringing in mud all over my clean carpets. Really, Neil's invited so many people. I told him we could never manage to entertain all those in the house. It's just daft I told him. People coming to a ploughing match don't expect to be entertained in the farm-house. But he would do it. Goodness, I wish sometimes that Neil wasn't so ambitious, for I don't seem able to keep up with him. He's invited Lord Mountarthur and Sir Alexander Romney and Sir John Peters of the Haughs and Mr Chalmers and—God knows how many more. Some are to be asked in for tea, and others are coming to lunch. Last night he said there would be ten for lunch, but this morning he says there'll be at least twelve. I don't know what to make of him. He doesn't seem to think his wife should know at all. I don't know what I'm going to do with only that stupid creature Hannah, and a cottar wifie in to help.'

You should be away getting on with the job just now instead of standing here yammering about it, old Mrs Dey said to herself. But a fat lot you'll do, you senseless neep, it'll be Hannah and the cottar wifie that 'll do everything, and it'll be you that'll get all the credit.

The old woman kept her eyes pressed to the spy-glasses, though she could see nothing. She wished it was her ears that were pressed against such a blankness. Oh, God, if only the stroke had made her deaf instead of dumb. . . .

'I'll be absolutely lost among such a crowd of strangers,' Rose nattered. 'They're all Neil's friends and I never have anything to say to them. I get quite bamboozled with all their farming talk. Thank goodness my two brothers are coming up from Edinburgh. I won't feel quite so lost when they're here.'

Annie Dey laughed sarcastically to herself. That was her daughter-in-law all over. She couldn't stand on her own feet. Whenever there was anything like this she always needed some members of her family there to give her moral support. What would she have done had she been an only child?

Finally, when the old woman wished she could scream in order to relieve her feelings, Rose rushed away to shout senseless directions at Hannah and the woman from the cottages who had come in to help. They would be made up with her, Annie Dey thought, trying to settle herself against the pillows that Rose had plumped up once again. But she failed to make herself comfortable. After a few minutes she rang her bell and kept on ringing it, hoping it would not be Rose who would answer.

Hannah galloped in, her red face even redder than usual. 'What are ye makin' all the noise about, ye auld limmer?' she cried. 'Do ye no' think there's plenty o' uproar in the house already without you makin' it any worse? I never saw such a stir. Young Mrs Dey's goin'about like a hen on a hot girdle. I'd need a dozen pair o' hands to do everythin' she yells at me. If she doesna pipe down I'm for handin' in my notice.'

'Mrs M'Kitterick's fair at boilin' point,' she said as she re-settled the old woman's pillows. 'I ken by the look o' her that it winna take much to make her up tail and awa' hame. And I dinna blame her either. Young Mrs Dey would make a brass monkey answer her back.'

'Never heed her,' Mrs Dey wrote on her pad. 'Sort the glasses for me.'

While Hannah was doing this, the old woman wrote: 'Where's Mr Neil?'

'Och, he's awa' out to superintend operations,' Hannah said. 'The tractors have all started to arrive for the match, but I dare say ye know that without me tellin' ye.'

The old woman blinked her eyelids to show that she had. For the past half-hour the rumble of tractors entering the close and careering down the farm road to the ploughing field had never stopped.

'Tell Mr Neil I want him,' she wrote on her pad.

'Want! Want! Want!' Hannah cried. 'Ye're aye wantin' somethin'. It would take a stationer's shop to keep ye goin' in writing-paper!'

While waiting for her son, the old woman shuddered every time she heard Rose's voice shrieking orders to Hannah or Mrs M'Kitterick. Why does she not talk less and do some of the things herself? Faith, that's what I'd have done. I'd have known then that they were done right, without lippening to the stupidity of a couple of glaikit quaens like that maidie and the M'Kittrick wifie.

'Well, Mother!'

Neil Dey blustered into the room. He was a tall, handsome young man of about thirty, with enormous shoulders and a brown face. The old shrunken woman in the bed, whose frame could scarcely be seen under the bedclothes, wondered again how she had managed to give birth to such a huge ox of a childe.

She pushed her pad towards him. On it she had written: 'See if your mechanical mind can't rig up these glasses so that I don't get another stroke with trying to hold them up.'

'Ay, Mother, but this is a fair problem you're giving me,' Neil grinned. 'Still, we'll see what we can do. I'll be back in a jiffy.'

Mrs Dey's sister, Miss Katie Soutar of the Barns of Kethnot, arrived at eleven o'clock. She was a small, sparse woman, aggressive in a bird-like way. 'Well, well, Annie woman,' she cried as she took off her fur-tippet and folded it carefully on a chair. 'And what kind of contraption's this your braw big son's riggit up for you? Faith, there must be something in his noddle after all besides scales!'

She examined the wires and tripod that Neil had constructed to hold up his mother's spy-glasses. 'Fine, woman, fine,' she said. 'This'll save you raxing to hold them up. Can you see all right?'

Mrs Dey signified that she did. The ploughing match was being held in a large field in front of the farm-house, stretching downhill at the foot of the lawn. Each competitior had got a bit of field marked off and they had already started to plough. 'There's a couple o' lassies amongst them,' Miss Katie said, standing at the window, touching the large cameo brooch fastened on the black velvet ribbon round her scraggy throat. 'Land girls! Dear knows what the world's coming to when quaens like that bid fair to outdo the men.'

Annie Dey pressed her eyes against the glasses. She could see each of the sixteen competing tractors, but mostly she watched the big red Allis-Chalmers driven by Geordie M'Kitterick, one of her own ploughmen. He was going along at a fine skelp, Geordie was, and even at this distance she could see that his rigs were trim and even. Although it was still early in the day a fair crowd of spectators had already arrived. And every minute more cars roared into the farm-close. 'It's a right car-park out there,' Miss Katie reported. 'If I was Neillie I'd charge ilka one of then a tanner a time for parking!'

Annie Dey ground her false teeth together. It was galling to think that her activities were limited to this square of window where she could get only a bird's-eye view. She ached to know what was happening in the house. She heard loud voices and laughter and the continual tramp of feet. A film of angry tears came between her and the panorama of the ploughing field, but she blinked her eyes rapidly to dispel them. And she sent Miss Katie out to report on what was happening.

While her scout was away. Mrs Dey keeked at herself in the hand-mirror Miss Katie had placed on the bed. She touched the neck of her pink silk nightdress, trying to pull it higher over the withered yellow skin of her throat. Miss Katie had done her hair for her. It wasn't as well arranged as Annie Dey would have done it herself, but faith, it was a sight better than either Rose or Hannah could have done. Ay, she looked not bad. A lot better than one would expect after six months in bed. Well enough, anyway, to receive visitors.

'What a stir there is in the house!' Miss Katie came back to report. 'That daughter-in-law of yours is racing about like a scalded cat. You'd think nobody had ever entertained a dozen folk to lunch from the mollygrant she's making.'

'Are you staying to lunch?' Mrs Dey wrote on the pad.

'I haven't been asked,' Miss Katie said. 'But I'm staying all the same. I'm staying until night, until the match is over and the last tractor's away home. I'll have to bide till then, anyway, for my grieve brought me in the car and he'll be staying until the bitter end. I'm not for missing any fun that's going. I doubt Lady Rose winna be pleased ava, but I'm not heeding her. My place is here beside my bedridden sister.' And Miss Katie winked and gave her head such a shake that her brown straw hat swathed in blue ostrich feathers almost fell from its precarious position on top of her thin grey hair.

Annie Dey smiled. She knew that not even an earthquake would budge Katie once she had made up her mind to stay. And suddenly for no reason at all she remembered something she hadn't thought about for years. Something that had happened long syne when she and Katie were young. They had been away for a jaunt in one of those new-fangled charabancs, and there had been an accident. The charabanc had coupit, and there had been a terrible stramash. Folk had been roaring and screaming, though most of them were unhurt, apart from minor bruises and shock. Above them all Katie's shrill voice kept shrieking: 'Save me and my sister first. For we're the Miss

Soutars of Kethnot.' And it had looked as though her persistence would win the day when suddenly from an obscure corner a little voice had piped: 'No, save me first, for I'm my mother's ain dear lambie.'

'Lord Mountarthur was just arriving,' Miss Soutar said. 'My faith, whaten a commotion! You'd think it was the King himself. Neillie and Rose bowing and scraping to him, and Lord Mountarthur this and Lord Mountarthur that. It fair gave me the grue to hear them. And him just a jimpit wee bit mannie with a game leg.'

'That's his car away down the field just now,' she said.

Mrs Dey watched the large black limousine crawl slowly down the farm-brae and into the ploughing field. She saw figures get out of it, her son Neil towering above the others. And she ground her teeth again, thinking that if she had been able she would have been with them.

Rose came rushing in. 'That was Lord Mountarthur,' she cried. 'He took a glass of sherry, and he's staying to lunch. Oh dear, I don't know whether I'm standing on my head or my hands! Can you see them all right, Mother?'

She plumped up Mrs Dey's pillows. The old woman watched her sourly, noting the way Rose was dressed. What a like ticket she was to be the hostess at an important affair like this! That old tweed skirt and that jumper that looked as if it hadn't cost more than three and elevenpence. And that necklace and ear-rings, cheap dirt she'd bought from the Chinese Jewel Shoppe in Princes Street the last time she'd been in Edinburgh. And those awful-like bangles that only a gipsy quaen would be found dead wearing.

Rose noticed that the old woman was looking at her bare legs, and she laughed. 'I haven't had time to put on my stockings yet,' she cried. 'Not that I have a decent pair to put on, anyway. I must away and ask Hannah if she can loan me a pair of hers. I know she's got two or three pairs of nylons that some G.I. sent her from America.'

'Oh, will you stay to lunch, Aunt Katie?' she said as she was going out.

'Ay, faith that was my intention,' Miss Soutar said.

'I—er—I wasn't expecting you,' Rose said. 'And the table's all set for twelve. I wonder if you'd mind having your lunch in here with Mother?'

'I'm sure you'd like that better, anyway,' she said. 'You'll be like me: you'll not be wanting to meet Lord Mountarthur and those other farming men.'

When she had gone, the two old women looked at each other. 'Sort my pillows,' Mrs Dey wrote on her pad. 'Rose always upsets them.'

All day Annie Dey kept her eyes fixed to the spy-glasses while she listened to the buzz and chatter from the hall. She looked often towards her door when she heard footsteps getting louder, but nobody knocked or came into the room. Several times when the expectant knock seemed imminent she fixed her mouth into a smile. But nobody came except Hannah, who galloped in at intervals with some fresh piece of news. And Miss Katie kept going out and in, bringing back her reports.

Neither Neil nor his wife appeared. 'She's awa' down to the field wearin' ma best silk stockings,' Hannah told her. 'Faith, if she gets them all glaur I'll be bonnie and mad!'

Rose appeared for a brief moment at tea-time. 'Oh, dear, what a day!' she cried. 'A lord and two baronets in my sitting-room! I'm so glad my two brothers were here to see for themselves, for they'd never have believed me!'

'Neil said I was to tell you he's never had time to come and see you,' she said. 'He's been so busy attending to everything. He's been fair rushed off his feet.'

Ay, sitting in the sitting-room, talking his head off, the old woman thought. He's never thought of rushing off his feet to come and see his poor old mother, anyway. I suppose he doesn't want any of his braw friends to see the skeleton in the Mains' cupboard.

'Is there anything you want, Mother?' Rose said.

But she had gone before old Mrs Dey could reach for her pad. Not that the old woman would have been capable of writing everything she felt. Her head was a cauldron of boiling words. Nothing she could have written would have had the salt tang of her tongue had she been able to speak.

Miss Katie was out on another reconnoitre. Presently Annie heard a tap at the window and she saw Katie making faces at her through the pane. You glaikit old devil, Mrs Dey said angrily to herself, what are you doing out there, acting like a clown? Remember you're a Miss Soutar of Kethnot. What if some of these orra ploughmen tinks saw you! Come in and tell me what's happenin' now. And she signed imperatively to her sister.

'Geordie M'Kitterick's won!' Miss Katie cried. 'And one of those land girls—the one that was driving that grey David Brown tractor—is second!'

Annie Dey sighed. Well, well, it was as it should be. It was only right that the prize should come to the Mains of Balfrithans. Dear God, if only she'd been fit enough to present the prizes herself. . . .

'Willie Sanderson, my grieve's son from Kethnot got third,' Miss Katie said. 'It's a pity he couldna have got second place instead of that quaen. There should be a law against letting lassies plough. I'm sure in our day no decent quaen would have dreamt of tackling it. Ploughing was always a man's ploy.'

The tractors were leaving the field. The farm road was like an ant-heap with spectators coming up for their cars. The first cars were revving up. . . . Surely now, Annie Dey thought, surely now some of them will come in and see me. Andrew Paton of the Bogs, or Tommy Leitch of the Burn, or some of those other childes that were aye so chief with Robert. They know I'm in bed. Surely some of them 'll come and pay their respects to an old woman who's given them hospitality manys a time in the past. . . .

The cars roared and backfired in the close. The tractors started to rumble up the brae. Miss Katie said: 'I expect my grieve'll be champing and ettling to be away, but he'll just have to wait for me. I'm not leaving yet.'

'It's a sore job when a body has to be beholding to her grieve to drive her home,' she said. 'Whiles I think I should fee one of those chauffeur mannies, but I say to myself: Get away ye daft auld tink, what would you be doing with a chauffeur!'

'Remember you're Miss Soutar of Kethnot', Annie wrote on her pad.

Miss Katie laughed, and Mrs Dey's lips twisted in sympathy, though no sound came from her throat.

'Ay, ay, lass, those were the days!' Miss Katie said. 'But us auld ones have to take a back seat nowadays.'

Rose rushed in, crying: 'Your grieve's waiting for you, Aunt Katie. He says he wants to get away in time to collect some wire-netting in Brechin on the way home.'

'And am I to share my car with a bundle of wire-netting?' Miss Katie Soutar said. 'Faith, but I'll give Jock Sanderson a flea in his ear. This on top of his soft son only getting third prize! I'll soon tell him I can easy get another grieve if he doesna watch his step.'

After her sister had gone, Annie Dey lay and listened to the sounds coming from the hall and sitting-room. She knew that Neil and his fellow farmers would be going over and over all the points of the match, arguing and criticising. She wondered if Lord Mountarthur and the two baronets had gone. Surely they would have asked for her. . . .

Twilight was beginning to stream through the window. The field that had been fallow that morning was ploughed. The rich red earth of the Mains gleamed in the light of the dying sun. The last competitor had gone and the sound of his tractor had faded in the distance.

The old woman rang her bell, wishing Hannah to draw the lace curtains. But although she rang and rang, nobody came. Hannah would be out in the barn, daffing with some ploughman lad no doubt, and there was such a speak in the sitting-room that none there would hear.

Annie Dey pushed away the spy-glasses and leaned her head weakly back on the pillow. It seemed no time since morning. The day had passed far too quickly for her taste. There had been such a commotion and such crowds of people as the Mains of Balfrithans had never seen before. It had been a day of triumph for the Dey family . . . and yet . . . and yet . . .

Occasionally she gave the bell a feeble ring, but hopelessly. And it was almost a shock to her when Hannah's red face peered round the door. 'What is't?' the girl cried.

She switched on the light and drew the curtains. 'Have ye heard the latest?' she said. 'Young Mrs Dey is for wantin' to buy the silver cake-stand that Geordie M'Kitterick won as the first prize. "Buy it from Geordie, dear," she says to Mr Neil. "I'm sure Mrs M'Kitterick will not want to be bothered with a silver cake-stand. She'd rather have the money, I know. What would a ploughman's wife be wanting with a silver cake-stand?"'

'I think she has a right cheek,' Hannah said. 'Don't you? After all, Geordie won it fair and square and his wife has every right to it.'

'Who's all here?' Mrs Dey wrote on her pad.

Hannah recited a list of names. Annie Dey closed her eyes at the end. All of them were people who might conceivably have come into her room to pass the time of day. 'They're all drinking and joking in the sitting-room,' Hannah said. 'My faith, but the whisky and sherry's got a bonnie fright!'

'Young Mrs Dey told me to tell ye she's for bringing her two brothers in to see ye later on,' she said. 'So will I give ye a bit tosh up?'

'Tell her not to bother,' Mrs Dey wrote on her pad. 'I don't want to see anybody now.'

'Well, is there anythin' else ye want?' Hannah said. 'I'm for away out-by to have a bit chaff with some o' the lads in the tractor-shed. I've done more than my fair share o' work the day, I'm tellin' ye. It's time I had a bit o' fun.'

'Put off the light'. Mrs Dey wrote.

When Hannah had gone she lay in the gloom, watching the light fade through the drawn curtains. The pattern of the lace was like a gigantic army of spiders enmeshing her in an enormous web. A tear—of rage, self-pity or loneliness, the old woman did not know which, and now she was beyond caring—rolled down her cheek and she made no move to wipe it away. The laughter and voices from the sitting-room swelled and ebbed, swelled and faded. The old woman, propped on her pillows, began to doze. Scenes passed before her eyes. scenes for which she needed no spy-glass to see more clearly. Scenes from the past swirled through the shadows of the sick-room. Scenes of that ploughing match long, long ago. . . . The horses arched their necks and pranced. The sunlight gleamed on their shiny rumps and lit up the gay ribbons on their manes and tails. The gentry folk bowed and came forward to shake her by the hand. Fine upstanding farmer-childes lifted their hats and shouted their congratulations as she passed through them, leaning on Robert Dey's arm. Lord Mountarthur himself was walking beside her, hat in hand. And there were cheers and loud hand-clapping as she took the silver cake-stand and presented it to Geordie M'Kitterick. . . . Ay, faith, Annie Dey was the queen of them all this day, and she bowed and smiled to right and left, knowing that at last her greatest ambition had come true. . . .

THE PLOUGHING MATCH was written in March–April 1947. It was published by Robert Herring in *Life & Letters Today* in November 1947, and then in John Pudney's anthology *The Pick of Today's Short Stories* (Odhams Press, 1949). It was in the collection *The Last Sister* (Methuen, 1950) and was the title story of volume two of Urquhart's *Collected Stories* (Rupert Hart-Davis, 1968). Its most recent appearance in print was in Ronald Blythe's anthology *My Favourite Village Stories* (Lutterworth Press, 1979).

15 *Elephants, Bairns and Old Men*

OLD WILLIAM PETRIE of Duncraggie Mains had five daughters, a son and a horse. After his son was killed at Dunkirk the horse became old Petrie's dearest possession. He had a number of horses, for although his farm was nearly seven hundred acres it was completely unmechanised. But he had only one Horse. It was never called the Stallion. Sometimes it was called the Staig, but mostly just the Horse. The other horses, except an occasional mare for breeding, were beneath old Petrie's attention, except when his daughters and sons-in-laws tried to get him to turn to tractors. Then he would defend his horses passionately and say that no tractor would ever come to Duncraggie unless it was over his dead body.

Old Petrie's daughters were a disappointment to him. They all nagged. The two oldest were unmarried, and now that each of them was well over forty they were likely to remain so. They ran his house, and they tried to run his farm and him. The other three were married to neighbouring farmers and they came regularly to Duncraggie Mains with their large quiet husbands and large noisy families. And when they got together the five sisters shrieked and rampaged about so much that old Petrie was always driven outside. Usually he took refuge in the Horse's box where he would sit plaiting straw between his rheumatic-twisted fingers.

He was sitting there late in the afternoon of one Hogmanay. The Horse munched oats placidly, and as old Petrie gazed at its gleaming haunches he was thinking of his son. It was eleven years almost since Alec had been killed on the beaches of Dunkirk. Eleven years. . . . Ay, man, but it was a long time. He had never thought when he got the news that he would live all this time to remember it. But the years had slipped by and now here they were at another Hogmanay. . . .

They were expecting the Family. Jenny and Margaret and their husbands were coming for tea and supper, and they would stay until the small hours of the morning after they had seen the New Year in. But Nellie and her husband, Dick Jeffreys, were bringing their children with them to spend the night. 'The bairnies'll brighten Grandpa up,' Nellie had said. 'He must have his dear ones around him at a time like this.'

Dick Jeffreys had aye been the old man's favourite son-in-law, although he was the most strident about the supremacy of machinery over horse-flesh. But he had been Alec's great friend, and this in the old man's view made up for his other shortcomings. Besides, he was a big fine handsome loon, the kind of man Alec had aye shown promise of growing into. They had been at school together, and it was Alec who had first brought Dick to the house. Every Saturday afternoon the two youths had played rugby, and Dick had aye come back for his tea, and they had gone to the cinema together.

The old man sighed now at the remembrance of those Saturday afternoons of so long ago. Fifteen . . . ay, going on for twenty years ago. Mrs Petrie had been living then, and many a chuckle she and he had had together when Dick had begun to grow up and the lassies had got their eyes on him. He had been that big and quiet, with never a word to say for himself when the lassies had chaffed and daffed with him. Ay, there had been a fell stramash amongst them to see which was to get him, and it was funny when you thought that it was wee Nellie that had finally nabbed him. Wee Nellie, the quiet one that had aye had her head buried in a book . . .

The roaring of a high-powered car through the farm-yard disturbed the old man's thoughts. He hoisted himself onto the corn-bin and peered through the dusty cobweb-smeared window. That was Margaret and Bill Johnston, no need to move just yet. 'I can have another quarter of an hour's peace until the whole circus comes, laddie,' he said to the stallion, reseating himself on the corn-bin.

But a few seconds later there was the roaring of another car, then the banging of doors, the high voices of the children, and Nellie's skirls of welcome. The old man sighed and looked at his watch. 'Ay, man, I wonder . . .' he said to the Horse, and he moved over and stroked the beast's neck. Maybe it was better to face them and be done with it? 'Tib and Molly ken I'm deaf,' he muttered. 'But they ken I'm no' so deaf as no' to hear our Nellie!'

'So you're there, Father dear!' Nellie screamed when he poked his head hesitantly around the kitchen door. 'I was just saying to the Girls where on earth could you be at this time of day when there's no work being done on the farm. Come away in and get warmed up. You must be freezing.'

'Ay, where have you been?' Tibby, the eldest girl, snapped, sweeping a lock of grey hair away from her eyes as she bent over the table, cutting sandwiches. 'Sittin' out there on your lone in that smelly horse-box I'll be bound! You'll catch your death of cold, and then who's goin' to nurse you?'

'Ach. I'm fine,' old Petrie said, but he suffered himself to be almost smothered by a hug and kiss from Nellie before he said: 'I'll awa' ben to the sittin'-room and ha'e a crack with the lads.'

His oldest grandchild, Sandy Jeffreys, a loon of ten, was sliding up and down the bannisters as the old man went through the hall. 'Ay there, Granddaddy!' he yelled. 'Look at me!'

'I'm lookin' at ye, my man,' old Petrie said. 'And I'll do more than look at ye if ye scratch these bannisters. I'll warm your hide for ye.'

He scowled as he opened the sitting-room door. He had always disliked Nellie's eldest, perhaps because she had named him after Alec—hoping by this to win the old man's heart and a good share of his fortune—and then decided to call him Sandy. The old man had often pondered upon this. Once in a moment of lucidity he had thought it was because the child was being conceived when Alec was fighting for his life on a foreign beach that he could not bear the sight of him, but he had thrust this quickly from his mind, and now he preferred to think it was because the boy was wild and uncouth.

Dick Jeffreys was standing with his back to the fire, warming his bottom. Bill Johnston was sitting in his father-in-law's favourite easy chair, but neither of them made any show of moving when the old man entered. 'Ay there, Mr Petrie,' Dick boomed. 'I was just saying to Bill that my new Allis-Chalmers is making a grand job of the ploughing. Especially yon stiff field at the burnside. Man, ye should see it spankin' along. It fair knocks all your horses into a cocked hat!'

'Now, bairnies, run away and play!' old Petrie said to little Rose and George, who had rushed screaming from the dining-room and clutched him round the legs. 'Granddaddy wants a rest.'

The children, however, took no heed of him, but, followed by Sandy, they ran ahead of their grandfather into the room, where Sandy immediately threw himself into the only other easy chair.

Old Petrie sat on a stiff-backed chair in front of the piano. He leaned his elbow with a bang on the open keys, but nobody paid the slightest attention to the discordant jangle. 'Have you got all your ploughin' done, Mr Petrie?' Bill asked, taking little Rose between his legs and dancing her up and down.

Dick laughed and stepped away from the fire. He pulled Sandy out of the easy chair and sprawled into it, one enormous tweed-covered thigh dangling over one arm. 'Not him!' he laughed. 'Do ye expect a man that works wi' horses to be done afore the likes of you and me?'

'This was my chair,' Sandy whined, punching his father's arm. 'I was here before you.'

'Get away, loon!' Dick thrust him aside and settled himself more comfortably. 'Get away, all you bairns. Away out of here and give us some peace!'

'Ach, leave the bairnies alone,' Bill said, throwing Rose into the air and laughing with delight at her screech of mock terror. 'They want to see all they can see. Isn't that right, m'dear? You've come to see your Uncle William.'

'Have you got any sweeties?' Sandy said.

'No, Sandy loon, I haven't got any sweeties. Your Uncle William is a poor man and canna afford to buy sweeties.'

'I think I'll put wheat in that field beside the mill,' Dick said. 'It hasna had wheat for two three years, and I had a right guid crop off it the last time.'

'Daddy ate all our sweeties comin' in the car,' Sandy said.

'Whisht, loon, whisht,' Bill said, taking out his cigarette-case. 'Ye manna speak when Daddy's talkin'.' He put a cigarette in his mouth and raked in his waistcoat pocket for his lighter. Dick reached out and gripped his knee. 'Here, you greedy devil!' he said. He took a cigarette from Bill's case but kept a grip on his brother-in-law's knee until he had got a light. Then he leaned back, puffing contentedly, and said: 'I think I'll put in ten acres o' sugar beet this year. It's a lot of work, but the country's needing sugar. And, man, it's a profitable concern.'

'Ay, but it'll nae be you that has the workin' of it,' Bill grinned. 'Ay, lad, but it must be fine to be a gentleman farmer! I wonder how you'd get on if you just had a wee croftie like me?'

'A wee croftie!' Dick grinned boyishly, and he wriggled about in his chair until the springs squeaked. 'Four hundred acres a croftie!' He guffawed and said: 'Man, that's made me feel right thirsty. What about a wee dram out o' your bottle, Mr Petrie?'

'Ay, let's have a wee dram before that drunken brute, Walter Innes, comes and takes it all,' Bill said.

'You're gettin' nothin' to drink until after tea.' Molly, the second Petrie daughter, had bounced in and heard his remark. 'The idea! Wantin' to deprive poor dear Wattie of his fair share!' And she shook her short dyed-brown bob which fell around her red face like an O-Cedar mop and switched on the radio. 'There that's better!' she cried, and she rushed out again, not listening to the blares of jazz mingled with disjointed talk and laughter which comprised a popular so-called comedy programme.

Old William Petrie picked his nose meditatively, looking from the group between him and the fire to the Family Gallery on top of the piano. There were photographs of all the children and grandchildren at different stages of their development. A large studio portrait of Alec in his captain's uniform made the old man look quickly to the three wedding groups arranged near it. The photograph of Nellie and Dick recalled something he thought he had forgotten. *Ay, Alec, loon,* he thought, *you were maybe right when you said yon to him. I was the only one that heard you, and I aye have it up my sleeve to tell her in case our Nellie gets outrageous . . .* He closed his eyes, remembering how Alec had been the best man at the wedding. He had walked around Dick before they set off for the church, smoothing imaginary dust off his enormous shoulders, resetting the carnation in his buttonhole. And old Petrie, peering unobserved through the doorway, had seen him flick the silver horse-shoe hung beneath the flower and heard him say: 'Christ, what does Nellie want you to wear this for? She's got you trickit out like a prize stallion, loon, and faith, she'll ride you to death.' And he had given Dick a friendly smack on the bottom and said: 'For the last time as a single man!' before they had clattered downstairs and into the waiting car.

The old man sighed and opened his eyes. He peered at the photograph. Nellie with her head held coyly to the side, was trying to the last to carry on being a Shy Little Thing, her hand clutching Dick's arm firmly, her fingers twined through his. But the camera had caught the twist of triumph in her smile, and had caught too, the uneasiness behind Dick's boyish grin.

'Here, Sandy!' the old man said. 'Go and ask your mammy if the tea's nae near ready.'

'I will not,' Sandy said.

'Go and do what your grandfather tells you,' Bill said. 'Go on now! See who'll be first!'

But none of the children moved. Sandy leaned against the arm of his father's chair, breathing down the back of his neck and whining. Rose and George looked at each other and giggled.

'Go on now like good bairnies!' Bill said. 'Go on, and Uncle William'll give you all a treat when you come back!'

Sandy rushed to the door, and the two smaller children followed. 'Ay, but I dinna ken what I'm to bribe them with,' Bill sighed, bending down and unlacing his boots. 'I must think up something by the time they come back.'

'Do you think I should try Yielder oats in yon field at the back o' the wood?' Dick said, slapping his knee. 'Man, it's kind of sandy, but I think it might give a fair good crop. What do you think, Bill?'

'I dinna ken,' Bill said, putting his boots beside his chair and stretching out his stockinged feet to the fire. 'What I'm worried about is what I'm to give those bairns when they come back.'

'Tea's nearly ready! Tea's nearly ready! Auntie Tibby's seen Uncle Walter's car comin' up the loan!' The children rushed in, howling, and crowded around Bill. 'You were goin' to give us something, Uncle Bill!'

'Elephants and bairns!' Bill muttered. 'Well now what was Uncle William goin' to give you? Oh, ay!' He grinned and winked at Dick, then he stretched out his feet. 'Now who would like to smell Uncle William's feet? Who wants the first smell? Come on now, bairnies, I'm only going to charge you a penny each. A penny for a delectable smell of Uncle William's delectable feet!'

The chidren giggled, nudging each other and shuffling about, feeling that the grown-ups were laughing at them. It was little George who made the first move. 'Give me a penny, Daddy,' he said to Dick.

Without taking his feet off his chair where he sat like an enormous Buddha, Dick squirmed and shuffled until he had brought out some money from his hip-pocket. 'Here,' he said. 'Here's a penny for each of you, then get to the devil out of here.'

George dealt out the pennies, but the children all stood giggling, and again it was George who made the first move. He handed Bill the penny. then he knelt and solemnly sniffed Bill's foot. 'I've smelled it!' he cried. 'I've smelled it!'

The others followed. Bill laughed, poking his feet in their faces. 'That's a grand smell, isn't it?' he cried, pinching Sandy's bottom. 'Ye couldna make a smell like that, loon!' He counted the pennies they'd given him. 'Threepence! Man, I never knew there was such a fortune in my feet before.'

'I want another penny, Daddy,' Sandy cried.

'Go to the devil!' Dick said. 'Go on, get out of here, the whole lot of you.'

'I want another penny,' Rose cried.

'Man, I never thought my feet would be so popular,' Bill said. 'I must capitalise this. No, no,' he cried pushing little George away. 'No smells for nothing! Go on now, the whole lot of you, the fun's finished!'

'Tea's ready!' Tibby screamed, poking her head around the door. 'Come and get it!'

All through tea old William Petrie sat as though mesmerised. Tibby shrieked at one end of the table, dispensing food, and Molly ranted at the other end. All around him his grandchildren whined and snuffled; his sons-in-law told each other about their crops, and his daughters yelled at the pitch of their voices. The old man scarcely ate; he sank deeper and deeper into a reverie, remembering tea-parties of long ago. Life hadn't seemed so noisy then. His wife had sat at one end of the table, and he had sat at the other. And Alec had been there . . .

Ay, it was changed days. The young men that Alec had brought in about had aye been quiet and deferential, saying 'What do you think I should do with this field, Mr Petrie?' or 'Do you think I could be doing with another six kye, Mr Petrie?' And his daughters had not been so much in evidence. They had been so busy watching the lads that they hadn't had time to talk. Ay, and wee Nellie there, that was roaring her head off just now, had been the quietest of the lot. Her head had aye been buried in a book. The only times she had looked up had been when Dick came to the house after a rugby match, and then she had watched him with adoring eyes. . . . Ay, but she had aye made certain when they piled into two or three cars on a Saturday evening to go to the pictures in the nearest town that she had been crushed against Dick, holding his arm . . .

After tea the children were put to bed much against their will, and their mother and aunts screamed even more than they did. The three young men sat down to play three-handed bridge. Their wives and sisters-in-law congregated around the fire, some with knitting, and Nellie, sitting close to the blaring wireless, held a book firmly against her face. The old man sat on the chair beside the piano, sipping the meagre glass of watered whisky which Tibby had handed him.

'Can ye nae get another programme, Nellie?' he said after a while.

'What's wrong with this, Father dear?' Nellie glanced up from her book, then looked down quickly again in case she missed anything. 'I'm sure we all like this. Don't we, Girls?'

'Ay, this is a fine programme,' Tibby said, craning her neck over the shoulders of the card-players. 'I'm fair enjoyin' it. It's a real fine programme for a Hogmanay night.'

'What about another dram, Tib?' Bill said.

'Ach, have ye nae had enough?' Tibby laughed and went to the sideboard. 'Mind, you lads, this bottle's got to last us till twelve o'clock.'

'Ay, but ye've plenty more in the cupboard!' Bill winked and threw down his ace. 'There, ma bonnie loons, this is my game again! Now, let's see now!' He began to count his score. 'How much is that you both owe me?'

'Och, leave the payin' up till the end,' Walter Innes cried. 'We've got plenty time for a wheen more games yet. Dinna you think that I'm lettin' you get away with this. I'll have my money back from you and more before the New Year's in!'

'Playin' cards on Hogmanay!' Margaret cried. 'And nae only a Hogmanay, but a Sabbath into the bargain! My faith, what would my mother have thought if she'd seen ye?'

'Ach, haud your tongue, wife! The better the day the better the deed!' Bill grinned. 'And Mrs Petrie liked her wee gamie as much as anybody else!'

Old William held out his empty glass to Molly, but she cried: 'Oh no, Father, you've had enough. You've had three nips already, and you ken what the doctor-mannie said. No, no, Father dear, you'll get another one to bring in the New Year and no more!'

The old man hunched in his chair, glancing from the card-players to the clock. Ten o'clock . . . half past . . . Bill was winning, and his howls of glee drowned his brothers-in-law's groans of exasperation. Eleven o'clock. . . . Ay, eleven years ago. The old man looked up at his son's photograph and wondered once again what would have been happening here tonight had Alec been alive. Alec would never have held with all this talk of tractors, and he would never have let Tib and Molly interfere with the running of the farm. Alec had aye been a lad after his own heart . . . fond of horses, not like his brothers-in-law who kept saying that they 'couldn't abide the brutes . . .'.

Half past eleven. . . . He looked again at his son's photograph, then he rose. He was making his way unsteadily to the door when Tibby cried sharply:

'Where are you going, Father?'

'Damn it all,' the old man spluttered. 'Can a man nae ging for a wee walk in his ain hoose?'

He went to the lavatory beside the kitchen, then after a few minutes, listening to see that the coast was clear, he unsnecked the back door and slipped out. It was a clear, frosty night, and the waning moon shone on the rime on the cart-tracks. The old man sniffed, his head lifted to the sky. From the nearby cottar houses he could hear the sounds of singing and merriment. Ay, they were all awake tonight, ready to drink their drams, if they had them, and see the New Year in.

He hobbled across the yard and opened the door of the stable. As he went into the Horse's box, there was a scuffling of straw and snorting as the stallion lumbered to his feet.'It's only me, laddie,' the old man said softly, and the beast gave a low nicker of welcome.

For a long time he stood, rubbing his hand gently up and down the stallion's nose, leaning his thin body against the beast's massive chest for warmth and company. 'Ay, laddie,' he murmured. 'Another year's near gone by, and where are we? How much longer, man, will it be?' He sighed, and the stallion nosed his shoulder in sympathy. 'How long will it be before we're both nae here?' the old man said. And a little later as he heard the ringing of church bells borne on the cold night air from the nearest village, welcoming in the New Year, he muttered: 'Elephants and bairns, Bill said. Ay, and he might well have said "and old men . . .".'

ELEPHANTS, BAIRNS AND OLD MEN was published in *Colophon* in September 1950. It was in Urquhart's seventh collection *The Laundry Girl and The Pole* (Arco Publishers, July, 1955), and was one of the three stories included in *A Third Book of Modern Scottish Stories* edited by Robert Miller and J T Low (Heinemann Educational Books, 1979). The story was broadcast on Scottish BBC in a programme about Fred Urquhart, produced by Gordon Emslie and read by John Shedden on 23 January 1975. It also appeared in 1975 in Denys Val Baker's anthology *Stories of Country Life* (William Kimber).

16 *Maggie Logie and the National Health*

MAGGIE LOGIE WAS a poor, simple but well thought of widow body in the village of Cairncolm. She was liked because she was aye pleasant and not a one to talk behind her neighbours' backs. After her man was killed in the sawmill in 1928, she cleaned the school, did odd bits of washing and cleaning for the minister's wife, and what with that and her widow's pension she managed to get by.

Tam Dodds, the beadle, who had been a mate of Andra Logie's visited her every Saturday afternoon and split a bit of kindling for her fire. He brought a bundle of wood from the mill with him, and after he'd split it, Maggie would give him his tea and they'd have a wee crack in front of the fire.

Usually there was only a bit handful of coal in the grate, but Maggie's big range was aye so highly polished that it gave the impression that the fire was bigger and brighter than it was. The steel fender shone like silver, and Maggie spent a lot of time and elbow-grease on the designs she squiggled with white and red pipeclay on the hearth. A couple of red china dogs with bold black eyes—Pomeranians they were, and they'd belonged to Maggie's Granny—sat on either corner of the mantelpiece; and there was a blue china clock with panels of Greek goddesses with very little on standing in the middle. It had been a wedding present, but it had never gone right since Andra was killed. Occasionally Tam tinkered with it and it went for a few hours, but it aye stopped again. Tam didn't seem to have the knack.

It wasn't long, of course, before the village jaloused that there was something between Tam and Maggie, and gossip was rife. But whenever folk asked about Tam, saying: 'Is it no' high time he was puttin' up the banns for ye baith?' Maggie would simper and say: 'There's nothin' definite, but he's aye comin' aboot.'

Things went on like this for a long time. Tam was thirty-four when Andra died—a couple of years older than Maggie—but he lived with his mother, a cantankerous old body who demanded a lot of

126

attention, and so he was never able to pop the question. By the time the war started he still hadn't popped it, and the auld wife seemed to renew her youth like the eagles when evacuees were billeted in the village. Mrs Dodds made sure she wouldn't get any evacuees herself, for she was bad with phlebitis in the leg and the doctor gave her a certificate to say she mustn't be trauchled with extra work. But this didn't stop her from having wee tea-parties and even taking the bus to Stranraer to go to the pictures with some of the wifies from Glasgow. Maggie got evacuees, of course, and a bairn broke one of the china dogs. Tam patched it together again with secotine, but it never looked the same.

By the end of the war the whole village was changed. The RAF and the Yanks had left their mark, and what with bigger money coming into nearly every house, folk were on a wave of prosperity, the likes of which they'd never dreamed of. Women that used to have just one good frock for Sundays and Women's Rural meetings and that had never even had enough clouts to use as dusters, began to talk about getting washing-machines. And nearly everybody had Hoovers or Electroluxes to keep their new carpets clean. Maggie Logie was now the only one who still hung her bit rugs over the fence in the back garden and walloped them with a stick. Although she'd had a wheen RAF boys and Yanks billeted on her, like most of the village folk, Maggie's house looked much the same as it was that day Andra Logie was brought home feet first.

Whiles Tam asked if she didn't think a wee modern fire would be more economical and easier to work, but Maggie aye said she couldn't be fashed with anything new-fangled. 'And if it's saving the kindlin' you're thinkin' about, Tam Dodds,' she said, 'a modern grate'll take as long to light and need as much wood as that yin.'

And so Tibby the cat, the great-great-great-granddaughter of the first Tibby that Maggie had had when Tam first came about the house, still sat in front of the old-fashioned range. She aye sat there, with her eyes half-shut, on the rag-rug that Maggie had made before she got married. Throughout the years it had got worn with the scuffle of army boots and the claws of Tibby's forebears, and every now and then Maggie would repair it with rags she got from the folks she worked for. The original pattern had disappeared long syne.

Mrs Dodds died the year after the war finished, but it made no difference to Maggie. Tam stayed on in the cottage behind the old smiddy and still came regularly every Saturday afternoon to break Maggie's kindling. Folk said: 'When's he goin' to hang up his hat wi' ye?' but Maggie would just give a bit skirl and say: 'There's nothin' definite yet. He's aye comin' aboot.'

The only thing different that happened was that Tam branched out and bought a motor-bike on the proceeds of his old mother's insurance money. And now every Saturday, after he'd split the kindling, Tam would reive away for a bit hurl with Maggie on the pillion. Whiles they went to Stranraer to the pictures, and whiles they'd go farther afield as far as Glenluce or Port Logan. When folk saw the bike whizzing past with Maggie in her Sunday coat and brown felt hat sitting bolt upright behind Tam, they'd give a bit grin and say things like: 'Love's young dream had better get their skates on before they baith land up in a ditch!' For Maggie was busy with the change, and Tam was a douce, settled man without a black hair left in his head.

At first Tam wore a cap and goggles when cycling, but after a while he got one of these berets that had been so popular with sodgers in the war. It suited him gey well, and when some of the younger lassies in the village felt skittish they'd tell him: 'Ye look a real smasher!' But Maggie aye kept wearing her old brown hat, though by this time she'd sewn some feathers on to it that she'd got from the minister's wife.

Well, the years went by, and still the villagers were speculating about orange blossom—though fine they kenned this wouldn't be likely at Maggie's age—and a slap-bang tea and drinks in the Women's Rural Institute, which was the place most weddings were held. But the only thing that happened was that Tom got rid of his old motor-bike and bought a new one with a side-car. And so he and Maggie now looked quite genteel going about the country, with Maggie sitting fair jecko in the side-car and giving Tam directions occasionally. 'She's gettin' a bit long in the tooth to ride pillion, onyway,' folk said, and it aye gave them something to natter about before some sat down to listen to the Saturday night play and the lucky ones watched the telly. They never went out on the bike on Sundays, for Tam said the minister wouldn't like it, him being the Beadle and near enough to being an Elder of the Kirk, and he must set a good example to the gormless young men of the village, some of whom were little better than these terrible teddy boys you read about in the papers.

But although there was no great change in the way they'd been going on for years, there was a change in Maggie.

When the Welfare State started in 1947, Maggie, like a lot of folk, was quite unaware that it had come into being. She hardly ever read the newspapers and she had no wireless.

'What would I be wantin' wi' a wireless for?' she had said to Tam when he'd urged her to be modern and upsides with everybody else. 'I havenie time to listen til't.' And so it was quite a whilie before Maggie learned how kind Mr Bevan and other big bugs like him had been to poor folk like herself. It was the minister who eventually explained to her all about the National Health Insurance Act. She couldn't take it all in, but she took in enough to understand that from now on she wouldn't need to pay for the doctor or the dentist, that she could get spectacles for nothing, she could even get an artificial limb free, if necessary, and she could get a wig.

'And what would I be wantin' a wig for?' Maggie said.

The minister looked gey taken aback, but he gave a bit laugh and said: 'Well, it happens to all of us in time, Mrs Logie. Nature, you know! The flow of oil to our roots gets clogged and we all—men *and* women—tend to get a little thin on top. Some more than others, of course,' he added quickly.

This talk garred Maggie think a lot more than usual. She hardly ever needed the doctor and she'd never been to a dentist in her life. She knew that she had an insurance card which the schoolmistress kept, for every now and again she'd have to wash her hands and sign it. But she'd never thought anything about it, not missing the ninepence or whatever it was a week that came off her school wages. But she thought about it all right when she found one week that her wages were less than they should have been. 'It's the new insurance stamps, Mrs Logie,' the schoolmistress explained. 'We've all got to pay more now—but look at the *wonderful* benefits we get!'

The schoolmissy was Labour and some folk said she put a lot of tosh into the bairns' heads. She explained all about the virtues of the National Health Insurance Act to Maggie, stressing what a good thing it was for the likes of her. But Maggie wasn't much wiser than she'd been when the minister explained it. One thing she did understand, however, and that was: that every week she was to pay more money to the Government and that for it she would get free medicine, free teeth, free operations, free specs and free hair.

And so, after chewing it over, Maggie made up her mind that she must get her money's worth. She started to go to the doctor's regularly, and it wasn't long before other folk that had aye been considered the standbys of his Panel were fair put in the shade. They got tired of saying: 'What's wrong wi' ye this time, Maggie?' when they went into the waiting-room and found her sitting first in the queue. And they were gey ill pleased when she began to outdo them with her ailments, for Maggie got hold of a medical book in the minister's library and studied it that well that it wasn't long before even the poor old doctor got a bit flummoxed. But he soon discovered that it didn't really matter whether he was able to diagnose the odd complaints or not—though Maggie was aye willing to give him the

benefit of what she'd read about them in the medical book—so long
as she got a prescription to take away with her. Whenever the doctor
was in doubt, Maggie would say: 'What about a nice tonic, doctor? As
well as everthin' else, I feel a wee thing run doon.' And so it wasn't
long before the cupboard in Maggie's back bedroom was filled to
overflowing with full, near-full and half-empty bottles of coloured
water, as well as with boxes of pills of all shapes and colours.

But being the doctor's star patient wasn't enough. Maggie paid a
visit to the dentist and had her teeth seen to. The dentist told her they
weren't at all bad considering her age and that all that was necessary
was a filling here and there, as well as 'a scrape and a polish'. All of
which he did, and all of which meant that Maggie traipsed out and in
to his surgery once a fortnight for two or three months. But not long
after the final polish, Maggie found that the price of insurance stamps
was going up and that another shilling or two would be coming off
her wages. And so she decided to get her money's worth and have all
her teeth out.

The dentist pleaded with her till he was near black in the face, but
Maggie wouldn't take 'No' for an answer. 'Out they come,' she said.
'It'll save me a lot o' trouble in the long run.'

Well, after being toothless for a wheen weeks and having trouble
when she masticated, Maggie got her brand new upper and lower
sets. But even then she wasn't pleased. She didn't think they fitted her
just right, and she was in and out of the dentist's for a good while
having them filed here and filed there. And then when the poor man,
near demented, told her that was the best he could do, she decided
that really the teeth were ower valuable to wear, except on special
occasions. So she kept them in a box on her chiffonier and only
popped them in her mouth when she went to the kirk on Sundays.
She didn't dare wear them when she was out on the bike with Tam
for fear a sudden bump would make her swallow them, so she got
into the habit of winding a white woollen scarf round her face. It was
a gey wide scarf, and only Maggie's eyes could be seen between it and
the rim of her brown hat, and it made an impudent village bairn ask if
she had joined the Ku Klux Klan.

Insurance stamps went up again, so Maggie decided she'd have her
appendix out. The doctor told her it was worse than idiotic, for the
truth of the matter was that the poor old man didn't think that
Maggie had such an organ in her body. But she insisted on her rights,
and the upshot was that she spent a fortnight in hospital and—
although she didn't care for it over much, thinking the nurses were
flibbertigibbets and a bit uppish—she wondered what other
operations she could have.

Now Maggie wasn't what you'd call a reader, except for the times when she pored over the minister's medical book. When she did read the papers on a Sunday afternoon she aye fell asleep ower them before she'd read more than some of the headlines. There was nothing wrong with her eyesight. She could thread a needle quicker than most folk, and could aye tell when she looked out her window what was going on at the other end of the village. But she decided that she'd have to get spectacles, and spectacles she got—a brand new National Health pair with light yellow frames and bits of glass sparkling like jewels just above her eyebrows. She didn't wear them in the house, of course; nor could she wear them when she was working, for they hindered her something dreadful. But she aye wore them when she went out on the motor-bike.

At first Tam didn't pay much heed to what he called Maggie's capers, but when she started to flight on him to go to the doctor's he put his foot down. 'Why should I?' he said. 'In the first place, there's nothin' wrang wi' me. And in the second, if there was, I could cure it quicker masel' instead o' wastin' my time sittin' among a' thae hippykondricks. Time was when ye went to the doctor, there was nobody waitin' but folk that were really ill. But now every man, woman and bairn in Cairncolm's sittin' there waitin' for a free dose o' cough-mixture.'

'But ye must get yer money's worth, Tam,' said Maggie.

'Money's worth!' Tam spat. 'That's a' folk think aboot nowadays.'

But Tam had a lot more to say when Maggie decided she must have a wig.

'A wig! Good God, woman!' he cried. 'Dinnie talk such damned nonsense. Ye've a grand head o' hair o' yer ain. I never heard such havers.'

'My hair's gettin' thin,' Maggie said. 'The minister tellt me that when ye get to oor age the flow o' oil to the roots gets clogged. I dinnie see why I shouldnie have a wig. I've paid for it.'

The doctor was as flabbergasted as Tam when she went to him for a certificate. 'Really, Mrs Logie,' he said, 'this is something I just can't do for you. There's no sign of baldness on your scalp.'

Maggie pled and pled with him, but he wouldn't budge. He even went the length of saying that he'd be more likely to sign a certificate consigning her to the loony bin if she didn't get away home and stop wasting his time.

But Maggie wasn't to be beat. Her mind was made up. The price of the Health Stamps was still rising, and she saw no reason why she shouldn't get all she could while the going was good. So she did a bit of experimenting with the scissors, and finally she cut off nearly all her hair, even going to the length of shaving her head in places. By the time she'd finished plowtering about, it looked as if she'd had a bad case of ringworm. And so she popped on an old dust-cap that had belonged to her mother and wore that for a few days so that folk couldn't but see and ask what was wrong. And, of course, they were all sorry to hear her health was so bad that her hair was falling out, and one and all said: 'Why don't ye see Dr Crombie aboot it?'

That was what Maggie was waiting for, but she didn't go right there and then. She waited for a week so that the doctor would be deeved by other folk saying: 'Isn't it terrible aboot puir Maggie Logie losin' her hair? She's run doon, puir soul, and nae wonder wi' a' the hard work she has to do. It's high time auld Tam Dodds popped the question and took some o' the burden off her. No' that he's likely to dae that now wi' her lookin' like a witch in a mutch. Puir cratur', what she's needin' is a wig.'

Maggie's own hair had been black, though lately it had got gey streaked with grey. But the wig she chose was a bright ginger one. When Tam saw it he was that dumbfounded that all he could say was: 'What next? Dinnie tell me ye're hankerin' after a gammy leg now!'

But Tam had more on his mind than Maggie's wig. His motor-bike and side-car were ten years old and had seen their day and generation. He thought about it for a long time—the better part of a year—and then plucked up his courage and sold them in part-exchange for a new bike and side-car, what the smart-alec in the garage called an up-to-date combination. 'Though I'm thinkin' maybe I should ha'e bocht new combinations for ma auld legs,' Tam said. 'I whiles doot I'm gettin' ower auld for dug-dancin' aboot the country-side on a bike. Especially wi' the traffic bein' so bad and me not bein' able to take the risks a' these young flibbertigibbets take.'

Maggie had been thinking about this, too. And after she read in the papers (for she'd taken to reading the papers to get full use of her new specs) that crash-helmets were necessary and should be made compulsory, she got another bee in her bonnet. If the National Health could give free wigs and free specs and free operations, why could they not give free crash-helmets? And so she paid a visit to the Insurance folk and the upshot was that after she had fair worn them out, so that extra cups of tea had to be made, and there was quite a lot of jookerypawkery, she came away with a certificate.

The following Saturday, when Tam came to the door and shouted 'Keeky-boo!' as he aye did to show Maggie that he was ready, it was a whilie before she appeared. And when she did, Tam stood like a stooky with his mouth wide open.

'Good God!' he said at last.

Maggie had her white woollen scarf wound round her neck and jaws as usual, and on top of them was sitting a muckle white crash-helmet.

'Good God!' Tam said again. 'The woman from Mars!'

Maggie had to pull down her scarf a bit to say: 'Less o' yer sauce, Tam Dodds. If you want to land a cropper and break yer neck, I dinnie. Crash-helmets are very necessary. The papers say so.'

When Tam had recovered and Maggie was sitting in the side-car, he put his leg ower the bike, and they bugbeetled off through the village. A wheen folk saw them whizz by, and one woman said to another: 'Did ye see that daft auld limmer? What next, I wonder!'

That was what Maggie was thinking herself as she sat in the side-car, bolt upright for fear she'd miss anything. She had one cupboard full of medicine, and another cupboard half-full, she had specs, she had teeth, she had a wig and she had a crash-helmet. What could she get next? There must be something. She didn't fancy another operation—though it would aye be a rest. But she was near sixty now, and there seemed to be little else to look forward to but the old age pension. For by now she kenned full well that Tam would never take the plunge and ask her to move into the old cottage behind the smiddy. Not that she wanted to do that, anyway. She was gey content with her own wee house.

There must be something, she thought, as they sped through Stranraer and down the road to Portpatrick. 'Mind that car in front, Tam!' she shouted, for the big black Zodiac was going at a fair lick and it looked as if Tam was ettling to pass it. She was going to add something else, but she jaloused that Tam couldn't hear her for the wind. And just at that moment she had a sudden thought. She'd minded what Tam had once said to her about a gammy leg.

A gammy leg! Now, that was something she'd never managed to get. And it was something she was entitled to, especially with the way these Health stamps kept rising in price. But what would ye do with a gammy leg, Maggie Logie, she asked herself. It would be no good to ye, for ye've got two good pins of your own. Mind you, what with your bunions and sore feet in general, it might be not a bad idea to have a leg sawn off and an artificial one from the Health folk in its place. It would maybe save the wear and tear on stockings . . .

Maggie was that pleased with the idea that she half-raised herself out of her seat and leaned towards Tam to tell him. 'What would ye say if I appeared wi' a gammy leg, auld yin?' she shouted.

But what Tam would say, Maggie never knew. For when she raised herself, Tam was trying to pass the black Zodiac, and what with the wind and the speed, Maggie lost her balance and lurched against him. The next minute the motor-bike-combination had skidded across the road and landed tapsalteerie in the ditch.

When the folk from the black Zodiac came back, they found Tam pinned under the motor-bike. All that was wrong with him was a broken leg, a dislocated shoulder and some scratches. Maggie was lying about five yards away. Her wig and her crash-helmet had come off, and the driver of the Zodiac stared with open mouth at Maggie's cropped head before he bent down to see what was wrong with her. It only needed a bit glance to see she was dead.

Puir Tam. Maggie had never bothered to make a will, so the seven hundred pounds she had in the Post Office and in Savings Certificates all went to her second cousin, who soon made short shrift of all the medicine in the house by filling the ash-bucket with bottles and boxes. Forby taking puir Tibby to the vet to be put to sleep.

MAGGIE LOGIE AND THE NATIONAL HEALTH was written in February 1958 and published in the November–December 1959 issue of *Envoy*. It was in *The Dying Stallion*, the first volume of Urquhart's *Collected Stories* (Rupert Hart-Davis, 1967). It was broadcast by the Scottish BBC on 19 February 1970, produced by Stewart Conn and read by Gudrun Ure.

17 *Pretty Prickly English Rose*

I WAS BUT ELEVEN when I was appointit maid in waiting to the young Queen Joan. I should have been still at home learning my letters in our castle in Angus, yon dreich cauld place on a crag jutting into the North Sea, but my grandfather, the auld earl, said it was time I went to court to learn deportment. He was aye called the auld earl to differentiate him from my father, who was an earl too, having inherited the title from his mother. My grandsire, the Earl of Auchencairn, had married the Countess of Bervie, uniting two great houses.

Phemie, my nurse who had been my mother's maid, protested it was not fitting that I go to court. 'The puir bairn should bide here among the folk she kens, not among strangers, where she'll be laughed at.'

'Blethers, wifie,' the auld earl said. 'She maun face up to her disability sometime, and the sooner the better.'

'She's nae fit yet to ging into the great wide world, and don't you try to force her, Geordie Hepburn,' said Phemie, who was a Hepburn too, though born on the wrong side of the blanket; although it was seldom admitted, she was, in truth, my grandsire's half-sister. 'Ye'll live to regret it.'

'Regret? What is regret, woman? 'Tis a word that means nothing to me. Or any Hepburn.'

'To any male Hepburn mayhap,' Phemie said. 'Ye can speak for yersel', ye stiff-neckit auld blaggart. But I'm speakin' for this bairn, who's nae auld enough yet to speak for hersel', I tell ye, if she gings to the coort she'll be laughed at.'

'She'll live long after she's laughed at,' he said, smoothing my hair. 'Will ye no', Grizel, my wee doo?'

And so indeed it has come to pass. I'm an auld woman now, aulder far than Phemie was then, and I have learnit to thole folks' spite and malice and their cruel laughter. I have lived long after a wheen of them that mockit me are dead and gone. Yet it was hard when first I came among strangers to keep a proud face and smile as Phemie and my grandsire had tellt me.

It was because she was never among the mockers that I loved and worshipped Joan Beaufort. I saw her first at Falkland Palace when my grandsire brought me into her presence. My father, Lord Bervie, was a hostage in England at the time: like several other great Scottish lords he had been sent to the court of Henry VI to languish there while our King James tried by divers new taxations to pay the money for his own ransom. So it fell upon my grandsire to introduce me into the court of King James and Queen Joan.

I mind fine how there was a silence as awesome as the tolling of the death bell as the auld earl led me down the length of the great hall to where she was sitting. We walkit slowly. This was not because of my grandsire's great age but because I could not move at a quicker pace. Seldom have I been more aware than I was yon day of my dragging leg, my long arms reaching to ablow my knees, my right shoulder higher than the other one, and my twisted body. The expanse of polished floor seemed endless as I hirpled along, crab-like, one hand in my grandsire's, the other holding the ebony stick that is aye my truest assistant.

The silence was broken by some titters from the half-dozen braw ladies surrounding Queen Joan. I could feel the blush burning my cheek-bones, but I keepit my head as high as I could manage because of my hunch. My grandsire pressit my hand so hard that it hurt, and I bared my teeth in a smile to keep from yelping.

The Queen turned and glowered at her ladies, but before they became quiet a voice I recognised as my cousin Kate's said clearly. 'I declare to Our Lady, 'tis wee humpy Hep!'

The Queen rose and came to greet us. 'Welcome, Lady Grizel,' she said, bending to kiss me on both cheeks. 'I heard tell from my Lord Auchencairn that you were bonnie, but I scarce expectit you to be as bonnie as this. You have a most beautiful face, my love.'

'Your Majesty is very beautiful yourself,' I said. And I blushit at having been so bold, and I hid my face against my shoulder.

Truly she was the brawest lady. I need not describe her, except to affirm that she had the longest, the most beautiful golden hair and a milk-and-roseblush complexion, for King James has proclaimed rightly to the world in the long poem he scribed after he first saw her from his prison window in Windsor Castle that she was his 'milk white dove' and 'the fairest and the freshest young flower that ever I saw'.

'I am glad, Lord Auchencairn, that you have placed this little maid in my care.' Queen Joan said, giving her hand to my grandsire to kiss. 'I shall nurture her right well and see no harm comes to sully her innocence.'

My grandsire bowed fell deeply and said, 'I can never thank Your Majesty enough.'

There was a skirl from amidst the assembled ladies, and Lady Catherine Douglas rushit forth in a swirl of green silk skirts, swept Queen Joan a bit curtsey, saying. 'By your leave, madam,' and then flung her arms about me and cried, 'Sweet coz! So ye have come to grace the Queen's court?'

My mother and Kate Douglas's were sisters. I never likit Kate, and she never likit me. She is dead now, and it ill befits me to decry her memory. She was hailed as a heroine at one time, and although I have my doubts about her heroics, thinking them false, I will not stoop to hinder her from being given some merit in the history of our native land.

In that year 1424, when I came to court, Kate was nineteen years auld: a big sonsy quaen with an outthrust bust, copper-coloured hair and sandy eyelashes. Her eyes were as green as her gown. She kissit me and said to the Queen. 'She's my puir wee coz, madam, and by your leave I will take her under my wing.'

'Ay, she's your wee coz, Kate,' my grandsire said. 'I trust you will remember that and aye treat her with decorum. I trust too that ye will never forget the honour of the houses of Hepburn and Douglas.'

'There will be scant need for you to take Lady Grizel under your wing, Lady Catherine,' the Queen said. 'She is already under mine, and she shall remain there.' And she took my hand and said, 'Come, my love, bid farewell to your grandfather and then I will show you the apartments that have been assigned for you and your attendants.'

Can it be wondered that I loved Joan Beaufort then? She was aye the kindest and most considerate of mistresses, and never once did she give me a harsh word. Others were not so kind. For longer years than I care to remember, I was ridiculed and never called anything but 'Wee humpy Hep'. It is only in recent times that folk have startit to call me 'the auld crookit Countess'. In those early days, though, apart from the servants, and they were nae often sae polite, the only folk that ever called me 'Lady Grizel' were the Queen and Master Oswald Graham.

Oswald was a big fine-looking childe of nineteen or twenty when I first set eyes on him and fell in love. My heart has been turned by divers braw bucks in my long lifetime—not that it has ever done me any good, for who could look at me without scorn or repulsion or, less often, pity when nothing preventit me from wearing my heart on my sleeve? The fact that I was of great wealth and the owner of vast estates, and a Countess forby, made not a blade of difference to them. But Oswald was a man apart, and he aye treatit me with gentleness and courtesy, and there was never any glint of pity or patronage in his manner towards me. I fell in love with him that first day, and although he has been dead now for these many years I love him still, and I shall never forget his dreadful death. Oft times I awaken throughout the night and a great wave of horror engulfs me, so that I cannot sleep again, and I lie for hours in stomach-churning misery.

Oswald was a gentleman-in-waiting to King James. His Majesty himself I scarce ever saw in my first weeks at court. When I did he was aye fell polite and treatit me as if I looked like everyone else. He was that occupied, though, with affairs of state that he had little time for any of his courtiers, above all a misshapit bairn. He was a handsome man, King James, and in that first year when he came home from long captivity in England after marrying the Lady Joan Beaufort, a cousin of King Henry V, he gladdened the eyes of all beholders. But he did not gladden their hearts when he imposed a tax of twelve pennies on ilka pound of the wealth of his subjects. This tax was levied to help pay his ransom to the rapacious English. No tax had ever been levied in the regency of the King's uncle, the auld Duke of Albany, so even the most loyal courtiers winced and whinged about paying, for loyalty is stricken hard when it comes to the purse and the pocket.

Fewer ladies cast lovesick eyes at the King's broad shoulders and there was fainter applause when he showed his strength at the games he was fond of playing. And there were many murmurs of discontent when he arrestit the auld Earl of Lennox and Sir Robert Graham of Kincardine and castit them intil prison. What King James had against Sir Robert, a fine upright gentleman and a cousin of Master Oswald Graham, nobody knew but His Majesty himself, though many folk made wild conjectures. But it was evident to all that what he had agin Lord Lennox, who was sib to me on my mother's side, was his relationship to the House of Albany. Lord Lennox's daughter was married to Duke Murdoch of Albany, the King's cousin, and it was against the Albany door that the King laid his capture by the English when, a bit lad of twelve, he was on his way to France to receive further education. The King blamit his uncle, the auld Duke, who ruled Scotland for most of the seventeen years James was a prisoner, for not paying a ransom to free him instead of garring him pay this ransom on his lone after he wed Lady Joan, which was what he truly believed although it was the whole Scottish nation that bore the brunt of it. So there was small doubt that his spite against the Albany family causit him to take it out on Lord Lennox, who was a harmless enough auld childe but owned great estates that King James coveted.

I was fond of Lord Lennox, whom I had been brought up to call Uncle Duncan, and I was fell upset at his incarceration. I was in attendance on Queen Joan when she pleadit with the King for him and Sir Robert, and well I remember how the King lookit at her with a hard eye and said, 'I would be grateful, my dearest wife, if ye would not question my authority. Do not fash your sweet head with affairs of state. Now, loveliest of all the English roses, if I summon Master Oswald to attend me at the tennis court, will you and your ladies pleasure us by watching our game?'

But Master Oswald sent back the servant to crave His Majesty's pardon. He was ill abed and unable to play. A day or two afterwards Oswald's illness causit him to leave the palace and ging to his estate near Dunfermline to recuperate. He did not come back to court for a goodly while, by which time Sir Robert Graham had been given his freedom. My puir auld Uncle Duncan was not given his, however, and a wheen months later—six or seven if I recollect properly— the King's hatred for the House of Albany was given full rein and he arrestit Duke Murdoch and his sons, Walter and Alexander. The Albanys and Lord Lennox were tried before an assize of noblemen and, sib though they were to the King himself as well as to most of those that sat in judgement upon them, they were proclaimed guilty of divers false charges. When they were led out to have their heads choppit off on the Heading Hill at Stirling there was much weeping among the spectators and there was no doubt that the King was the most unpopular man in his ain kingdom yon day.

I weepit sore for my Uncle Duncan, especially when King James seized his estates and the Lennox earldom and keepit them for himself. Still anon, folk forget things quickly: far ower quickly it seems to me. Before long the King was popular again, and ladies like my glaikit cousin, Kate Douglas, never stoppit talking about his good looks and his great strength. Even then Kate could not help but show she was in love with His Majesty. It was not seemly to show sic an unbridled passion, howsomever, and so Kate was forced to dissemble and act as though she were in love with divers other young gallants of the court.

If I never knew the blessings of marriage, neither did the Lady Catherine Douglas, who was sic a braw hussy. Kate had an eye for the lads, and the lads had an eye for Kate. Yet though they daffit often enough with her none was ever willing to offer his hand in wedlock. Kate was ower bold even for the boldest of them. She was a domineering wench, and her clippit tongue made the callants steer clear of entering into any long alliance with her. Besides, she had little tocher. However much some of her sweethearts may have lusted after her, none was willing for wedlock when all she had to offer was a small estate in Perthshire and a wee pickle siller.

Yet, though I was resigned to the fate of being an auld maid, me that had great wealth. Kate was not. Like myself, she turned her gaze and the full force of her passion upon Master Oswald Graham when he returned to court after the long mysterious malady that folk whispered about ahint their hands. None ever whispered about it to me, and it was not until long after that I learnit that Master Oswald's illness had been a diplomatic one, him being fell fond of both King James and his cousin Sir Robert and not wanting to take sides with either in whatever was the cause of the strife between them.

Master Oswald found himself in just as sore a pickle when both Lady Kate and I set our caps at him. Puir Oswald, he was hard put to it whiles to keep his dignity and not take to flight like a hare fornent the hunter. Not that he was worriet about myself. After all, I was little more than a bairn, and disabled forby, so all he needit to do was treat me like a favourite sister. And this he did by teaching me the French tongue, playing chess with me for hours on end, reading aloud when I was ower tired to hold the volume myself, and singing ballads in his sweet tenor voice. But when it came to dealing with Kate Douglas, he was like a flounder in deeper, stronger and darker waters. Kate was not content to be treatit like a favourite sister. She hankered not only for Oswald's bonnie countenance and big, braw body; she had her eyes on his wealth and great estates, and both of her grasping hands were ready to stretch out and hold them. Howsomever, Oswald was no fool, and after polite dalliance with Kate, which he could not well prevent since they were in sic close contact at court, he was forced to show that if he was for wedlock, Lady Catherine Douglas was not the lady he would share it with.

Kate was sic a brazent limmer she could not comprehend that Master Oswald was not hers for the plucking, and he had to spell it out in large ciphers. Kate took the rebuff with an ill grace. She had had rebuffs before, and she was to have rebuffs aplenty in the years to come; but this ane from Master Oswald she took extreme sore to heart. From gey near swooning with ecstasy whenever she was in his presence, she startit to behave like a cock at a grossit, doing her utmost to damage him with tongue, teeth and claws.

I shall never forget one instance of Kate's unrelenting hatred of Oswald Graham. This is partly because it showed me for the first time that Joan Beaufort was not the gentle, sweet creature she had aye appeared hitherto. The Queen had occasion to borrow one of Master Oswald's grooms to tend her favourite horse for a week while its regular attendant was sick. The groom tended the beast well but, alas, one hot morning when he led it into the palace yard for the Queen to mount, the horse misbehavit badly, prancing and rearing. The groom, a fair-headed young childe who was also suffering from the heat, lost his temper and struck the beast across the hurdies with his whip. Little did he ken that the Queen was already standing inside the palace door, in the shade, waiting for her favourite.

'How dare you presume to correct our palfrey, serf!' Queen Joan cried. 'For this effrontery you will receive correction from your own whip.'

And she called the seneschal and ordered the groom to be given twelve stripes. She then mountit her horse and her ladies mounted theirs. I was, of course, unable to ride, so I was helpit intil my litter. As I settled myself I heard Lady Catherine Douglas say, 'The knave has neither beggit Your Majesty's pardon nor pleadit for clemency.'

In truth the groom had not uttered a word, though his face flamed with shame at his nakitness being exposed fornent so many fine ladies when he was held by two of the palace guards, his hose were tooken down and he was bendit over.

The Queen said, 'Neither he has. Good seneschal, give the varlet as many stripes as you wish until he begs for mercy.'

And she urgit on her palfrey. As she did so, Lady Kate said with a sly glance through the curtains of my litter, ''Tis a pity the knave's master is not in his place. It would serve him well for allowing sic a scurvy creature to attend til Your Majesty's valuable palfrey.'

'Have no fear, Kate,' the Queen said. 'Master Graham will feel the lash of my tongue ere this day is out.'

'Guidsakes, madam, I never did think ye were sae prickly,' Kate said with a skirl.

'I can be far pricklier than this gin I have the provocation,' the Queen said.

When she came back from her ride the Queen sent for Master Oswald. Howsomever, he had forestalled her. King James himself appeared with Oswald when he came that even to her summons, the King, who was the shorter, with his arm around Oswald's waist.

'What ails ye, my lovely rose?' said King James in a silky voice. 'This is not a bonnie tale I hear from our Oswald. Was the heat ower strong to withhold my lady's ire this forenoon? Oswald tells me his serf is in a fell bad way and will need doctoring for a good wheen weeks.'

The Queen said nothing. She turnit the side of her face to him and said to Kate. 'Lady Catherine, will ye be good enough to read us some stanzas from His Majesty's long poem? Yon poem he wrote to me when he was a poor prisoner in the tower at Windsor?'

And so we all had perforce to listen to Kate mouthing the lines we were ower often deeved with. I watched the Queen's face when Kate recited:

> *And therewith cast I down mine eyes again*
> *Where as I saw, walking under the Tower,*
> *Full secretly new coming here to Pleyne,*
> *The fairest or the freshest young flower*
> *That ever I saw, me thought, before that hour,*
> *For which, sudden abate, anon astart*
> *The blood of all my body to my heart.*

Without looking in the King's direction, the Queen interruptit, 'Mayhap the King's grace does not recollect that Tower? 'Twas so many years ago, and times and feelings change.'

The King laughed heartily and said, 'I recollect yon Tower full well, my lovely English rose. My feelings havena changit with the years, even though we are in a caulder climate now. This was ower het a day for Scotland's clime, and 'tis a great pity that your ladyship's humour was nettled by sic a trivial occurrence. Will ye forget it, my love, and dance a measure?'

He clappit his hands and the musicians struck up a gay, lilting tune. The King walkit smilingly towards Kate, saying, 'If the Queen's Majesty will give her hand to Master Oswald, I will give mine to Lady Catherine. Come, my loves!'

As I watchit Queen Joan treading the steps of the dance with Oswald I realised for the first time that, under all her sweetness, she was as ruthless as the King; and her ruthlessness was stronger and more subtle than his. Besides, she was more devious and this fooled folk the more easily into thinking she was as beautiful inside as she was out. It was the first time I ever criticised my mistress in my mind, but it was not to be the last.

And so in this way the years went by. The court moved from Falkland to Stirling, from Dunfermline to Edinburgh, from Jedburgh to Linlithgow. We bided for a few months in ilka palace or castle, and then movit on to another when the effluvium from the privvies became ower noxious for our noble nostrils. In between whiles I would ging home to Angus for a wheen weeks, sometimes months, to supervise the running of my estates. My father died in his English captivity when I was thirteen and I became Countess of Bervie. My grandfather died of a broken heart seven months afterwards, and so I became Countess of Auchencairn as well. Often after that I was aware of King James looking at me with a speculative eye, and fine I knew he was considering whether it might not be worth his while for something to happen to me, an accident mayhap, so that, since I had no close kin and he was my guardian, he could appropriate my estates and the two earldoms as he had already appropriated the earldoms of Lennox, Mar, Fife and Strathearn, all of which had been forfeit it to the Crown because of divers mishaps.

But I am thankful to say that whatever evil may have passit through His Majesty's mind it never came to fruition, and I hirpled on happily, devoted to the Queen and her bairns, and aye in love with Master Oswald and grateful for every small crumb of comfort and joy he gavit me.

During all this time the Queen gave birth ilka year, except in those in which she had miscarriages. By the time I was three and twenty, in the year 1436, she and King James had six daughters, but only the one son, little Jamie, who was the delight of his mother's and his father's eyes and mine.

And during all these years, too, Kate Douglas nurtured her viperish spite against Oswald Graham, a spite that came to sic a woeful pass in the hinterend. She and I hatit each other more and more until, after it was all over, I would gladly have stranglit her—except that strangling was ower gentle a death for sic a spawn of the Devil.

I was sixteen when Phemie died of an ailment of the breast that she had striven to hide from everybody until the last few weeks when the puir soul was in agony and could not prevent herself from crying out at odd moments when she thought nobody was hearkening til her. Another by-blow of the Hepburns took her place as my maid and companion and faithful guardian. Elspeth was three or four years aulder than me, and we never doubtit that my father and hers were one and the same; but Elspeth, thanks to the blessings of the Lord, was not burdened by any of my infirmities, and she had a nippier tongue than mine intil the bargain. She was aye as able as Phemie had been to protect me from folks' backbitings until she died three years syne.

And as Elspeth was a never-failing prop, against which I leanit with safety, so was I, for a long time, a prop for my favourite next to Prince Jamie, of all the royal bairns, the Lady Joan Stuart. Joan is the third daughter of King James and Queen Joan and, like myself, she is sore afflictit; she is deaf and dumb, puir bairn, even though of unsurpassable beauty like her mother. Since she marriet James Douglas, Lord Dalkeith, a second or third cousin of my own and Kate's, in 1458, I have seen little of her; for after Dalkeith was made

Earl of Morton on their wedding day, she has chosen to settle in his
castle at Dunbar and cloister herself far from court life. But when she
was a bairn she and I were aye together, sic close companions that
my dear coz Kate usit often to skirl to her cronies, ''Tis a question of
the blind leading the lame. Or is it the dumb leading the half-daft? 'Tis
certain anyway that the two dafties seem to crave no other company
than their own. Doubtless 'twould be a guid thing if they would hie
intil a nunnery thegither—'twould be a great blessing to their
families.'

Yet neither Princess Joan nor I had any notion to comply with
Lady Kate's wish. As she grew older Joan did not lippen so much on
my help and company, for a deaf and dumb bairn of her own age was
brought to court to be her maid-in-waiting. This was only as it should
be. I was fell glad for Joan's sake, and it enablit me to turn and fasten
all my affection on her brother Jamie, who was also afflictit with the
strawberry birthmark that, later, made folk call him James of the fiery
face.

Like me, Oswald Graham was devoted to the royal bairns, and he
dandled them in his arms when they were wee, wipit their noses and
their bottoms, helpit to teach them to walk and read and talk, and
held them on their ponies and taught them games, later on, when
their father was ower busy with affairs of state to attend til his
parental duties. Like me, too, Oswald had a favourite. His was the
auldest lassie, Margaret. He and she were fell chief. Often on wet and
snowy winter days, when the King and Queen were out on wolf
hunts and other ploys, and he and I were left ahint to play with the
bairns I have heard the Princess Margaret say, 'I full intend to marry
ye, Oswald, when I grow up. I'd fain be your wee wifie.'

This was not to be, howsomever. Whilst still a bairn Margaret was
affianced to the Dauphin of France. Although she was tellt at the time
that she would be going to Paris one day to be a Queen, Margaret as
often as not forgot it and keepit on saying she would marry Oswald.
Then in 1436, the time came for her to ging to France to be wed. She
was but twelve years auld. She gret full sore when she was told and, I
think she kent then, puir lambie, she would never see Scotland nor
any of us again. Queen Joan was wishful for me to accompany the
Princess to be her chief lady-in-waiting, and I was agreeable, for I
would have likit fine to see Paris. But the King objectit because he did
not consider me auld enough nor experienced enough to be
Margaret's guardian. King James and Queen Joan argued about this,
but the matter was settled with finality when the royal physician
decreed that I would never have the strength to survive the long sea
voyage, far less the stamina and cunning necessary to combat the

rigours and intrigues of the French court. Oft times I have thought King James garred the physician give this verdict because he was feared I might have the wrong kind of influence over the Princess or that I might die and leave the lassie alone and defenceless in yon foreign clime—though this, doubtless, would have givit him a grand opportunity to seize my estates and titles for himself. It is a pity His Majesty thought so poorly of me, for disablit though I am with my hunch and my lameness, I am yet of fell strong constitution, witness the fact that now, as I tell this tale, I am in my eighty-eighth year.

Master Oswald Graham was also wishful to accompany the Princess to Paris, but here again King James puttit down his foot. He tellt Oswald his proper place was here in Scotland to attend on himself, and he refusit to give him permission to ging with Margaret. When Oswald objectit, saying he was Margaret's auldest friend of mature years and near like being her foster-father, and that he felt it only right he should guide her through the mazes of the French Valois family and all their complicated alliances, King James said he would hear no more of it. His Majesty waxed so wroth that he said if Oswald persistit he would bring down upon him the law he had made forbidding certain folk, mainly clerics addicted to the Pope in Rome, to leave Scotland and take their siller to a foreign clime. Master Oswald said he was no cleric and that if he wantit to bide for a while in France he saw no reason why he should be stoppit. Because of this the King and Oswald castit out, and Oswald retired in a huff to his estates in Galloway, swearing he would never show face at court again. Puir man, 'tis a great pity he never keepit that vow.

Howsomever, after a couple of months he and the King's Majesty became reconcilit, and Oswald came back to court in time to see young Margaret set sail from Leith for her new life as the Dauphin's bride. Puir Margaret, like Oswald she was born under an evil star, for she was illservit by yon awful-like man who was to become King Louis XI of France and has aye been known, rightly, as the Spider King. His treatment of the puir lassie was devilish, and it was a blessing in a way that she did not live long enough to become Queen of France.

And so in this fashion, we came to the last winter of the King's reign. By then, after all their catterbattering about Margaret's marriage to the Dauphin, King James and Queen Joan were not cohabiting. And for a while now Kate Douglas had achievit her ambition and was become the King's mistress. Queen Joan Beaufort consolit herself with

Sir James Stewart, who was aye called 'The Black Knight of Lorn'. And I will say in her favour that she was more discreet about her dealings with Sir James than the King was about his with Lady Kate.

What the King's feelings were about Sir James I know not. On the surface he aye greetit him in a friendly manner, and they oft played tennis thegither. Indeed, it was Sir James now that the King played with more often than he played with Master Oswald. As for the Queen and Kate, they were like sisters, living in each other's laps and seldom apart, except when Kate was in the King's bed.

I, alas, had nobody to console myself with. Although Oswald had come back from Galloway, his manner and way of life seemed to have changit. He was not so gay and blithe as was his wont in past years. He broodit greatly, and he was prone to sudden fits of black rage that ill became him. Mark ye, he seldom showed this ill-humour fornent me; we still played chess, and he would sing and read to me as of yore. Yet I could not but notice that every wee while he would appear to forget what he was doing and stare into vacancy like a bullock in a pen waiting for the slaughterman's mallet.

In December 1436 the court movit to Perth where the King was to preside over a council receiving a papal legate. Perth Castle was in a sorry state, so we took up residence in the Black Friars' monastery outside the town. The monastery was a bit crampit for sic a large assembly, even though the friars cooried six and seven in a cell to give the courtiers more space. I shared a room with Kate Douglas and Elspeth and Kate's maid, Kirsten. It was a fell squeeze, but the weather was cauld and, the firing in the monastery being austere, none of us mindit much, except Kate who was aware of the rest of us watching ilka time she slippit out to ging to the King's chamber.

Whilst waiting for the great council to start, the King amusit himself by playing tennis with Oswald and the Black Knight of Lorn and his private chamberlain, Sir Robert Stuart, the grandson of the auld Earl of Atholl, who was of the blood royal and some folk said should have been king instead of King James. The King had gotten ower stout for his age—he was but thirty-eight— and he gave himself over to the tennis in an attempt to lessen his corpulence. He and his three attendants appeared to get on full well while playing their games, but they played with sic vigour, especially the King's grace, who did not seem aware of his own great strength, that they keepit sending the tennis-balls into an underground vault where they rolled down a drain intil the stagnant waters of the moat. So, incensed at losing sae many balls, for he was a most parsimonious childe, the King had the drain vault closit up. This was an act that was to cost him unco dear in the long run.

Another manner the King found of amusing himself was to visit a
Celtic seeress to have his fortune told. But he was not so amusit when
she tellt him he would be kilt before long and that his body would
have sixteen wounds. He tried to laugh off her warning, gave her a
paltry pickle siller for her pains, and in a gay court that Christmastide
His Majesty was the gayest person.

In the New Year I fell ill. I shivered with cauld and was hot with
fever, turn and turn about, and so perforce I had to take to my bed.
Day after day, week after week, I lay there wishing I could have this
illness in the wider space of my own chamber in my dreich castle in
Angus. But I could not quit the court, for by then snow had fallen
heavily and the roads were blocked. It would have been ill advisit for
me to travel in sic a feeble state, even though I would have been well
happit in a litter. Sometimes Oswald came to see me, and he would sit
and glower in atween reading or singing to me. He would give me
some news of the court's ongoings: how many were away on a wolf
hunt, what had been said at the last meeting of the great council,
news of the royal bairns who had been forbiddit to come and see me
in case they caught an infection, and sic like bits of homely gossip.
But most of my news was gleanit from Elspeth, who keepit me well
nourished with titbits.

And so it was she who came bursting into my room about
midnight on 21 February and tellt me that King James had been
murdered.

'Oh, my leddy!' she cried, for she never took advantage of being
born on the wrong side of the blanket. 'Sic terrible ongoings there has
been this nicht. The puir King has been stabbit to death. 'Tis a wonder
ye didna hear all the fearsome clamour. 'Twas enough to waken the
dead—though nothing will waken the King now, puir unfortunate
gentleman. His Majesty was preparin' to retire, and the Queen and
Lady Kate were helpin' to remove his harness—for he'd been joustin'
this even with Master Oswald on horseback in the tilt-yard ootby—
and me and Lady Kate's maidie, Kirsten, were helpin' and wonderin',
I micht as well say, which o' the ladies the King was for beddin' down
with, when there was an unco clamour outside. Sic clashin' o' swords
and armour clankin' and blood-curdlin' shoutin'. Lady Kate rushit to
the door to bar it, but lo and behold there was no bar til it. Some
callant had removit the bar aforehand. Lady Kate tried to sneck the
door by puttin' her arm where the bar should be, but she wasna long
in snatchin' it awa' and skirlin' like a scaddit cat when the first sword
came through the opening and gave her a bit cut.

'Meantime the King had tore up the boards leading down intil the
vault and squeezit through the hole. The Queen and Kirsten and me

put back the boards and stood on them, and Kirsten and me startit to unplait Her Majesty's hair as though it was the maist natural thing to do: us gettin' her ready for her bed, like. Sir Robert Graham and Sir Robert Stuart and some other callants came burstin' intil the room."Whaur's the King?" demandit Sir Robert Graham. "His hour has come." "His Majesty has retired to bed," says Queen Joan. "And how dare ye burst like this, sir, intil a lady's chamber? I shall have you arrestit at once. Call the guard, Lady Catherine." But Lady Kate was that fashed with the cut on her airm she took no notice. She kept skirlin': "Oh, my puir airm! Oh, my bonnie airm! I'll be scarred for life." '

Elspeth paused to draw breath. I was sitting up in bed, my hands clutchit to my throat. 'What happened next?' I managed to croak.

'The twa Sir Roberts and the other callants withdrew,' Elspeth said. 'They rushit away to the King's bedchamber, and we could hear them yowlin' like werewolves. Oh, 'twas unco uncanny, my leddy, and I hope I'll never live to experience the like again. The Queen says to me, "Elspeth, go and rouse the palace guard. And you, Kirsten, ging doon intil the vault and see that His Majesty has managed to escape through the drain intil the moat." But before we could move a foot's turn the King came back up through the hole in the floor. He hadna been able to get out intil the moat, he had forgotten he had blockit up the drain on account o' his lost tennis balls.'

Elspeth put her hands to her forehead and swayit from side to side, 'Oh, my leddy!' she keened. 'I hardly daur tell ye what happened next. Sir Robert Graham and the other callants came rushin' back intil the room, and whing they fell upon him and startit to hack intil him with their swords. At that moment, too, Master Oswald Graham came burstin' into the chamber, wavin' his sword and shoutin' "Stop! Stop!" And he thrust himself fornent the King and tried to parry the sword thrusts. The Queen, too, got atween the King and the murderers, and she got a sair cut on the shoulder. But 'twas of no avail. The King was struck doon, and he is lyin' there now as dead as an auld stag, with sixteen wounds in his body.'

'Sweet Christ in Heaven,' I whispered, and I crossed myself. 'What happened next?'

'I havena finished, my leddy,' Elspeth said. 'Ye have not heard the half o' it. And this ye will never believe.'

'They have not killt the Queen, too?' I cried.

'No, she is well enough except for the cut on her shoother, and it will heal in time.'

'Well, what?' I shouted. 'Tell me, woman!'

Elspeth bowed her head and claspit her hands thegither. 'Ye must be brave, my lambie,' she said. ''Tis dreadful news I am about to tell ye.'

'What?' I sank back against the pillows, sweat pouring down my face.

''Tis Master Oswald,' Elspeth whispered. 'The puir gentleman. He has been arrestit and cast intil a dungeon. Lady Kate has accusit him of being in tow with the King's murderers. In troth, she vows he is the one who arrangit the whole affair, and that he appearit at the last minute to pretend he wasna in league with them. Lady Kate vows 'twas he who put the planks across the moat to help the murderers get intil the monastery, and 'twas he took all the bars offen the doors. She doesna seem to think it might have been Sir Robert Stuart, who, God kens has mair cause for wantin' the King out of the way.'

'Kate said that?' I cried. 'How does she . . .?'

'Ye may weel ask, my lambie,' Elspeth said. 'Kate Douglas—and even though she's your ain cousin—is an ill-gettit trollop who'll stop at nothin' once she has got her knife in. And she has got her knife intil Master Oswald right up til the verra hilt. And forby, she has the Queen's ear. Why she should have is beyond my puir feeble comprehension, for I would ha'e thocht Queen Joan would have loathit the sicht o' her for flauntin' herself sae blatant-like as the King's light o' love. But women are kittle-cattle, as you and I ken full well. Anyways, Kate's lyin' tongue has won the day, and puir Master Oswald is chainit up in ain o' the cells.'

Oswald protestit his innocence time and time again, but Joan Beaufort was adamant. I realised then that she had aye been jealous of poor Oswald. And Kate Douglas was there at her side, whispering foul lies into her lug. Within a week or two Sir Robert Graham and Sir Robert Stuart and the five others who had helpit to stab the King's grace were roundit up and lodged in the dungeons of Edinburgh Castle. For Queen Joan and her court quittit Perth immediately after the murder, and preparations were made to crown wee Jamie, who was just six years auld, as King James II in Holyrood Abbey.

I was still ill, and I was sore of heart because of Oswald. Kate Douglas kept coming to my chamber and telling me about his guilt. Time after time I tellt the lying limmer to begone from my sight, but she keepit on pricking at me, skirling like a loonie-wifie when I pressed my hands ower my ears to shut out her taunts.

A month after the murder the auld Earl of Atholl, who was near seventy, was arrestit because folk said he aspired to be king and was at the head of the conspiracy to put himself on the throne. He was draggit in chains at a horse's tail to Edinburgh, and a couple of days after that he and Sir Robert Stuart, Sir Robert Graham and Master Oswald Graham and the five others were put on trial.

By this time I was out of bed and hirpling about, but my heart was heavy and I would fain have been a thousand miles from Edinburgh town. I askit Queen Joan if I could have her gracious permission to retire to Angus so that I might recover from my long illness. But before Her Majesty could say anything, the bold Kate Douglas cried, 'And is Wee Humpy not to be in attendance on Your Grace on the great day, madam?'

'I fear Lady Grizel is too delicate and too gentle-natured to watch the proceedings,' the Queen said.

'Havers, madam!' said Kate. 'Wee Grizel is a Hepburn, and the Hepburns are well kent for their toughness. Am I not sib to them? Fine I ken how hard yon family can be, and if I can watch the trial so can she.'

'Lady Grizel has had the flux,' the Queen said. 'We deem it hardly fit that she should witness . . .'

Kate cried, 'Oswald Graham spurnit puir wee Grizel, my lady. 'Tis only right she should see the blaggart suffer his just punishment.'

'In that case,' the Queen said, 'you will attend upon us tomorrow morn, Lady Grizel, when the culprits are brought to justice.'

I pleadit and pleadit, but next morning at eleven o'clock, the bitterest morning of my life, I was in the Queen's train when we went into the great hall of the castle. I stood behind Her Majesty's chair. Kate Douglas, who had her arm full covered with bandages, was allowed to sit on a stool beside the Queen. There was no need for her arm to be bandaged, for her wound had healit up, Kirsten had tellt Elspeth. Yet Kate was full determined to make the most of it, to appear the heroine that earnit her the nickname 'Kate Bar The Door' till the end of her days.

I was sae weak with sorrow I had to lean heavy on my stick with one hand and cling to Elspeth's arm with the other. I near swooned when the prisoners were brought up from the dungeons. My poor Oswald lookit like a ghost, with a growth of beard on his white, hollow-cheekit face. I shut my eyes and hopit he would not see me coorying there ahint the Queen's chair.

Sir William Crichton, the Keeper of Edinburgh Castle, a perfidious rogue who had aye lackeyed to King James, then read out the charges against the nine gentlemen. He endit his harangue with, 'Ye shall suffer the utmost rigours of execution, and may God have mercy on your souls—for not a body in Scotland has.'

Sir William bowed to the Queen. She inclined her head graciously to him, and she said, 'Let the trial begin.'

While a lawyer-mannie, brought there to give an air of versimilitude to the proceedings, was pleading for the prisoners, I heard Kate Douglas say, 'You remember, madam, the end of King Edward the Second of England? Remember what his wife causit to be done til him when he displeasit her with yon callant Hugh Despenser? It seems a goodly fate for Master Oswald Graham.'

'Am I likely to forget it, Lady Catherine?' Joan Beaufort said. 'King Edward was my great-great-grandsire.'

I did not think of it then, for I was that overwhelmit by pain and misery, but oft I have thought about it since. King Edward may have been Queen Joan's great-great-grandsire, but equally his wife, Queen Isabella, her that folk cried 'The She Wolf of France', was Queen Joan's great-great-grandmother. Is there small wonder then that from that day I hatit Joan Beaufort with a hatred that corroded my entire being?

Suddenly there were screams, and it was me that was screaming. I screamed and screamed. When I came to, I was in my own bed, with Elspeth attending to me. The tears streamed down her face as she tellt me what had happened to the prisoners, as tellt to her by some castle guard who had been in the torture chamber after the trial.

And that eve Kate Douglas came and repeatit the tale, telling me that a red-hot crown had been placed on Lord Atholl's head. I buried my head ablow the bed-clothes and refusit to listen. Elspeth said afterwards that the common folk who, God kens, are not over blessit with the finer feelings, were outragit at the cruelties perpetrated on the murderers, and many said that when Sir Robert Graham cried in his death agony that they had killed James Stuart because he was a cruel king, he might well have addit that James had been wed to an even crueller queen.

A wheen weeks later when I was riding with the Queen in a litter through the gate of Edinburgh Castle I saw Lord Atholl's skull, with the iron crown embeddit intil it, stuck on a spike above the portcullis. I spewed all over Joan Beaufort's rose-pink satin gown.

Ye may wonder why I continued in the service of that foul woman for so many years afterwards. She had been sae nice to me when I was a bairn I could scarce credit yon lovely rose-bloom face could hide sic a charnel house of horror. I never forgave her for what she causit to be done to Oswald, that kindly gentle soul, and I hatit her ever after. Yet the truth is that I was full fond of her poor afflictit bairn, wee Jamie with the fiery birthmark on his face, the new King, and I felt it was my bounden duty to bide beside him and try to instil some goodness intil him, hoping he would not inherit the cruel streaks of his mother and her ancestress, Isabella of France. And I regret to say that I gloatit with the fullest pleasure when, a year or two afterwards, Joan Beaufort was glaikit enough to destroy her own position as the Queen Dowager of Scotland by taking her paramour, Sir James Stewart, the Black Knight of Lorn, as her second husband. I had not the least pickle of pity for her downfall.

PRETTY PRICKLY ENGLISH ROSE was written in 1975 and printed in Fred Urquhart's collection of historical stories *Proud Lady in A Cage* (Paul Harris, 1980).

18 A Diver in China Seas

NOW THAT I FEEL death's cauld hand crawling over me every night I keep turning my mind to the corpses I've seen in my day. Not that I have seen that many. I have aye tried to give them a wide berth, and I can mind of a few I declined to look at, though hard pressed by their nearest. In all, I've seen maybe seven or eight.

The first was Bobby Leitch. It was when he was eighteen or nineteen that I remember him best. He was a braw lad with yellow hair and big sad-like eyes that would suddenly light up and blaze like blue lamps when he saw a joke. Not that it was often he saw a joke; he was awful serious, and I mind him best with a sad face. When I was sixteen I took a great fancy to him. He was a shunter on the railway down at Granton. I was working myself then as a nursemaid to some swells at Trinity, so whenever I got the chance I hurled the pram with the two wee Ritchies in their white fur bonnets along to Granton, and I would parade beside the railway lines between the Middle pier and the West pier in the hope of seeing Bobby. Whenever I did he would just give a bit wave and cry: 'Hey, Carrie! How're ye gettin' on in the pugs' parlour then? Are ye still eatin' vinegar with a fork and holdin' out yer pinkie when ye sup yer tea?' And then he would laugh and give a string of wagons a shunt with his pole. He would leap on the nearside buffer of the last wagon and ride away with a wave.

Whiles it seemed senseless to walk all that way to Granton, putting up with the greeting of the Ritchie bairns, who were terrified of the steaming engines and the rattling of the long goods trains, just for the sake of hearing Bobby make the same auld joke and give the same wee wave. But I was in love, and when you're in love you'll put up with a lot.

And then one day my Auntie Annie brought the news that Bobby had been killed. When he was coupling some loose wagons onto an engine pulling other wagons the engine had come quicker than he'd expected and it had crushed him between the wagons. My Auntie Annie took me to see Bobby in his coffin. There was upwards of a dozen folk in the Leitch's house. Most were women, but there were some men too, and Mrs Leitch was dispensing tea to the women and

drams to the men with a lavish hand. 'He's a lovely corpse,' Auntie
Annie said when we looked at Bobby with his smooth bonnie face and
his yellow hair brushed like a golden helmet. 'He's beautiful.'

Mrs Leitch, like a good hostess, agreed with her guest. She even
went a bit farther. She said Bobby was that lovely she could have sat
and looked at him all day.

I was fell taken with Bobby's corpse, and I've never forgotten it,
though I can't rightly see his features after all this time. It must be
sixty years syne, and you can't blame a body for forgetting the face of
the first lad she fancied. It's only because I tell myself so often about
his blue eyes and yellow hair that I remember them.

The corpse I mind best is auld Jessie Meiklejohn's. It must be about
forty years since she passed on. It was before the war, anyway, in the
days when it was not so fashionable to be cremated or for the corpse
to be taken away to the undertaker's mortuary.

I was married to Harry Henderson when I became acquainted with
Nora and Jessie Meiklejohn. They were a couple of auld maids living
in a basement in a street off Leith Walk. I met Nora because of an
accident. Harry and me were living in a tenement near there, and one
forenoon coming out of the Co-op grocery this elderly body who'd
gone out in front of me suddenly slipped on dog-shit and went down
with a wallop. I was the first to reach her, and I helped her up and
put the packet of tea and a few other things that had fallen out back
in her basket for her. 'There ye are, missis,' I said. 'Are ye all right,
hen?'

'I've twisted my ankle,' she said.

'Lord love us!' I said. 'Will ye be able to walk at all?'

She took a wee step and fell against me. 'I doot I can just hirple,'
she said 'Can you give me your arm as far as my door, dear? It's not
far. It's just the next street, about a hundred yards away.'

I took her home, and I met her sister Jessie, and we all got very
friendly over a cup of tea and a slice of Dundee cake. After that we
became pals-a'-bubbly and I was as often in their house as I was in
our own. Harry was unemployed at the time, and there wasn't room
in our pokey wee but and ben for both him and me. So I used to leave
him alone with his grievances and his eternal wireless—he switched
it on loud as soon as he came in, and I believe he would have nicked
me with his razor if I'd as much as raised a hand to put it off. There
was no wireless at the Meiklejohns. A wireless would never have
stood a look-in there. Nora and Jessie often talked thegither and they
hardly ever seemed to draw breath—except when they were listening
to me. They were aye delighted to see me. 'It's fine to have a bit of
young life about the house,' Jessie said.

Young life! Me that was turned thirty-four at the time and feeling every day of fifty. My mother and father died when I was a bit bairn and I had no recollection of them or their corpses. I was brought up by my Auntie Annie. I'm never likely to forget her, the sanctimonious auld bitch, forever grasping for every penny I earned. So I was fell glad to have two decent women like the Meiklejohns to be friends with, even though they were getting on for forty years aulder than me. Their father had had a wee plumber's business and had left a bit of money. They weren't rich, nothing to put up bills about, but they were quite comfortable. They were very good to me. One or other used to slip me five bob or a ten shilling note nearly every time I saw them, telling me to buy something nice for myself. Not that I ever did. Anything they gave me aye went on food or on fags for Harry. It was their company I liked best. They were a lively pair of auld besoms.

When Harry was unemployed the first time I did some charring in the West End, and even after he got other jobs I kept it on, for the extra money was very handy. I cleaned a lawyer's office in the early mornings, then after I'd had a cup of tea and a natter at what used to be called a cabby's shelter near the Caley Station, I did the rough work at some gentry's house in Randolph Crescent. On the way back from my work I usually looked in at the Meiklejohns before going home. By the time I'd kent them a couple of years this was a daily habit. There was aye a bite waiting for me. They either kept something warm in the oven or they waited till I arrived to have their own lunch. I never needed to hurry home till it was time to make Harry's tea.

And then when Harry died after he got pneumonia through getting soaked one night in the last job he took as a night-watchman at a brewery the Meiklejohns were kindness itself. They wanted me to give up the but and ben and go and live with them. 'This is sic a big flat there's plenty of room for three,' Nora said. 'Especially since we all agree with each other so well.' But I put my foot down about this; I felt it was better to have a haven of my own, even though it did seem a waste to pay rent when it wasn't necessary. Still anon, it was better to be independent.

But sleeping in my own house was my only independence; otherwise the Meiklejohns and me lived in each others' pockets till Jessie died. I ate all my meals at their house, except my breakfast and that was just a couple of cups of tea and bap spread with marge. They wouldn't take anything for my keep, but in return I did all their shopping and most of their housework. And I kept them entertained.

The Miss Meiklejohns liked a joke. When I met them first Jessie said: 'I don't hold with jokes that are dirty for dirtiness' sake. But I don't mind if a joke's not clean so long as I get a guid laugh.' I remembered this, and I was aye careful not to go over the score when I told them anything I'd heard in the cabby's shelter. Some of the jokes the taxi-drivers and the other chars told were gey near the knuckle, but as time went on and the two auld maids and me were letting our hair down more and more, I repeated some of these jokes when they pressed me. And we had so many good laughs that by and by I didn't trouble to beat about the bush but told them everything I heard.

One day I told yon one about the kilted sodger running like mad to catch a tram, and the auld English lady who clapped her hands and cried; 'Heah! Heah!' when he caught it. Jessie laughed that much at the kiltie's reply she complained afterwards of a pain in her back. 'I shouldn't have laughed so hearty,' she said. 'But oh, that's a guid yin, isn't it? Ye're a right comic, Carrie. I don't know how you mind them all, but I'm glad you're not blate in comin' out with them.'

Next afternoon Jessie was in bed complaining about her back, saying the awful pain in her left shoulder wouldn't go away and she felt a kind of numbness spreading from it. But bad though she was, she asked if I'd heard any good jokes that day. 'I've been laughin' again at yon yin ye tellt yesterday,' she said. 'I can just hear the kiltie sayin' "What did ye think ye'd see, mem? Ostrich feathers!"' And she laughed and laughed again, and gey near choked herself. At night she got that bad I went for the doctor. She died a wee while after he arrived.

I went then for Mrs Forsyth, the laying-out woman, and I let the undertakers know. I stayed the night with poor auld Nora. Next morning I didn't go to my work; I phoned one of the snooty wee typists in the lawyer's and told her I wouldn't be in because of a death in the family. Then I chummed Nora who was beginning to revive, to Patrick Thomson's to buy some black clothes. We had lunch afterwards at Mackie's in Princes Street.

When we got back in the late afternoon Mrs Forsyth was there again. The undertakers had been and Jessie, in her best blue nightgown, was in her coffin on the bed. 'She looks right bonnie,' Mrs Forsyth said, admiring her own handiwork.

Nora gave a few wee snuffles, then she said: 'Ay, our Jessie was aye a bonnie lassie. She could've married, y'know. There was no call for her to be an auld maid. She had plenty of flames and several guid offers.'

'Why did she turn them doon then?' Mrs Forsyth asked.

Nora said: 'God alone knows.' And she went to the dressing-table and tried on the black hat we'd chosen in PT's. She stood back and looked at herself, cocking her head from side to side. 'D'you know,' she said, 'I don't think I like this hat. I don't think it suits me.'

'But ye liked it in the shop,' I said. 'Ye look lovely in it.'

'That's what yon sales-lassie said, but I'm beginning to think she was telling a lie. Not that I'm accusing you of bein' a liar, too, Carrie. I just don't fancy myself in it.'

Mrs Forsyth said: 'Ye look awful nice in it, Miss Meiklejohn.'

'It's the kind of hat that would've suited Jessie,' Nora said.

'Ach, ye look jist as nice as yer sister in it.' Mrs Forsyth's hand went to her mouth. 'Ye ken what I mean, Miss Meiklejohn.'

Nora raked her with a fish-like eye.

'See how it goes with the coat,' I said.

Nora put on the new black coat and paraded up and down, preening herself. 'How does it look, Carrie?' she asked.

'I tellt ye in the shop,' I said. 'It's a right braw rigout.'

'It doesn't go with this hat,' she said. 'I wonder if Jessie's mourning hat would go with it?'

She brought Jessie's black velour from the press and put it on. 'There!' she cried. 'This is the very dab. It suits me better. In fact, though it's myself that says it, it suits me a damn sight better than it ever suited Jessie.'

'Puir Miss Jessie,' Mrs Forsyth said, giving her bleary eyes a bit dicht with a dirty hankie. 'She'll never wear a hat again.'

'Ah well, she'll have a halo instead,' Nora said. 'Like enough, anyway, if all we read in the Bible is true.'

She took another turn up and down in the coat and the black velour, then she sat down forenent the mirror and admired herself.

'One of Jessie's auld beaux was a diver in China seas,' she said. 'Davie Nasmyth. He went there after she'd turned him down three times. But he's back bidin' in Edinburgh. At Tollcross. He came home five years ago, and we saw him once or twice. But he stopped comin' when Jessie refused him again.'

Mrs Forsyth looked into the coffin, sighing: 'Oh, Miss Jessie, if ye'd jist played yer cards right you could've been a lady of leisure in China and them other foreign places. Ye would jist've needed to clap yer hands and the wee blackies would've come runnin' to do yer biddin'.'

'It's more likely that it would've been Davie Nasmyth that was clappin' his hands and Jessie that would've been runnin' at his bidding,' Nora said. 'Though, mind you, if Jessie had been the marrying kind I don't think she'd have chosen Davie. She had plenty of better flames.'

I had heard of this man Nasmyth before. 'Will he be comin' to the funeral?' I asked.

'I don't know. I suppose I'd better invite him. I'm sure he'd want to see Jessie off on her last journey.' Nora sighed. 'It must be four years since we saw him. I wonder if he's changed much. He's just a year aulder than me.'

'Ye should hang up yer hat with him, Nora,' I chaffed her.

'Ay, ye should grab him while the goin's good,' Mrs Forsyth said with a laugh. 'There's nothin' like a funeral for bringin' folk thegither. It's wonderful what a few tears on a lassie's cheek'll do to the menfolk.'

'I'd never thocht o' it,' Nora simpered. 'But it's an idea, isn't it? He must be lonely. As for me, God kens what I'm going to do without Jessie. Ay, I suppose I've got to the age when I need a man's strong hand behind me and his broad shoulders to fall back on.'

'Well, ye'd better get in touch with him right away,' I said. 'If ye write him a letter I'll go out and post it. We cannie depend upon him seein' the funeral notice in tonight's *News*. No' everybody reads the hatches, matches and despatches.'

'Ach, I cannie be fashed writing,' Nora said. 'I'm too tired and worn out. Maybe you could phone him tomorrow morning, Carrie, from your work? I'll be glad to have a man's support at the funeral. Davie hasn't got a phone himself, but if you phone the newsagent three doors away they'll give him a message.'

Next morning when I set off for the West End I was intending to phone this newsagent as soon as I got into the office, but on the way I decided phoning would be an awful trauchle. I decided, too, I wasn't going to bother about going to work. A death in the family was surely good for three days off.

I went to the big Co-op drapery in Bread Street and bought a pair of winter drawers. I knew how cauld it could be standing beside graves and hanging around churchyards. Then I went to Tollcross. I was curious to see what a diver looked like; to the best of my knowledge I'd never seen one.

Mr Nasmyth was tall and very thin, with a terribly wrinkled face the colour of cold coffee. He looked ninety but I knew that, if Nora was telling the truth, he was only seventy-three. His hands trembled. He looked a right gawk, but there was nothing gawky about his voice. It was loud and very self-confident and sounded as though he was used to giving commands.

I told him Nora was wondering if he'd like to come and see Jessie before she was nailed down. 'No, no, no!' he cried. 'I've seen enough corpses in my day, Mrs Henderson. I have no desire to see any more.' Nor would he accept Nora's bidding to the funeral. 'I'm feared of funerals,' he said. 'Will you give Miss Meiklejohn my apologies and say—well, I can hardly say a previous appointment, can I? Better say I'm not well. Tell her it's my malaria. It's not really a lie. I'm liable to get my malaria at any time without much warning. I hope, Mrs Henderson, you won't mind telling a wee fib for me?'

'Of course no',' I said. 'I'm delighted to be of any service to ye, Mr Nasmyth. Ye've jist to say the word.'

'Well, maybe you'll not mind coming back and telling me how the funeral goes?' he said. 'Will you come to tea the day after?'

In those times women didn't often go to the graveside, but if there had been no women there would have been hardly anybody at Jessie Meiklejohn's. Besides the undertaker's men, there were only two old men cousins. And seven women, all competing with each other to see who wept the most.

I told Mr Nasmyth this the next day when I went to tea, and what with this and other things I garred him laugh a lot. He was like auld Jessie, he liked a joke. He asked me to tell Nora he'd pay her a wee visit soon to offer his condolences.

I don't think he ever made that visit, though. Soon after the funeral I stopped seeing Nora so often, and stepping in only occasionally instead of every day meant that I didn't hear about everything that she was doing, except that she was out on the ran-dan a lot. She joined a Whist Club and got very pally with another auld maid like herself.

Neither did Mr Nasmyth ever mention he'd been to see her, and as he took me into his confidence it doesn't look as if he had. Not that I cared whether he saw her or not. It was Jessie that was really my friend. And Mr Nasmyth's too, if it came to that.

After we'd been courting for about six months me and Mr Nasmyth got married. He died when he was seventy-six, the same age as I am now, and left me a good pickle siller. His was the last corpse I saw. I did hear that Nora Meiklejohn lived until she was ninety, but I never saw her after I married Davie, nor did I see her corpse or go to her funeral. And now I'm thinking, with death's cauld fingers plucking at me, how lucky she was to live till ninety, even though she wasn't lucky enough to hang up her hat with Mr Nasmyth.

A DIVER IN CHINA SEAS was written in February 1976 at the invitation of Maurice Lindsay, who published it in Number 2 of *The Scottish Review*. It was then published in *The Texas Quarterly* (USA) in its issue of Autumn 1977, and also in Denys Val Baker's anthology *Stories of Horror and Suspense* (William Kimber, 1977). It was the title story of Fred Urquhart's eleventh collection of stories and novellas, published by Quartet Books in August 1980.

19 *Witch's Kitten*

CYN AND I SAT ON TOP of her coffin and watched the mourners enter the kirk. Muriel Brunton and Nurse Abernethy sat in a back pew. In a wee while Bessie Dodds crept in and sidled down beside them. I had never seen Mrs Dodds wearing a hat before. She had worn the same green and red headscarf over her curlers all the years I'd known her. Two women from the village that I knew only by sight had a confabulation just inside the door, then they chose a pew about the middle of the aisle where they could miss nothing. Old Mr Nisbet who used to do the garden before he had to give up with his rheumatics, hirpled down near the front on his stick. He sat with head down, biting his straggly smoke-browned moustache. A couple of middle-aged women I didn't know sat behind him and studied their hymn books.

'They were great pals of Kathy's,' Cyn said. 'I can't see why they've come—except from curiosity. They're women I never liked.'

I could not resist a merry mew when Mrs Drummond and Mrs Jarvis-Waddell, two great galleons full of importance, sailed slowly down the aisle to the front pew as chief mourners. Nan Drummond, all solicitude, hovered over her friend like a mother hen, holding her elbow and settling her as she'd set precious porcelain. I mewed again hysterically, knowing the Jarvis-Waddell woman needed no help, knowing only too well to what lengths of devilment she would go.

'Wheesht!' Cyn hissed.

'They cannie hear me,' I said.

'How do you know?' she said. 'You haven't been dead long enough yet to know what they can hear and what they can't.'

I was a few months short of eleven when Cyn died. The vet did me in, at Mrs Jarvis-Waddell's command, the same day. So I missed becoming seventy years and seven, which I would have attained if he'd left me alone. I knew how old I was because often in the last year I had heard Cyn say: 'Anne of Austria is seventy. She has reached her allotted three score years and ten.' And always I'd heard her give a sad wee cackle after that, implying that it woudn't be long now before the fairies got me. She never seemed to remember that she herself had

160

long since passed the same life-mark. It is true that she'd said from time to time, on her 85th, her 88th and her 89th birthdays: 'I'll not see another birthday.' But a year ago, on her 90th, I'd noticed she hadn't repeated this.

I looked around the kirk with interest, while we waited for the minister. I had never been in a kirk before. Cyn had not set foot in a kirk for many years either, and this was the Drummonds' way of getting their own back on her instead of having the funeral service at the graveside like other decent Presbyterian bodies.

'Not a bad turn out,' Cyn said. 'Ten mourners. Better than I expected. Though I'm surprised the lawyer-mannie isn't here to grace the festive board.'

'Surely you don't want him?' I said.

'Why not? I'd like him to see the damage he's done. It would be something to nag at his conscience for the rest of his days.'

'I doubt he's got a conscience,' I said.

'You should have more faith in human nature, Annie,' she said.

'How can I? I'm only a poor wee cat that's been ill done by.'

I could not help giving another skirling mew when Miss Beanie Gilmour garred the organ give an extra loud peal, and the Reverend Snotty Drummond came sweeping in from the vestry wearing his long black gownie with its purple and white accessories. I had never seen him in his Sunday togs before. I looked close to see if he had the usual snotter at the end of his neb, the reason for Cyn christening him this. She thought the nickname was a secret between her and me, but one day, in excitement, she let it out to Bessie Dodds, and it hadn't been long before the whole village knew and the minister got it back. It did not endear Cyn any more to him and nosey Nan.

'Wheesht!' Cyn cried again. 'Be quiet and you may learn something that'll be of advantage to you in the after-life.'

Cyn's name was Miss Cynthia Isobel Mackenzie, and she was a poet. It was because she was a poet and didn't give two hoots for them that Nan and Snotty Drummond disliked her. She never tried to hide her contempt and anger for their manipulation of Miss Kathy and their responsibility for her dreadful Will. The Drummonds came religiously once a week to visit her after Miss Kathy died, and Cyn always received them with icy politeness, but they never dared call her anything but Miss Mackenzie. Only a few folk close to her called her Cyn. They were all lady-bodies of her own generation, and most were dead now, too. Some folk called her Miss Mac. She didn't like this, saying she was Miss Mackenzie to the *hoi polloi* or nothing.

So Miss Mackenzie she'd been to everybody for years. Except to Mrs Bessie Dodds, the cleaning-lady whose husband drove a tractor at the Barns of Dalbogie. Mrs Dodds called her Miss Mac behind her back, and often to her face. It was a kind of running battle between them. When first she came to be the daily at Seven Yewtrees, Mrs Dodds, a sonsy young farm-wifie, had been what Cyn called over-familiar and had kept calling her 'Miss Mac, hen,' and 'Miss Mac, m'dear' every half dozen words until Cyn had put her foot down. 'My name, Mrs Dodds,' she said in that loud upper-class voice of hers that could have filled a drill-hall, 'is Mackenzie. MACKENZIE Miss Mackenzie to you, if you please. And if you don't please, you can ask Miss Brunton for your wages and depart in peace. But if you do please, you must mind not to say "Miss Mackenzie" ower often. There's nothing worse than having one's name continually deeved in one's lugs.'

'Okay, Miss Mac hen,' Mrs Dodds said, fell affronted. And she tossed her head with such abandon that the curlers she always wore ablow her headscarf rattled. Mrs Dodds was a great head-tosser, and when she was having her mid morning cup of coffee and biscuits in the kitchen with Miss Brunton and Nurse Abernethy her curlers clattered about so much you'd have thought she was conducting an orchestra. And they always rattled waur than usual after she and Miss Cynthia Mackenzie had a bit tiff about names.

Years long syne Cyn had been in love with a sailor called 'Sin', short for Sinbad. They had called themselves 'The Two Sins' and said it was a film they were starring in. They were introduced by an admiral, for Sin was a high ranking officer, and so they'd had their great love story. But it was a story that turned out badly for Cyn Mackenzie. Sin was drowned at Jutland. I never heard what his real name was.

I got mine when I was a month old. I used to be a twin. My sister and I were called Penny and Twopence by the village wifie whose black cat had kittened us. Miss Mackenzie bought us when she heard we'd been born in May. 'In olden days,' she said to the scandalised village wifie, 'witches would never have any but May kittens. They vowed they made the best familiars. They're stronger and more cunning than most cats. I hope these two will help to keep my broomstick   in   control   whe   a   high   wind.'

Cyn's sister, Miss Kathy, was still alive then. She was as scandalised as the village wifie when Cyn, a keen student of history, rechristened us Anne of Austria and Caroline of Naples. 'It's more in keeping with your new status as gentry,' Cyn told us.

'Havers,' said Miss Kathy, a bossy body who kept laying down the law. 'Carrie and Annie they'll be from henceforth. And I'll have you know, Cynthia Mackenzie, that your royal ladies will have to be a lot cleaner in their habits if they're to remain in my house.'

Miss Kathy always called Seven Yewtrees 'my' house. She would never have dreamed of saying 'our', although truthfully it was as much Miss Cyn's as hers. Seven Yewtrees was built in the early eighteenth century to house a large family, and it had stood in the middle of an estate of several hundred acres. But the acreage had dwindled like the family fortunes, and by the time Miss Cyn and Miss Kathy were born it was standing in a garden of three acres and a paddock. It was occupied then by the girls' parents, General 'Buffy' and Mrs Mackenzie and a staff of five indoor servants, a nanny and a coachman. By the time I came to it as a kitten the paddock had been sold; the house was well weatherbeaten and needed repairs; most of the garden was just rough grass; and only the two old sisters and their housekeeper, Miss Muriel Brunton, lived in a few rooms, the rest of the house being dust-sheeted and deserted.

When the General died at the age of ninety-four he hadn't mentioned the house in his Will. Miss Kathy had been Buffy's favourite, for he couldn't abide Miss Cynthia and her poetry and what he called her whimsy-whamsies; so he left seven thousand pounds to Miss Kathy, and the remainder of his possessions to be divided equally between her and Miss Cyn. But Miss Kathy always chose to forget that Seven Yewtrees and everything in it belonged to both of them. Since she was ten years younger than Cyn—there had been a wheen miscarriages and two babies that died in between—Miss Kathy fully expected to live long after Cyn, who was delicate and had a bad heart. Cyn was encouraged, therefore, to spend her money by paying all the household bills. Kathy hung onto her own.

Miss Kathy was seventy when Carrie and I came to bide in 'her' house: the age I am now, the age I suppose I'll be for all eternity. She was seventy-three when she died, so I had plenty of opprtunities to watch her in action; I ken how true it was that Cyn did all the paying-out while Miss Katherine, as she insisted on being called by Mrs Bessie Dodds and others of the lower orders, sat back jocose and watched her own bank balance rise higher and higher. Miss Katherine, who deemed herself appointed by God to manage her older sister's affairs, was absolutely certain that Cyn would die long, long before her. Cyn would not be able to take her money with her, and nearly all of what she left would be taken by a rapacious government; so it was only sensible, right and proper that Cyn should pay the household bills, the gardener's wages, Miss Brunton's wages, the charwoman's wages, and the rates and taxes and insurance, forby the income tax, so that Kathy could hang onto her own money, and it would be there, in readiness, when the time came and she was left to cope on her lone-some.

Not that she would ever be on her lonesome. She would have her dear cousin, Willie Jarvis-Waddell, to be her staff and prop for the rest of her days. Willie Jarvis-Waddell was a third cousin of the Mackenzie sisters' mother. He was a big bug in the Foreign Office and had a mansion in Yorkshire and a house in Belgravia, which Cyn told me is a fashionable part of London. The Mackenzies' money had dwindled through the decades, but the Jarvis-Waddells had kept an iron grip on theirs. They were what Cyn called stinking rich.

Willie visited Seven Yewtrees twice or thrice when he was a bairn; then they didn't see him until Buffy's funeral. He was a good looking young man of twenty then, and Miss Kathy, aged fifty-four, a repressed spinster though she would never have admitted it, fell in love with him. For the rest of her life Cousin Willie was her god. Even when he married, it didn't make any difference to Kathy's great pash. She kept inviting him and his wife Bertha for holidays, which were paid for, of course, by Cyn. Nothing was too good for Cousin Willie and Dear Bertha. Crates of champagne were stocked. Expensive foodstuffs were sent up from Harrods and Fortnum & Mason. All on the account of Miss Cynthia Mackenzie, who had to hide it from Kathy if she was rash enough to buy a book that wasn't a paperback. A lot of the wines and foodstuffs got wasted, for Willie and Bertha never stayed for the full term that Miss Kathy had invited and expected them for; they always had some excuse and, after a couple of days, would hasten away farther north into the Highlands so that Willie could do a little fishing and shooting on some great estate. Yet, no matter how they abused her hospitality and invitations, Kathy always gushed about, 'My cousin Willie in the FO—such a brilliant administrator who's always travelling abroad with the Foreign Secretary.' If Cyn spoke about him she only said he was a distant cousin—'a very distant one, and the more distance there is between him and me the better I'll like it.' Cyn called him and his wife 'Waddling Willie' and 'Bitchy-faced Bertha'. They did not like Cyn either.

I heard all this from Cyn in the long hours she used to lie in her bed with nobody to talk to. And over and over again she told me about the time Willie and Bertha came for a week and stayed only the one night because Willie had to dash—he said—to Balmoral to confab with the Queen. This was a memorable night in Cyn's life, the night all the evil and damage was done.

That night Miss Kathy had invited the Rev Snotty and Mrs Drummond to dinner to meet her famous cousin. The Drummonds had just come to the village, and a great all-absorbing friendship had sprung up between Nan Drummond and Miss Mackenzie of Seven Yewtrees. Nan Drummond was a big stout body with a big damp face that always had beads of sweat on the temples and upper lip. Her large protruding eyes had great bags under them; the irises were so pale a grey and the whites were so unhealthily yellow, they looked like cold poached eggs that had got stale from lying in the pantry. Nan Drummond fair oozed sympathy and affection for those she thought in want of it. Kathy Mackenzie was a natural target.

When she wasn't directing Miss Kathy's life, Nan Drummond was tripping over with good works. In olden times she'd have been able to use up all her energy in saving village girls in trouble, poking her nose in where it wasn't wanted when they had bastard weans; but in our day the village girls wouldn't admit to belonging to the village at all, and they were all on the pill and too cute to get caught. So Nan Drummond would have had a very lean time in our parish if it hadn't been for Miss Katherine Mackenzie.

It was she who egged on Kathy to make yon Wicked Will.

This was after she met Waddling Willie and Bitchy-faced Bertha. Mrs Drummond was tremendously impressed by Willie, who hadn't started to run to fat yet. Like her buddy, Kathy, she fell for his diplomatic palavers. And when he was called to the phone in the middle of dinner and came back to say Lillibet wanted him to go to Balmoral the first thing next morning to help her and Tinker sort out a crisis in the Middle East, she was that overwhelmed by joy and pride at sitting next to a man who was on such intimate terms with Her Majesty and the Foreign Secretary that she never once thought of the inconvenience and the waste and the cost caused by Willie's shortened visit. Nor did Miss Kathy.

She beamed at her cousin and said: 'We'll be so glad to look after Bertha while you're away, dear. Rest assured she'll be safe with us.'

'Bertha is coming with me,' Willie said. 'Lillibet insisted on it.'

Only Miss Cyn failed to be impressed. She neither believed that Willie had been summoned to Balmoral nor that he was on Christian name terms with the Queen. 'I jaloused that he and Bitchy-Face were going to a hotel in Aberdeen or Strathpeffer or to the home of whatever man Willie had got to phone him,' she told me. 'They couldn't bear biding at Seven Yewtrees for any longer than I could bear having them in the house.'

Like Kathy, Nan Drummond was so unsuspicious of Waddling Willie's deceit that he and Bertha could scarcely have reached whatever haven they'd chosen before she started to agitate for Kathy to make her Will in Willie's favour. The whiff of Willie's presence, the powerful scent of a man who could speak so nonchalantly about his Sovereign Lady, was like gunpowder in a charger's nostrils to Nan Drummond. She saw herself becoming one of Willie's bosom pals. If she could be so chief with Willie's cousin, then she could be as chief with Willie himself—*and* his wife. Already Mrs Drummond saw that when Miss Kathy joined her ancestors—Miss Cyn would be away long before that, needless to say—she would become the greatest pal of the Jarvis-Waddells when they settled down in Seven Yewtrees, and—who knew?— she might become intimate with the Queen too.

Until Nan Drummond broached the subject, Kathy Mackenzie had not thought about her Will since the time thirty years ago when Buffy, straight-backed and bristly-moustached, had ordered his lawyer to make Wills in which each daughter made the other her sole heir and executor. Now, with Nan breathing so vehemently in her lug, pointing out that Cynthia couldn't last much longer with her weak heart, Miss Kathy was only too ready to summon the family lawyer.

The lawyer who'd drawn up their own and Buffy's Wills was dead. His place had been taken over by his son, Mr Ronald Glossop-Macleod, a smart young man who took a fancy to Cyn, but with Nan oozing advice at Kathy's elbow he was conned into drawing up what Miss Cyn always called the Wickedest Will in the World.

In this will Kathy left Seven Yewtrees (forgetting half of it belonged to Cyn) and her jewels and all her money—except for two thousand pounds to her dear friend Mrs Nan Drummond—to her beloved cousin William Eric Jarvis-Waddell, appointing him her sole executor. Then Mr Ronald Glossop-Macleod said that *maybe* she had better make the Will a little longer than this. 'All of us are at risk, Miss Mackenzie,' he said (these were his exact words, Cyn told me, for she'd sat there in the drawing-room and heard it all from A to Z). 'It isn't at all likely, but there is always the possibility, of course, that Miss Cynthia *might* outlive you,' and he gave Cyn a wink and a special heart-warming smile, like a melting marshmallow—'so I suggest that in case this happens you leave your property and money to her in trust for her lifetime, allowing her the income from your funds but not allowing her to touch the capital, until such time as she, in turn, will hand them over—and her own funds too, I trust—to Mr William Jarvis-Waddell.'

Cyn protested that she had no intention of leaving Waddling Willie a halfpenny, but she was ignored. Miss Katherine said she agreed wholeheartedly with Glossop-Macleod, and she thought that maybe as her sister's own capital would be depleted should Cyn outlive her (and here she shook her head affectionately at Cyn to signify that, naturally, she didn't believe this) she would make it a condition of Cyn being allowed to stay on at Seven Yewtrees and to utilise the income from her own estate if Cyn would leave certain sums to charities in which she (Kathy) was interested. And she gave Master Ronald a list of these charities, saying she would have left them the money out of her own estate, except that she wanted as much as possible to go to her dearest cousin Willie.

Ronald most reluctantly put this conditional clause in Miss Katherine's Will and she signed it, despite all Cyn's protestations. 'I can't see why you're making all the fuss, Cynthia,' she said. 'You'll be dead long before me, so it doesn't need to worry you. Willie will see that the charities get their legacies from what money you've left to me.'

Nobody knew how really wicked the Will was until Miss Katherine Mackenzie kicked the bucket a great many years before it was expected. Cyn knew right away how dire it was when Willie and Bertha came to Kathy's funeral, and Bertha collected all the jewels. The sisters had some very precious ones that had belonged to their grandmother, who had bequeathed them equally to both sisters, though Kathy always claimed the lot. Bertha put the jewel case under her oxter, saying: 'Legally, I shouldn't take them till you die, Cynthia, but I know you'll never want to wear them—it's hardly likely in the short time you've got left—so I might as well have them now. Jewels improve with wearing.'

Miss Cyn never stopped talking about these jewels and the Will for the next seven years. Day after day, night after night, when she couldn't sleep, she went over the Will and what it was doing to herself and her dependants. ''And that means you, Annie,' she would say. 'You're my chief dependant now that your poor sister like my own sister is away.' For my twin, so grandly called after Queen Caroline of Naples, had been killed when she was only a year old by an Alsatian dog belonging to one of the village brats. 'You and Muriel Brunton and Bessie and Nurse Biscuits, you're all my dependants and I want to provide for you all after the fairies take me away. You can rest assured that Waddling Willie won't provide for you.'

The only thing that gave Cyn any joy over Miss Katherine's Will was the fact that Waddling Willie and his avaricious wife couldn't lay hands on Seven Yewtrees and the rest of his legacy until she died. 'It's what keeps me alive, Annie,' she said. 'Just to spite Willie I've told the fairies I won't be ready to go with them for a long time yet. Though, mind you, I'd fain often be away to join my dearest Sin, it's the thought of doing Willie down that keeps me here.'

She talked like this not only to me but to Miss Brunton and Mrs

Bessie Dodds and Nurse Abernethy, the district nurse who, in the last years of Cyn's life, came in every morning to attend to her. There was always a tussle when 'Biscuits' gave Miss Cyn a blanket bath. Cyn hated anybody washing her face, and poor Abernethy had to keep saying: 'Now be a guid lassie, Miss Mackenzie , and let me give your phisog a wee dicht. Surely ye don't want to look like a smoked-out tinker when the doctor comes?' 'I don't care what I look like,' Cyn would say. 'The doctor'll just have to thole it. Better folk than him have seen me with a smut on my nose. I remember once when the Countess of Dalwhinnan came to call on my mother . . .'

When she wasn't talking about the Wicked Will and how little siller she had left in the Bank and how it would be depleted even more when yon charities got what by rights should come out of Kathy's or Waddling Willie's money, Miss Cyn recited poetry. She would recite her own poems, and she would recite screeds and screeds by a man called Browning. But her favourite poets were Emily Dickinson and Alice Meynell. Hardly anything ever happened without giving occasion for her to remember some apposite quotation from one or the other.

A morning came when she was talking about Sin, her sailor laddie, and the good times he and she had had, and she said: 'Maybe Emily Dickinson kent more about sailors than any of us when she wrote: "Can the sailor understand / the divine intoxication / of the first league out from land?" '

And then she sighed and said: 'Now, let's be quiet for a wee while, Annie. I'm going to sleep.'

I went to sleep too. When I woke, Miss Cyn was still sleeping, so I slipped through the open window and foraged in the garden. When I returned she was lying on her back, very straight and stretched out, and there was a hankie over her face. I sprang up on the bed, but I didn't curl up beside her. I was debating whether I'd have another wee nap or whether I'd go and see if Bessie Dodds had a tit-bit for me when Miss Cyn said: 'Annie! Now that I'm away, I want you to be a good wee cattie until your own time comes. And I want you to give Waddling Willie's fat legs a real good scratching when he comes to the funeral. But mind he doesn't kick you!'

I looked round and there was Miss Mackenzie standing there in her nightgown behind me. She was that thin and worn-away I could see right through her. I looked from her to the Miss Mackenzie on the bed, and I cried: 'Guidsakes, mistress, what's ado?'

'A stupid question, Annie,' she said. 'You ken fine what's happened to me. You ken that I'm a ghost just as well as I ken that you can speak like this when you feel like it.'

It was then that voices made me notice that the door, which was always open, was now shut. Nurse Abernethy and Dr Duncan came in. Dr Duncan walked through Miss Cyn and bent over Cyn on the bed. 'I'm glad, she went so quietly,' he said. 'Her old ticker just conked out.'

'I'll old ticker him!' Cyn said to me. 'When I think of all the heart pills that gowk's garred me swallow in my time!'

After the undertaker and his men had carried out Miss-Mackenzie-on-the-bed in a funny-looking purple blanket-box affair, Cyn and I joined Miss Brunton and Bessie Dodds and Nurse Biscuits in the kitchen. Miss Brunton and Bessie were still snivelling, putting their hankies to their eyes, and Abernethy kept trying to jolly them. She cracked a wee joke, and after a while Mrs Dodds tucked her hankie into her apron-pocket saying: 'Ah well, it has to come to us all. Puir Miss Mac, rather her than me, though. I'm no' ready yet.'

Biscuits cracked another wee joke, and they were laughing when the phone rang. Miss Brunton answered it. Cyn and I could hear every word that Bitchy Bertha said at the other end. 'Mrs Drummond has just phoned to tell me that Miss Mackenzie died last night,' she said. 'Why was I not informed earlier?'

'Miss Mackenzie died only two hours ago,' Miss Brunton said. 'I phoned Mrs Drummond at once, and she came to look at Miss Mackenzie before the undertaker took her away to the mortuary.'

'Who are you?' Bertha demanded.

'You know perfectly well who I am. If you had deigned to visit Miss Mackenzie even once in the seven years since her sister died you'd perhaps have known me better. I'm Miss Muriel Brunton, the housekeeper.'

'Why haven't you left? You've no right to be in the house now that the body's gone. I asked Mrs Drummond to give you notice. You will lock up the house at once and give Mrs Drummond the keys.'

'I'm staying until Sunday to look after the cat.'

'Have the cat destroyed', the voice said. 'Immediately.'

'Miss Mackenzie wanted the cat to go to a good home,' Muriel said. 'We're going to find one for her, and I don't leave this house until we do. We haven't decided which day the funeral is to be yet, but no doubt your friend Mrs Drummond will keep you well informed.'

And she banged down the phone. She and Bessie and Nurse Abernethy started to discuss me. Mrs Dodds said she'd be more than glad to have me, but there were some collies at the Barns and she didn't think I'd take kindly to them.

'I'd have her,' Biscuits said. 'But a district nurse's house is no place for a cat. There are always interfering folk who'd complain about it being insanitary.'

They were still arguing back and forth when the phone rang again. 'If it's that woman,' Muriel Brunton said, 'tell her I've left for Hong Kong.'

'Hello,' Biscuits shouted into the mouthpiece.

'This is Mr Glossop-Macleod. I'm so sorry to hear about Miss Mackenzie's death. Who are you? I've just had Mrs Jarvis-Waddell on the blower—all the way from Yorkshire. She says there are strangers trespassing in her husband's house, and she orders you all to be gone before this evening. Will you kindly hand the keys to Mrs Drummond? Mrs Jarvis-Waddell also told me to inform you that she has a complete inventory of all the furniture and valuables in the house and she will check this with the contents as soon as she arrives for the funeral.'

'She's feared we nick something,' Biscuits said. 'I've aye had my eye on yon picture of the wifie in the red cloak in the hall, but I doubt, I doubt . . .'

'It's in the inventory,' Miss Brunton said. 'I went round with the agent at the time, and I remember him taking notice of it. It's not worth anything, but it's better not to take any chances with that woman.'

Mrs Dodds said: 'I'd have liked a wee memento. Could I no' take yon wee blue jug that's ahint Buffy's photy on the drawing-room mantelpiece? It would never be missed. I deserve somethin' after workin' here for donkey's years.'

'That jug's lapis lazuli,' Muriel Brunton said. 'It's one of the first things she'd spot. Anyway, you've been left a good few hundreds in Cynthia's Will.'

'Ay, if Waddlin' Willie lets me have it,' Bessie said. 'I bet he'll try to stop us all gettin' what Miss Mac put in the Will she made last year.'

Biscuits said: 'He can't do that. She was in her right mind, and what money's left of her own has nothing whatever to do with him.'

They were having lunch when Alick Buchanan, the vet, arrived and said a strange wifie had phoned from England and told him the cat was to be put to sleep. 'Instanter,' he said, lifting me and giving me a cuddle. 'It'll be all right, Annie my wee doo, one prick and Bob's your uncle.'

The three women set up a great hue and cry, but Alick was adamant. 'It breaks my heart,' he said. 'But orders is orders. I not only had the strange wifie. I had Mrs Drummond on the blower forby, telling me to get on with it.'

The vet didn't come to the funeral, but the lawyer did. He arrived as the coffin was being carried out of the kirk. Ronald Glossop-Macleod was carrying a wreath. He held it behind his back, not knowing what else to do with it, when they all gathered round the open grave and Snotty said a long prayer. I had a keek at the wreath, and it said 'To Cynthia with deep affection from Ronald'. She had never called the man 'Ronald' in all her life. She had called him a lot of names, but never Ronald.

The undertaker began to dish out the cords so that the coffin could get lowered. He handed the first cord, with a bow, to Mrs Jarvis-Waddell; then he handed the second to Mrs Drummond. The third went to Mr Glossop-Macleod. Then the undertaker hesitated, looking about to see which other mourner seemed most worthy to get the fourth, and after a pause he handed it to Mrs Bessie Dodds. But he didn't bother to bow to her. He was busy looking at his men to give them the signal to let the big ropes drop, which they did in a fell hurry, and so Cyn's coffin tumbled down into its last resting-place.

'I'm sorry Waddling Willie wasn't able to come because he's in some Bongo-Bongoland with the Foreign Secretary,' Cyn said. 'I'd have liked fine to put a cold hand on the nape of his neck when he was kneeling in the front pew.'

'Never mind,' I said. 'Maybe the Blacks'll pop him in a pot.'

'No such luck,' she said.

'Would you like me to rub against Bertha's leg and make her topple into the grave?' I asked. 'I'd fain like some revenge.'

'No, no, Annie,' she said. 'We must think of something better than that. Something more lasting.'

For the next two days Cyn and I watched Bitchy-faced Bertha and Nan Drummond rake through Cynthia's and the family's papers, screwing them up and throwing them into cartons that they carried out and emptied in a heap on the lawn. Drawer after drawer, cupboard after cupboard were emptied and the contents carried out. All the family photographs, their birth certificates and wedding licences, photographs of friends, letters that went away back to Cyn's great-grandparents—for the Mackenzies had been great hoarders—were picked up, glanced at and thrown onto the scrap heap. All the manuscripts of Cyn's poems and the letters Sin had sent her were laughed at and torn into smithereens. And while they destroyed several generations of family love and pride, the two women talked and talked. Bertha kept telling Nan Drummond about all the grand times they would have when she and Waddling Willie took residence in Seven Yewtrees, but Cyn and I, who could see right into her evil mind now that we were ghosts, knew this was just a ruse to keep Nan sweet in the meantime, for Bertha planned to sell the house and all its antique furniture and pictures as soon as she could make the arrangements with a big firm of London auctioneers.

By the second evening the two women were exhausted by their rummaging and destruction, and an enormous bonfire of papers, letters, birthday and Christmas cards, old clothes, children's broken toys, photographs, postcards, all kinds of cherished keepsakes, everything that had gone into the creation of three or four generations of Mackenzies, was standing six or seven feet high on the rough grass that once had been a well-kept lawn. And as the sun was almost setting over the Grampians, Bertha went to the scullery and brought out a can of paraffin oil. She sprinkled about half of it over the wreckage. Then both women struck matches and threw them onto the pyre. The bonfire flared up and was soon going merrily.

Bertha said: 'Well, that's a good day's work done.'

'It is that,' Nan said. 'Now, dear, let's go home to supper and a nice wee drinkie to celebrate your inheritance.'

Cyn stood by the bonfire, moaning and wringing her hands. 'The years of love,' she cried, 'the years of joy that are going up in smoke!' I spat venomously in the direction of the manse, and went to find something to eat. I hadn't known ghosts got hungry. I was enjoying the remains of some fish when I noticed the half-empty oil-can left on the back-door step. The stopper wasn't screwed on properly.

I don't know where the idea came from. But I acted at once. I leaned against the can and knocked it off the step. In a jiffy I had got off the cap with my paws and teeth; then I started to roll the can towards the bonfire. The paraffin spurted out everytime the can rolled over.

Cyn stopped moaning and watched my efforts to trundle the can. At first she watched with sad amusement; then she watched with irritation. 'You'll hurt yourself, you silly wee pussy,' she said. 'Aren't we in enough trouble without you doing that?' And then, suddenly, the purpose of my activity dawned on her.

'Oh, what a wonderful idea!' She clapped her hands and laughed. 'What a smashing idea, as your friend and my friend. Mrs Elizabeth Dodds would say. "Right smashin' guid, eh, Miss Mac hen?" I do wish our good friend was here to shout encouragement from the side-lines. And maybe to help kick the can!'

Cyn shot out her foot, newly rejuvenated by death, and sent the oil-can two feet nearer the bonfire. I dunted it with my head and pushed with my forepaws, sending it another inch towards its destination. Cyn gave a wild screech of laughter and gave it another kick.

'It breaks my heart,' she said. 'Poor old Seven Yewtrees! I feel like the Vandals and the Visigoths sacking Rome.'

In a few seconds the fire rushed along the oily tracks I'd left and licked the back door. It was not long before the flames were thrusting into the house. The sun went down as the kitchen became one big fiery oven. Before it had been dark for an hour Seven Yewtrees was a blazing mass.

Cyn and I flew up and sat on the roof. I was nervous of the flames licking up towards us, but Cyn said: 'Don't be a feared-gowk. You must remember you're a ghostie now and you can't be harmed by fire, water, heat, snow, any of the elements you like to name. You're invincible and invisible.'

Still, I was nervous, and so I pranced about, thinking I could feel the heat seeping through my paws. It was all very well being a witch's kitten, but I didn't care for fire. At first Cyn said: 'Stop dug-dancing about.' Then she began to get excited, too, when the flames got higher and folk from the village started to arrive. Some of them stood and watched the blaze, standing like stookies and doing nothing. Others rushed away to get the police and the fire brigade and pails of water that they flung on the fire—as if their paltry contributions could help quench such a gigantic furnace.

By the time three fire brigades came Cyn and I were dancing sky-high above what was left of the roof, gurgling with glee at the sight of Bitchy-faced Bertha and Nan Drummond holding onto each other and wailing in the front of a crowd of villagers, which, by this time had swelled to well over a hundred. Cyn took higher and higher leaps in the air, and she shouted down to them: 'An eye for an eye and a tooth for a tooth! Greet awa', my bonnie dearies. I aye knew I'd have the last laugh on you.'

They couldn't hear her of course. But that didn't make her revenge any less sweet. 'Even if they do get the insurance to cough up,' she said, 'it'll not be as much as the property was worth. And I'm not sure that the insurance will pay. The insurance folk may say it's arson, for there's that oil-can in the middle of the bonfire. I wonder if their fingerprints are still on it? Wouldn't it be fun if Bitchy-faced Bertha and Nosey Nan were stood up in the dock and sentenced to twelve months hard! It would serve Nan right for wanting so much to be a guest of Her Majesty.'

Cyn gave a skirl and a few leaps, then she cried: 'I feel just like Anton Dolin! What a pity it is that you never saw the ballet, Annie.

You'd have loved it. You'd have loved Dolin in *Hymn to the Sun*. But what am I havering about? It''s not Dolin I feel like. It's Nijinsky! I'll never forget him in *The Fire Bird* . . .'

WITCH'S KITTEN was written in the Spring of 1978 for James Hale's anthology *The Midnight Ghost Book* (Barrie and Jenkins, November 1978). It was then published in Denys Val Baker's anthology *Ghosts in Country Villages* (William Kimber, May 1983) and in Fred Urquhart's collection of pseudo-supernatural stories *Seven Ghosts in Search* (William Kimber, November 1983).

20 *Just What You'd Term a Simple Country Lass*

I USED TO HAVE a cousin, Bobby Shand, who was the biggest blow. He died years ago. I don't think I ever saw him after I was in my teens, but I've remembered a few things about him all my life. Our Ma couldn't bear him. Whenever his name was mentioned her tongue went like shears clipping clouts. 'That big bounce,' she'd say. 'All his eggs are double-yoked.' And then she'd get started. She never forgot the time he came to bide with us for a holiday in October 1922. 'He cut my best towels with his razor,' she said. 'And he never stopped talkin' about his wife being only a simple country lass.'

My Uncle Colin, Bobby's father, was a miner. But Bobby was too grand to be a miner. He was an insurance agent. I could never see, and neither could my mother, why it was considered grander to be a man going from door to door collecting a few pence each week and writing it down in his wee book than a man who did a hard day's work down the pit, getting his face and body black by howking coal. Bobby Shand thought so, though. 'My father'll never make a penny slaving his guts out for the coal-owners,' he used to say. 'You never get anywhere in this world if you work for other people. You've got to be independent and strike out for yourself.'

Our Ma said: 'If he calls being a door to door salesman strikin' out for himself, then I've another name for it. He lives on commission, ye ken. A real hand to mouth existence, if you ask me. He'd be better to have a good steady pay like his father. But of course that would mean gettin' his face and hands black, and Mr Big Head won't have that.'

I never saw my Uncle Colin, who was our Da's oldest brother. If it comes to that, I can almost say I never saw his other two brothers either; for Uncle Geordie was in his coffin when I saw him, and I got only a glimpse of Uncle Sandy, a bent-double auld skeleton, at the funeral. They all had big families, nine or ten bairns each, and our Da said they were inclined to be sniffy at him because he had only two—and both girls at that. You can see that I had a lot of cousins. Most of them were a lot older than me, and many are likely to be dead by this time. I never saw half of them, and I don't suppose any of them would have wanted to see me, with my reputation. Not that I could care. My heart's not broken. After all, a good part of my life has been spent in strict seclusion and I've been cut off from my relations by more than mere distance. I'm not what you'd call a family woman. Family trees and family get-togethers mean nothing to me.

I never met any of my cousins, except Bobby Shand, until I was fourteen or fifteen. All of them lived in the mining villages of Fife, and I spent my childhood in the Dumfriesshire hills, where our Da was head gamekeeper on a large estate. We lived a quiet country life among the gentry. There were no comings and goings between us and our Da's three brothers and their offspring. Ordinary folk did not have cars in those days, and trains were used only occasionally. Little travelling was done from place to place unless it was on important business like a family funeral or sometimes a wedding.

The way I came to meet Bobby Shand earlier than any of the others was because of a funeral. My Uncle Colin got killed in a pit disaster in 1922. Looking back, there aye seems to have been pit disasters when I was young. Our Ma and Da went to Cowdenbeath for the funeral. Da got three days off work, and he near had to get down on his hands and knees to get it. Cissie and I were left in the care of Mrs Sturrock, the head gardener's wife. Before she went away our Ma said to me: 'Now, Ivy, behave yourself and do everythin' Mrs Sturrock tells you. None of yours airs and graces, mind. Try to forget for once that you're the Duchess in *The Duke's Secret.*'

When they came back they said they'd invited Cousin Bobby to come for ten days or a fortnight. 'I asked him wi' a grudge,' our Ma said. 'He got my goat with all his bounce and the speech he made at the funeral tea. All about it being his place as the eldest son and hardly saying a word about his poor father being buried under tons of coal. Though in a way I couldn't help feelin' sorry for him. He's been ill with the bronchitis, and he looked that peely-wally the words were out before I could help myself.'

'You did the right thing, Gracie,' our Da said. 'I didn't take to the fellow either, but we couldn't do anything else for poor auld Colin's sake.'

I was ten or eleven at the time, maybe twelve. I forget. I've told that many lies about my age, and it's a long way to look back. Anyway, I was still a bairn—even though I was a gey knowing one and never missed a trick. I remember Bobby that first time fine. He would be about twenty-seven or twenty-eight. He wasn't a bad looking bloke, fairly tall with a good head of black hair and a wee toothbrush moustache. And he had a way with women. That I must say for him. He had Cissie and me near turning somersaults round him, and even our Ma was eating out of his hand, though it was much against her grain. 'He's a smarmy bit of goods,' our Da said that first night after Bobby had been sent off early to bed by our Ma who said he looked worn out after his long journey. 'I suppose he needs to be a bit of a sook in his line of business, but I wouldn't trust him with two bent halfpennies. I don't know where he gets all his palavers. He doesn't get it from our side anyway. Us Shands are a well-doing, straightforward bunch without any frills, though I do say it who shouldn't boast. My brother Colin was as honest as the day is long, so Bobby must get it off his mother's side.'

Cissie said: 'Get what, Da?'

'Mind your own business, miss,' our Ma said. 'Ask no questions and you'll be told no lies. It's high time you were in your bed.'

'Och, what's the hurry, Gracie?' our Da said. 'Tomorrow's Saturday, and the lassies can have a long lie. And why shouldn't they hear about Mary Ann's side of the family?'

And then he told us that when she was a girl our Auntie Mary Ann worked as a clerkess at the cash-desk of a butcher's shop and she was caught fiddling the till. 'It was neck or nothing she'd get put in the nick,' our Da said. 'It was lucky for her that the auld sheriff took a fancy to her after she'd run circles round him with her slavery tongue. He dismissed the case as not proven. Oh ay, Mary Ann had a lot to be thankful for that our Colin lowered himself to marry her after that. Mind you, I'm not saying anything against her. She was a good wife to our Colin and she's taken his death real badly. I thought she was never going to stop greeting when the minister had his say at the funeral tea.'

'Ay, she fairly went her mile,' our Ma said. 'If you ask me, she enjoyed being the centre of attraction. She was determined not to let Bobby have all the limelight.'

'Now, now, Gracie,' our Da said. 'There's no cause to make her out to be any worse than she is. I admit it wasn't like her to carry on like that, throwing her petticoats ower her head and wailing like a banshee. she's aye been such a cheery case, very jokey and all that.'

'That's what I'm gettin' at,' our Ma said. 'She's aye been so gallus that you'd have thought she'd have put on a bolder face, with the minister there and all. I ken that losin' her man was a sair blow, and such a good man at that. But there was no cause, it seems to me, to have behaved like she did. She was just playin' to the gallery. It just proves what I've aye thought: that there's something two-faced about her.'

'Well, I wouldn't exactly call Mary Ann two-faced,' our Da said.

'But there's something else I can never quite put my finger on. It isn't just sleekitness. Now I would say that Bobby's sleekit, and I'd leave it at that. There's something about his mother, though, that's deeper. She's not like our side of the family. Us Shands have good straight-growing roots. But Mary Ann . . . I'd go as far as to say that Mary Ann's not quite the clean potato.'

That first morning of his holiday our Ma gave Bobby his breakfast in bed. 'Poor soul, he needs feeding up,' she said. 'And the rest 'll do him good.'

Bobby didn't get up till about eleven o'clock. Seeing it was Saturday Cissie and I were at a loose end, so we hung around and watched him shave in the scullery and then sluice his face and neck with hot water in the enamel basin. We were going to follow him back to the spare room and we'd have stood, I'm sure, and watched him dress if our Ma hadn't shouted: 'Ivy, I want you to go and feed the hens for me. Cissie'll help you while I make us all some tea. I think your big cousin could be doin' with a cup.'

We were all drinking tea and eating slices of our Ma's speciality, vinegar cake, when she said: 'D'ye ken, Bobby, I've never met your wife. I never saw her at the funeral.'

'She wasn't there, Auntie,' he said. 'We have three children, and she had to stay at home and mind them.'

'Fancy! Three bairns!' our Ma said. 'And you just a young man yet. Little aulder than a bairn yourself. Dear, dear. And what's your wife like, Bobby? Is she bonnie?'

'She's all right,' he said. 'She's just what you'd term a simple country lass. She's not quite up to my standard, Auntie.'

That took the wind out of our Ma's sails, for all she said was: 'Well, well.' Then she said to me: 'Ivy, I want you to go to the village for some messages. Maybe you could take your big cousin with you? Would you like a wee walk, Bobby?'

The village shop was owned by old Mr Rowland. He was a widower and you hardly ever saw him, for he was usually pottering about in the back premises. The business was run by his daughters, Miss Rowland, Miss Meg and Miss Kitty, who were all quite good-looking young women. They were what they and the village thought slightly superior. Our Ma used to give imitations of them and their determination to be posh.

The shop was packed that Saturday morning. Cissie and I were real proud of Bobby as we went in, and the door bell clanged notice of our arrival. Bobby was swaggering like a peacock. He had on a pale grey homburg with a black band. It was stuck at a fair angle on the side of his head, and he gave the village women time to admire him before he took it off with a flourish and said: 'Excuse me, ladies.' Cissie gave a bit giggle, but I pretended not to hear her. Bobby kept his hat in his hand all the time we were in the shop. Miss Rowland, Miss Meg and Miss Kitty were all serving. 'Good morning,' Bobby said, bowing to them all. 'Lovely morning!'

When our turn came we got Miss Kitty. She was the bonniest of the sisters. While she was getting the messages on our Ma's list, Bobby kept up a flow of chatter with her. From the way he chaffed her you'd have thought he'd known her all his life. Miss Kitty primmed and pranced with delight, and she was slower at getting the sugar, bread, tin of corned beef, sultanas and other odds and ends than she needed to be. After I'd put them in the basket and Miss Kitty had entered them on our account, Bobby bought twopenny bars of Cadbury's milk chocolate for Cissie and me. He paid for them with sixpence from a purse he took out of his trouser pocket. I couldn't help staring. It was the first time I'd ever seen a man with a purse. Our Da wouldn't have been found dead with a purse in his pocket. Not that our Da ever had any money on him. He always let our Ma do the paying.

'My, aren't you girls lucky-bags to have such a nice big cousin,' Miss Kitty said, handing us the chocolate.

'Young ladies should always get what they like,' Bobby said. 'Don't you think so, Miss Kitty?'

'Too true, Mr Shand,' she said.

Us girls were all over Bobby that first couple of days, but by the time he'd been with us for a week the gilt had worn off. It started on the Monday after I came out of school.

Cissie had gone to Mrs McNeill's to get fitted for a new dress, and I was faced with the prospect of walking home on my own. I didn't really fancy that. Though I didn't fancy going to Mrs McNeill's and waiting for Cissie either, because the fitting might take well over an hour. Mrs McNeill, a widow body who took in sewing, was a great talker and was aye losing her specs or swallowing a pin or doing something else daft that made the fitting spin out far longer than it should. So I was fair delighted to see Bobby Shand going into the village shop. I thought I would have company on the way home and maybe a bar of milk chocolate or a whipped cream walnut into the bargain.

I looked into the shop window. I peered between the shelves holding glass jars of mint humbugs, dolly mixtures, jujubes, black balls, pralines and other kinds of sweets. There was nobody in the shop but Bobby. He was leaning on the counter talking to Miss Kitty. I could see he was chatting her up, as they call it nowadays. She was giggling.

She stopped when I went in, 'Yes, Ivy?' she said. 'Do you want something?'

'No,' I said. 'I just want to be with my cousin.'

'Well, I don't think your cousin wants to be with you at the moment, dear,' Bobby said. 'You go on home. Scoot!'

I stood still and leant on the counter. 'I think I'll have a bar of chocolate,' I said. 'What kind d'you think I should have, Miss Kitty?'

'Nestles Milk? Cadbury's? or Fry's Cream? They're all twopence. And then there's the penny bars of Fry's Plain. Which d'you want?'

'I can't make up my mind,' I said. 'I've just got threehalfpence.'

'Have a penny bar of Fry's,' Miss Kitty said. 'Keep the halfpenny for another time.'

'I don't really like Fry's Plain,' I said 'I'd rather have a twopenny bar of Fry's Cream.'

'Give her that,' Bobby said. He took two pennies from his purse and put them into Miss Kitty's outstretched palm, closed her fingers over them, and then held her hand. 'Now scoot, Ivy,' he said.

'You *are* kind, Mr Everest,' Miss Kitty said, 'Say thank you to your cousin, Ivy.'

'Ta, Bobby,' I said, and went slowly to the door. I stopped with my hand on the handle. 'Everest? Was that what you called him? You've got it wrong. It's Shand, the same as us.'

'Of course, it's Shand,' Bobby said, giving a high-pitched laugh. 'I always say Everest without thinking. Robert Everest is my nom dee plum. I'm a writer, y'know.'

'What do you write?' Miss Kitty said.

'I'll tell you in a minute,' he said. 'Hurry on home, Ivy. Your Ma wants you to go to Mrs Sturrock's for some vegetables. She told me to tell you to get your skates on.'

I went, but I thought a lot as I took the silver paper off my chocolate, screwed the paper up in a ball and threw it in a ditch before I went through the gates leading into the avenue of the Big House.

The next afternoon Cissie and I met Bobby coming towards the village. He crossed to the other side of the road and never looked at us. Cissie shouted 'Hello, Bobby!' but he never answered.

The same thing happened on the Wednesday, except that Miss

Kitty Rowland was with him, and she gave us a wee bow and a smile. Though she said nothing.

On Thursday we met him at the big gates. He was going to walk past again without speaking, but I gripped Cissie by the arm and made her stand still. 'Where're you going, Bobby?' I said.

'It's none of your business,' he said. 'I'm just going for a walk.'

'Would you like us to come with you?' Cissie said.

'No,' Bobby said. 'You go on home, like good girls.'

'We don't want to be good girls,' I said. 'We want to go with you.'

'You're not coming with me,' he said. 'Go on now when you're told.'

'We'll go home when we're good and ready, Mr Everest,' I said 'I think we'll chum you as far as the shop.'

'Do what you're told,' he said. 'If you were mine I'd take the skin off your backside.'

'Ay, but I'm no' yours,' I said. 'Thank God for that, too.'

He made a breenge at us, so we took to our heels. We stopped running after about ten yards, though, and I yelled: 'Who do you think you are? Charlie Chaplin with your wee mouser? Yah, your boots are cracked for the want o' blacknin'!'

I was encouraged to shout this because I knew our Ma had already had more than a bellyful of Master Bobby. She never stopped complaining. Her main complaint was that Bobby wouldn't get up in time to have breakfast with the rest of us, but lay in bed until our Ma was forced to take his upstairs on a tray so that she could get on with her work in peace.

'And then he comes down all lad-de-dah and ditters about among my feet,' she said. 'I can't get the floor swept or the dishes washed for him coming to my elbow and saying "Listen to this, Auntie," or "What do you thing of that, Auntie?" I'm fair deeved with his tongue. I've never been called "Auntie" so much in all my life, and I'll be honest and say I don't like it.'

The truth of the matter is, yon holiday was a big mistake. It was a mistake in the first place for our Ma to let funeral sentimentality get the better of her and invite Bobby; she wasn't a sentimental woman, and she knew as well as I do that blood is not thicker than water. And it was a mistake for Bobby to come to relatives who were complete strangers. He was a cocky small town boy by far happier standing at street corners or chatting up his women customers. He was out of his element. He had no idea what the real country meant to some people and how to behave in it.

To try to entertain him our Da took him shooting on the moors one day. All the walking and climbing tired Bobby out and gave him sore feet. And he didn't know one end of a gun from the other. Our Da shot some grouse and pheasants, but Bobby wouldn't draw a trigger. He said: 'I'm against shooting innocent birds so they can be eaten by the idle rich, Uncle.'

'But these are not going to be eaten by the idle rich, my man,' our Da said. 'You ken fine that the gentry are away in London. These are going to be eaten by us.'

Bobby was always going his mile about the idle rich. 'He's a right Bolshie,' our Ma said. 'He should be in Russia supervising the Grand Dukes and Grand Duchesses that have been sent to work in the salt mines.'

She wasn't surprised when he told her he was thinking of standing as a Labour candidate at the next election. 'I feel I'll become as great a Member of Parliament as Ramsay Macdonald and Willie Gallacher,' he said. 'You'll be proud to say you're related to me one of those days, Auntie.'

'Fancy that!' our Ma said. 'You're aiming high, aren't you?'

'You've got to aim high, Auntie, if you're going to shoot down the capitalists,' Bobby said.

'I thought you were against shootin',' she said. 'I thought you told me field sports are barbarous.'

'Well, I don't hold with shooting innocent birds, Auntie,' he said.

'I notice it didn't prevent you from eatin' them,' she said.

'It's really the gentry I don't hold with, Auntie,' he said, as smarmy as a rattlesnake. 'I'd line them all up against a wall and order the lads to pull the triggers.'

'Ye wouldn't pull a trigger yourself, I suppose?' she said. 'Are ye feared you would miss?'

Our Ma didn't hesitate to pull the trigger and she certainly didn't miss when the moment came. The moment came on the second Saturday. At ten o'clock Bobby was still in bed, so our Ma told me to take up his breakfast. 'Wake up, sleepy head!' I shouted, opening the door by dunting my bum against it and carrying in the tray. 'Where will I put this? Are you able to sit up and get it on your lap? Or are you still dreaming about Miss Kitty Rowland?'

I planked the tray on a chair, drew the curtains and then put the tray on his lap. 'Would you like me to comb your hair before you start to eat?' I said. 'Talk about a golliwog!'

'Go away, little girl,' Bobby said. 'Leave me to eat my breakfast in peace.'

I went out and slammed the door.

When he came downstairs in about an hour's time he didn't bother to bring the tray with him. Our Ma gave me a nod, and I went up and fetched it. By that time Bobby was shaving at the scullery sink. I put the dirty dishes on the draining board; then I stood and watched him sweeping off the shaving soap with his cut-throat and wiping the blade every few minutes on the towel. Cissie was leaning against the wall watching. Our Ma was out feeding the hens. I took my chance and slipped up again to the spare bedroom.

Bobby's wallet was on the dressing-table. I just thought I'd have a wee keek inside it to see if it had a photo of his wife. I wanted to know what a simple country lass looked like. There were no photos, though. There were his Oddfellows membership card, a couple of letters I didn't have time to read and seventeen pound notes.

Seventeen pounds! It was a fortune in those days. More anyway than I thought the likes of Bobby Shand had any right to have. What was a cheapskate like him doing with all that? I took a pound and slipped it under the elastic of my knickers. Later on I hid it behind a loose brick in the wall at the back of the kennels. As far as I knew, nobody knew about this loose brick but me. If our Da had known he would have got the under-keeper or one of the estate's handymen to have cemented it up long syne.

That night, after our high tea, when Cissie and I had settled down to do our home work on the kitchen table, Bobby came in in a great stew. He was all dressed up. There was a dance in the village hall, and I guessed he was going to take Miss Kitty Rowland.

He said: 'I've lost some money, Auntie. I wonder if you've seen it anywhere, lying around?'

'Oh dear!' our Ma said. 'What a catastrophe! How much have ye lost, Bobby? A half-crown? Or five shillings? I'm sure you haven't dropped it in your room. I'd have found it this mornin' when I gave it a good sweep, under the bed and everythin'.'

'It's not that kind of money, Auntie,' he said. 'And I'm sure I didn't drop it either outside or in. It's a pound note if you want to know the truth.'

'A pound note? Oh, God Almighty, what a loss!' Our Ma gasped like a fish on a hook. 'Are ye sure you've lost it? Have you looked in all your pockets?'

'It was in my wallet this morning,' he said. 'It's not there now.'

'How d'ye know?' she said. 'Have you counted it right?'

'Of course I've counted it right. I've counted it again and again.

There were seventeen pounds this morning, and now there are sixteen.'

'Seventeen pounds!' our Ma cried. 'What are ye doin' with all that money, Bobby Shand? Have ye robbed a Bank or somethin'?' And she gave a bit laugh to show that he wouldn't have the gumption to do anything as bold.

'I wouldn't have said anything about it,' Bobby said. 'But it's not all my money. Some of it belongs to my Insurance Book.'

'And now you're sayin' that somebody's pinched it?' she said.

'Now look, Auntie, I'm not accusing anybody.'

'What are you doing then?' she said. 'Comin' in here skirlin' like a cat with a red-hot firework tied to its tail and sayin' me or one of my lassies has stolen your money. I'll have you know, Bobby Shand, that our branch of the family's a very respectable one. Not like some branches I could mention.'

'I'm not accusing you, Auntie,' he said. 'I was just mentioning that I'd lost a pound.'

'And I'll just mention somethin' at the same time,' she said. 'I see you're ready to go courtin' Miss Kitty Rowland. Oh ay, I have my ears close to the ground, and I ken what's going on. High time it was put a stop to. Your poor wife. Even if she is a simple country lass she deserves a better man than you. I'm sorry for her. And I'm sorry for Miss Kitty too, being taken in by you, I don't suppose she kens you're a married man with three bairns? And what's this I hear about you bein' a writer and havin' a nom de ploom? It may fool Miss Kitty, but it doesn't fool me, Bobby Shand.'

'It was just a joke, like' he said.

'Some jokes have a queer way of back-firin',' our Ma said. 'And this joke's one of them. It's high time you ended your holiday, Bobby m'man. Your room's beginning to be preferred to your company.'

'If that's the way you want it, Auntie,' he said. 'I'd been banking on being here a bit longer, like.'

'Well, you've banked wrong,' she said. 'And while I'm at it, there's another thing I've been wantin' to mention, Bobby Shand. You can cut your throat with your own razor for all I care, but I won't have you cuttin' my best towels.'

That was aye a sore point with our Ma. For months after Bobby left she ranted on about those towels. 'You'd think when he made the first cut,' she told folk, 'he'd have taken care not to do it again. But not him, the big blow! He was aye that busy talkin' about the poor workin' man being downtrodden he had no time to look and see what he was doin'. One of the towels has that many cuts you'd think it was a venetian blind.'

I changed Bobby's note into half-crowns and hid them. They kept me going for a long time in twopenny bars of chocolate. Once Miss Kitty said that I seemed to get more pocket-money than Cissie, but I told her I got the extra by running messages for Mrs Sturrock and the maids in the Big House.

The following summer Bobby wrote to our Da and said he'd like to come for another holiday and bring his wife with him. She was anxious to meet Auntie and the girls. 'No thanks,' our Ma said. 'Auntie's not anxious to meet her. There are enough country jossers in this house already.'

I saw Bobby Shand once or twice again a good few years later. Once was at our Uncle Sandy's funeral, and once was at some cousin's wedding. I don't think I exchanged more than a couple of words with him.

Of course, he never got near being a Labour candidate. He was too big a bounce even for the comrades. But his wife blossomed forth in local politics, and she became a town councillor in some wee town in Fife, where she moved after Bobby was killed in a motorbike accident. She was a great one for shooting off her neck and became a big bug in the Labour Party. But I didn't hear this until long afterwards; I was that busy being headlines myself at the time she was elected that all my relations were terrified to see the name 'Shand' in the national newspapers. 'Scottish Con Girl Soaks New York Millionaire': that was the one I'll never forget. It was a lie, anyway. He was a small town banker from Tennessee and I only managed to get five thousand dollars off him. Mrs Councillor Shand said on a platform that Ivy Shand was not quite the clean potato and was a black burning disgrace to the entire Shand family. I'm sure they all followed my career with great interest after that, and they must all know exactly how many times I've been inside.

In a way I blame Bobby for what happened to me. He should never have put temptation in my way. I'll never forget him saying 'Go away, little girl' with a royal wave of his hand like King Tutankhamen. Who did he think he was speaking to? His simple country lass of a wife?

JUST WHAT YOU'D TERM A SIMPLE COUNTRY LASS was written in the Spring of 1981 and was published in *Scottish Short Stories 1982* (William Collins/Scottish Arts Council).